First to Blink

Also by Robin Lehman

PERSEVERANCE

First to Blink

A novel by

Robin Lehman

FOGDOG PRESS

FIRST TO BLINK

Cover design by Robert Aulicino

Library of Congress Control Number: 2013949458

ISBN 978-0-9841469-3-2

Printed in the United States of America

FOGDOG PRESS
Box 3510
Lawrence, KS 66046

www.fogdogpress.net

For Pat, Lindsay, & Regan,
whose love and support sustain me

and for Murphy, whose sweet doggy smile
lit up my life every day of our nine years together

1

SPECIAL AGENT Regan Manning hadn't felt this pumped since she brought down the vice president of the United States. She spotted her partner returning with a fresh cup of coffee and jumped up from her desk. "We got him!"

Nick jogged the rest of the way and high-fived her with such zeal that coffee splashed over the edge of the cup and onto his jeans. He didn't seem to notice the burning liquid on his thigh. "No *shit*? You got Lee to confess?"

"Yep, he'll sign an affidavit saying the congressman hired him to bribe Chinese officials," Regan said excitedly, bouncing up and down on her feet. After eight months of painstaking investigation—and then being stalled for the past month—the new development made her even more bubbly than usual.

"I swear you have magical powers, partner."

"Not magical, just relentless. I think Huang Lee confessed in order to shut me up."

"Man, I can't believe it. All those months of digging and putting the squeeze on people, and we finally got somebody to cave."

"Yep, and the DC media will have a field day," said Regan. "Hotshot congressman bites the dust."

Nick took a slurp of coffee and set the cup on his desk. "Let's go tell Roland."

Lisa Roland, assistant director of the Washington Field Office, was about to head out to a meeting just as they arrived. "I think you're going to want to hear this, ma'am," said Regan.

Roland nodded and waved them into her office. "What's up?"

Regan made a concerted effort to stand still. "We got our Chinese informant to implicate Haines—he's emailing me a signed affidavit today."

Roland's eyes lit up. "His story lines up with our other informant's?"

"Like a zipper."

"Excellent work, guys. Get with your contact in the Fraud Section and coordinate with the U.S. Attorney on charges."

"Then we pick him up for questioning?" Nick looked like he was ready to bounce, too.

Roland smiled. "Then you pick him up. If he knows the Justice Department is about to prosecute his company, he may do whatever it takes to save himself."

❧

ON THEIR way to see Adam Mohr, chief litigator in the Justice Department's Fraud Section, they got a call from Roland.

"You're not going to believe this," she said in a somber tone.

"What?" said Regan, fingers tightening on the steering wheel.

"CIRG just got called out to Congressman Haines' home in Montclair. There's a hostage situation."

Her heart picked up its pace. "Seriously? The family's being held by a gunman?"

"No—Haines *is* the gunman."

"*What?*" Regan felt like all the air had been sucked from her lungs; she looked at Nick, whose jaw had gone slack.

"The babysitter came this morning and couldn't get in. Both of their cars were in the garage, so she called the police. Haines apparently became extremely belligerent and ordered the responding officer to leave. He managed to get a look in the house through a side window, and Haines was holding a gun on his wife and little boy."

"Why? Why would he do that?" It was a question directed at the universe rather than her boss.

"I'm hoping our CIRG people will soon have an answer to that." The callout of the Critical Incident Response Group, based a short distance away at Quantico, probably meant the locals were afraid to touch it given Haines' notoriety.

"Okay, we're heading to the scene, ma'am," said Regan. "We'll give you a heads-up on the situation once we get there." Regan accelerated, the phaser siren and flashing grille lights on her black SUV parting the morning rush-hour traffic as neatly as a rat tail comb.

"I can't fucking believe it," said Nick. "We're *this* close." He held up his hand, thumb and trigger finger less than an inch apart.

Ten minutes later, the pair blew into Montclair, Virginia, a community that hunkered around a pristine lake and inspired thoughts of sleek boats and manicured golf courses.

"Whoa," Nick said, glancing around. "I think we just arrived in the Land of Deep Pockets."

Regan said, "Uh huh," but she barely noticed. She was trying to imagine what on earth would turn Jon Haines into a hostage taker.

They found the street where the congressman and his family lived, a quiet residential lane that had morphed into a parking lot for emergency vehicles and news vans. A chain of nervous cops held back a swarm of reporters and camera people jostling for the best vantage point in case bullets started to fly. They flashed their FBI creds and were waved through.

The modern two-story house sat nestled into the edge of the forest, cocooned in a protective embrace against the outside world. Unless, of course, the place was surrounded by enough armed cops to take down a small nation.

The agents strapped on their Kevlar and headed for the white command-post tent that dominated the sprawling front lawn, giving the scene something of a wedding party feel. Beneath the tent, instead of rounds draped with white tablecloths and dainty centerpieces, officers worked the computers and other electronic equipment that had been thrown into some semblance of order on long tables.

Not a party dress in sight.

Al Rinehart, head of CIRG's Crisis Negotiation Unit, spotted them. "I can't believe my eyes ... it's Manning and Jenesco! Did you guys have a change of heart and decide to come back to us?"

Regan smiled. "Nah...you've got your A-team on it. You don't need us."

Al leaned close to her ear and spoke in a low voice. "They're good, Pippi, but not as good as you."

She gave his arm an affectionate squeeze. Al was the only one who got away with calling her that—a throwback to Pippi Longstocking, a book he'd read to his daughter when she was little. Regan got tired of people commenting on her red hair and freckles, but she cut her old boss some slack because he'd been an amazing mentor. Told her more than once that he'd never seen a negotiator with such finely honed instincts and such "goddamn unwavering determination."

She *had* turned into a pretty good negotiator, had loved the challenge of getting into a guy's head and talking him back from the brink. Her success rate had been phenomenal—but then again, she'd never faced a well-known congressman who went postal.

And investigation was her true calling. She loved the complexity of it, the myriad twists and turns. Her assignment to the Washington Field Office's FCPA team, investigating violations of the Foreign Corrupt Practices Act, was her dream job. Somehow she'd managed to talk Nick into leaving CIRG, too, even though the anti-corruption team wasn't *his* dream job. He was a sniper at heart.

"Have they figured out what's motivating him?" said Regan.

"Nope," said Al. "So far all he's said is that he wants us to get the hell off his property."

"Knowing Haines, that's not surprising. But why point a gun at his wife and kid?" She shifted her gaze toward the house, struck by the tranquility of the setting. Apparently it was all a lovely façade.

"Whatever the reason, it should finish him politically," said Al. "But in this town, who the hell knows? He'll probably run for speaker next year and win." He rubbed a hand over his shaved head; he'd been balding for some time and recently decided to give up the fight. Regan was still getting used to his new look.

"Yeah, no, I don't think so, Al," said Regan.

He turned to look at her, his eyes narrowing. "I figured you guys might be here for more than a closer view. What's going on?"

"We've spent the last nine months investigating Jon Haines. We were hours away from bringing him in."

Al's eyes got wide again. "No shit? He bribed foreign officials?"

Regan nodded. "Up until he was elected to Congress two years ago."

"So you're here to make sure he comes out intact because you want your shot at him."

"You got it, boss. He's key to nabbing the bigger fish."

"Do you think he knew you were closing in on him? Maybe that's what pushed him over the edge."

"No, I don't think so," said Regan. "We've kept a tight lid on it."

"And our informants are too worried about their own hides to risk telling him," said Nick.

"So this standoff is a whole separate deal," said Al. "Boy, the congressman must think he's bulletproof."

Regan nodded. "He's going to find out he's about as bulletproof as a paper vest."

The trio stood in silence a moment, listening to the negotiator plead with Haines. Al said, "Hey, Pip?"

"Yes, sir?"

"You called me 'boss.' I think that deep down you really want to come back."

Regan grinned. "If the FCPA gig doesn't work out, I'll be sure to give you a call."

2

JULIA HAINES scanned her husband's face, searching for some remnant of the man she married. At what point, precisely, had he transformed from her sweet, sensitive Jon to the homicidal maniac standing before her?

"Look what you've done!" he roared. "The police are all over the goddamn place! You're trying to ruin me!" His hair, usually without a single strand askew, spiked at odd angles. Coupled with his wrinkled pajama bottoms and the "UVA Law" t-shirt with a hole under one arm, he looked more like a jacked-up college student than an esteemed member of Congress.

Julia took a deep breath and tried to keep her voice steady. "I'm not doing a thing to you, Jon."

"Why did Rosie call the police? We could've settled this on our own!" His face was flushed, the veins on his neck distended like ropey vines.

"Rosie called the police because we didn't answer the door and you wouldn't let me answer the land line or my cell phone. You shouldn't have threatened that officer, Jon; it only made things worse." Though her tone sounded remarkably level, even slightly disapproving, she had to fight the urge to vomit.

He moved closer, his face twisted in a nasty sneer. "He had no business being here—but thanks to you, we've now got an entire army on our front lawn."

Julia averted her gaze and remained silent. She didn't dare provoke him further.

He moved away, then spun around and came toward her again. "It's Peter, isn't it?"

"What? Don't be absurd," Julia replied, taking a step back. "He's just my colleague. I've told you that a thousand times."

"Then why were you leaving?" he screeched.

"Mama, why is Daddy so mad?" whimpered five-year-old Jackson. He'd been glued to her side ever since his dad found them in the garage hurriedly loading a suitcase into the car. Jon had forced them back inside, gun pointed at Julia's head.

For more than an hour after that, he'd paced stiffly back and forth, fury turning his face into a stony mask. Then he slumped in a chair, his rage slowly giving way to remorse. His eyes pleaded with her to understand his pain.

Now he was ramping up again, and Jackson obviously felt it, too.

"It's okay, honey. Daddy's just upset." She stroked the terrified boy's head and looked back at the husband she no longer recognized. "I was going to the townhouse, that's all. I needed some time to think." Julia stayed at their Georgetown residence when her work kept her in the lab for long hours.

"Think about what, Julia? Your Mexican lover? Was he planning to meet you there?"

Julia blanched; Jon's tone sounded more scornful of Peter Cordova's Hispanic heritage than the fact that she might even *have* a lover. He found it hard to believe that someone with Peter's humble beginnings could become the respected scientist he was without other people dragging him along.

You're one to talk, she thought angrily. But before she could reply, the metallic voice outside repeated, "Congressman? I need you to talk to me."

"I think you better respond to that officer before they storm the house and someone gets hurt. I'm sure their patience is running out." Julia didn't know much about hostage negotiation, but she did know it took more than a one-sided conversation to work. How long before they gave up and sent the SWAT team in?

His eyes widened in alarm, then grew narrow; he was a swirling vortex of emotions as he paced between the living room and foyer. It was like trying to reason with a tornado.

"I'm going to phone your home line, Congressman Haines," the female agent called out. "Let's just chat, and you can tell me what's going on. I want to help."

A moment later, the phone rang. Julia gave her husband an expectant look.

Jon glanced at the phone, then resumed pacing. The call went to the answering machine.

"Jon, please --"

"Shut *up!*" He pointed the gun at her.

Julia collapsed into a wingback chair and wrapped herself protectively around her son. She closed her eyes and tried to steel herself for an attack—if not by her husband, then by the snipers outside that surely had them in their crosshairs. Jackson dissolved into sobs; it took every ounce of self-control not to join in.

"Shh, it's okay, honey," she whispered, holding the boy tighter. She willed herself to stop shaking.

The phone rang again. Jon ignored it. He started muttering, hands held against his head.

With Jon momentarily distracted, she searched frantically for any possible means of escape. A moment later, she heard the agent's voice over the bullhorn again. "Congressman Haines? Please pick up the phone so we can resolve this situation without anybody getting hurt."

15

The phone rang. Jon snatched it up and said, "Everything's fine. There's just been a misunderstanding, that's all. Our babysitter thought something was wrong, but we're fine."

Julia saw her husband's jaw go rigid as he listened to the voice on the other end of the line. "I did not threaten the police officer, I just told him to leave," he barked. "And now I'm telling you. Pack up your circus tent and get the hell off my property."

3

SIERRA ONE, do you have the solution?" said Al. Clustered around him, along with Regan and Nick, were the tactical team supervisor and the on-scene intelligence officer.

"Intermittently, sir," came the reply. "We've got a constant visual on the wife and son, but the subject is moving back and forth between the living room and the front hallway. He looks pretty agitated. If it's a go, we'll have him in our sights the next time he steps into view."

"It's *not* a go, Sierra One. Repeat: do not take the shot. Stand by."

Al turned to the group. "Too much risk to the hostages if we attempt the shot with him moving around like that. I also don't like our odds if we try to enter the house right now. We need to get him calmed down first."

A young male agent came over with a satellite phone. "Call for you, sir; it's the deputy director."

Al took the call, mostly listening, and then said, "I understand, sir. We'll do our best." When he disconnected, he said, "Orders from the top: get this wrapped up."

Regan was confused; normally their protocol was to allow a lot more time for negotiation. "Why? Like you said, we need to calm him down. It's only been—"

"Because the speaker of the U. S. House of Representatives called Director Tate, that's why. He's alarmed about the protests

17

this thing is setting off in the district and he wants to get it shut down before things escalate further."

"Then maybe he should put in a direct call to his dutiful little soldier," said Nick. Haines had become a regular part of the backdrop every time Speaker Stallworth spoke to the press.

"Apparently the speaker's tried calling Haines, but he's not picking up."

The tac team supervisor said, "My team's ready whenever you are, Al." His eyes were bright with anticipation; Regan thought she could hear him pant, but it might have been her imagination.

The primary negotiator strode over from the negotiating area. "I can't get him to budge, boss. Hey, Regan. Any suggestions?"

"You're doing an awesome job, Tess." She pretended she hadn't heard the order from above. "It's just going to take more time; Haines thinks he's running the show."

"Yeah, well, so far he is." Tess tipped her head back and forth, loosening her shoulders.

"Not when one signal from you will have SWAT on him like bugs on a biscuit," said Nick.

"I guess there's that," said Tess, taking a long drink from her water bottle. "All right, I'm going back at him."

Al said, "Push him harder, Tess. We're about out of time."

A look of confusion flitted across her face, but she didn't argue. "Okay, boss." She marched back over to her designated spot behind a row of rose bushes and put her headphones back on.

"Bugs on a biscuit?" Regan whispered to Nick.

"That was the only metaphor I could think of off the top of my head."

"Simile."

"What?"

"It's a simile, not a metaphor."

"Oh, right, Professor Manning. I'm a big boob. How's *that* for a simile?"

"That's a metaphor."

Nick shook his head and moved away.

Al said, "I can give the negotiators another hour. Then we go tactical."

The tac team supervisor nodded enthusiastically. This time she was sure he was panting.

Regan saw their corruption case heading off the rails. She moved closer to her old boss and spoke in a low voice. "I know you've got a ton of heat on you, Al, but I'm just afraid of the risk to the hostages—and to the congressman—if the tac team goes in."

"The risk is high whether tac goes in or not. And I've been given a direct order."

Regan did a little pacing of her own, then she moved several yards away and put in a call to Roland. She filled her in on the situation.

"You want me to defy a direct order from Tate?" Roland made no effort to conceal her incredulity.

"Ma'am, you know how close we are on the corruption case," Regan pleaded. "We need Haines in order to bag the big guy."

Roland was quiet a moment. "How certain are you of Jennings' culpability? Because I don't have to point out to you, Regan, the disastrous consequences if you're wrong."

She was right. Winston Jennings, chairman and former CEO of the global security firm Imhoff-Greyson, former U.S. senator, and former defense secretary of the United States, was not someone you wanted to piss off.

"Absolutely certain of his culpability. Not certain we can prove it. That's why we need Haines."

"And what makes you think Haines would cooperate? His loyalty to Jennings is practically legendary."

"Haines is as ambitious as they come, and Jennings can only take him so far. We're betting that if he thinks he can get a deal that will make him look less guilty—like he was just following Jennings' orders—and maybe allow him to eventually salvage his political career, he's going to grab it. Even if it means his long-time mentor goes down."

"But taking his family hostage makes it a moot point, don't you think?" said Roland. "Even Haines, as self-important as he is, can't be delusional enough to think he'll just walk away from this unscathed."

"Unless he doesn't see it as a hostage incident. He probably views it as simply a domestic dispute, and it's nobody else's business. That's why he keeps telling our people to get off his property."

"And you think that with a few more hours, he can be coaxed out of there."

"Yes, ma'am, *if* he can be convinced that the FBI is just following procedure by staying onsite until they exit the house. I think the negotiators need to sound calm, take it slow, let him believe we think it's not that big a deal. My gut tells me if we push too hard too fast, he's going to escalate his behavior. And if he's suffering some kind of mental breakdown—as it appears he could be—he might kill them and then himself. The ultimate act of control."

Roland was quiet again. "You make a compelling case, Regan. Let's just see if I can persuade Director Tate that it's compelling enough to push back against the speaker of the House."

4

AN FIELDING saw it right away: this was anything but your typical hostage situation. No, this one involved a politician who was the darling of his party and a pre-eminent Georgetown University research scientist who happened to be his wife. Dr. Julia Haines was well-known for her cutting-edge work on Parkinson's disease, and some of her most promising results were obtained through the use of embryonic stem cells.

For most pro-lifers, embryonic stem cell research equaled abortion. So was this simply a domestic dispute or something much bigger and more ominous?

That was the central question he posed in today's political blog on NBCNews.com. He finished his final edits and hit the send button, then sat back and waited. The comments would start within minutes. It amazed him how many people had nothing better to do than hang out online and comment on stuff.

The investigative journalist's weekly show on NBC, *Fielding Questions*, had surged in popularity in recent months, garnering more than five million viewers and climbing. His inquisitiveness, along with his ability to neatly dissect people and their issues, earned him the nickname "Digger Dan." He relished the moniker.

The first comment popped up on his screen. "OMG! It's sickening to think Haines' right-wing politics take presidence over his marriage." Dan smiled; commenters tended to be creative spellers.

More comments appeared. One in particular caught his eye; Rusty0503 told him he was "scum" and that he had "no respect for life" because he had lauded Julia Haines and her research in the blog piece. *Apparently, old buddy, your pro-life views don't extend to Parkinson's sufferers.*

Dan was undaunted by haters like Rusty0503. They kept him on his toes, made him better at his job. Made him keenly aware of how important it was to be thorough in his investigations and avoid any kind of bias, regardless of his own views.

Truth was, he had been intrigued by the congressman long before the man pulled a gun on his wife. Two years ago, Haines seemed to have come out of nowhere and then surged ahead like a Kentucky Derby dark horse driven to beat the odds. His rise in the party had been almost meteoric.

It was no secret that Winston Jennings greased the skids for him. Ever since the powerful Senator Jennings, chairman of the Senate Armed Services Committee, gave him the plum job at Imhoff-Greyson and then anointed him as an assistant secretary at Defense, he had been an extension of the man.

Like a third arm on a guy that already had way too much reach.

At some point, though, wasn't Haines' success dependent on his own merit, his *own* political savvy? After all, Jennings couldn't be there twenty-four/seven, especially now that he had semi-retired to his ranch in Kansas.

In recent months, Dan had poked around the edges a little, had tried to elicit opinions from other politicians about the enigmatic Haines, but nobody bit. It was like the subject was taboo.

Which only stoked his curiosity even more.

And now the high-flying congressman had committed an apparent act of political suicide. Time for Digger Dan to get to work.

๛

WINSTON JENNINGS drove his pickup across the cattle guard and headed for home. He wanted to check in with Haines to make sure he was keeping a close eye on their legislation so everything could proceed on schedule.

Once Haines won reelection in a few months, the congressman would continue his skyward trajectory, propelled by Winston. But first Jon had to get that wife of his under control. Right now, Julia wasn't exactly helping things. In fact, she was hurting him, and that was a major problem. He would have another talk with Jon when he was in Washington next week.

He pulled around to the side of the sprawling country home that was Betty's pride and joy. Ever since they'd returned to Kansas from Washington eighteen months ago, she'd been on a remodeling frenzy. There wasn't one square inch of the place that hadn't been torn out or painted or spruced up in one way or another.

He'd gone along without complaint. Lord knew she'd had to put up with enough while they were swimming around in the DC fishbowl all those years.

"C'mon, Gert," he said to the yellow Lab that went everywhere with him. Winston loved all dogs, but Gertie was special; best bird dog he'd ever owned and a pretty good companion, too. Didn't yap all the time like Betty.

Gertie plopped down to take a nap in the sun. Winston entered the back door and took off his boots in the mud room.

23

"Win? Is that you?"

Who else would it be, Betty? The pool boy?

"Yeah, hon, it's me." He found her in the kitchen stirring up some sort of fancy concoction that involved whipped cream. "What's cooking?"

"Lemon icebox dessert. The girls are coming for bridge this afternoon."

He stuck his finger in the bowl and stole a lick. "Tell 'em not to get too wild. I have phone business to take care of."

"Okay, we'll try to keep it down. You wouldn't hear us way back there in your office anyway."

"I don't know, Betts. That Erma has a pretty good cackle when she gets going."

She gave his arm a playful swat. "You get going, old man."

Just shy of seventy, he *was* an old man—only two years younger than the age his father was when his heart called it quits. But unlike his dad at this age, Winston still had the energy and keen mind of a forty-year-old.

Well, maybe a *fifty*-year-old.

As he made his way to his inner sanctum, Winston reflected on the good life he had as a cattle rancher here in the Flint Hills, a world away from the Washington babble and the media that never slept.

But close enough to keep his finger firmly on the political pulse.

He turned on the TV to Fox News. The breaking-news banner that stretched across the bottom of the screen hit him like a sucker punch to the gut: "Virginia Congressman Holds Family at Gunpoint."

Even if he hadn't recognized the house, he'd have known it was Jon. More than once, Winston had overlooked odd ticks in the man's behavior. But Jon's unquestionable loyalty—and pliability—had trumped his occasional mental wobbliness.

Winston's hands began to shake as he watched the news coverage. The FBI had been on scene for two hours, and so far Jon refused to cooperate.

Winston couldn't comprehend such a thing. Was Jon really that far off his nut that he couldn't control himself? If he was, Winston's plan might be in serious jeopardy.

He placed a call to Jon's cell phone; no answer. He pulled an address book out of his desk drawer to locate the number for their home phone, but then he hesitated.

He needed to get to Washington *now*, not next week. He needed to be there for damage control.

5

"I HAVE to say, Pippi, you must have some serious pull with the assistant director if she's willing to ask Tate to reverse his order."

"It's not about my 'pull,' Al. It's about a huge case of public corruption that's about to go down. And it's about keeping the Haineses alive. Besides, we're not asking the director to reverse his order, just delay it."

"Well, since you're here, you may as well head over to the negotiating area and help out."

Regan smiled at her former boss. "I thought you'd never ask." She sprinted over to the negotiators before he had a chance to change his mind.

Tess looked surprised to see her. "What's up, Regan? Is Coach benching me?" Both women had been basketball standouts in their younger days; both were still as competitive as ever. But above all else, they were team players.

"No way, Tess. I'm just here to help you guys out." She greeted the other two negotiators and the mental health consultant standing by. "Haines still won't engage?"

"Right. He won't answer any of our questions, won't talk except to shout orders at us, and now he won't even answer the phone."

"That might actually be a good thing," said Regan. "Haines might not see this as a hostage incident, just a private dispute with his wife that we stuck our noses into. He thinks if he ignores us, we'll eventually give up and go away. According to the sniper-observers, he doesn't look nearly as wigged out as he did earlier. In fact, he seems to have settled down quite a bit."

"So how long do we give him?" asked one of the other negotiators.

"We're still waiting on word from Director Tate, but I expect we'll have just a few more hours."

Regan turned to Tess. "Why not try telling him that when he comes out, we're going to need to interview him briefly so we can wrap this up? *When* he comes out, not *if*. He doesn't have a choice—but give him the impression it's all going to be pretty low-key and routine. Tell him it's just a quick interview to make sure everything is A-OK and then we all go on about our business."

"And we tackle him the minute he steps out the door," Tess said with a grin.

"If he's cooperative, then we allow him to remain upright. If he's not, then Haines is going to get a close-up view of that gorgeous lawn."

❧

"CAN I go play?" said Jackson. His angst had subsided now that his dad had stopped ranting again.

Julia gave her husband a questioning look.

Jon sat at the bottom of the stairs that led to the second floor; he gave a nod. Jackson headed up the stairs, avoiding physical contact as he passed his dad.

Jon looked like he'd run out of steam. Was he ready to surrender?

"Honey, I'm sorry things haven't been very good between us lately," Julia began. "I know you're having a hard time with my work. But please try to understand, I'm—"

"Killing fetuses." He shifted his gaze to her.

She'd been going to say *fine-tuning a drug compound that will finally halt the progression of Parkinson's in patients, not just treat their symptoms.*

But she had tried to explain her work to him before, and if anything, the gulf between them had widened. She shouldn't have brought it up; with Jon's obvious mental state, it wasn't the right time to try to mend the cracks in their union. That would have to come later.

Or not.

Right now, her only goal was to get out of the house and away from him without getting Jackson or herself shot.

"Maybe you're right," she sighed.

He perked up. "Really? Or are you just saying that because I ... you know ..."

"Keep pointing your gun at my face? No, Jon. I admit I'm stressed and tired and I want this to end. But more than that, I want us to be *us* again, not acting like we're enemies at war. This is just so crazy."

He stood and moved to the living room, kneeling down by her chair. "Oh, Julia, that would make me so happy. I want us to go back to being the way we used to be, ready to take on the world. With you beside me, there's no limit to what I can do. I can run for—"

"Mommy?" Jackson appeared at the top of the stairs.

"What is it, sweetheart?"

"There are some men with big guns climbing up the trees. I can see them out my window."

Jon sprang to his feet. "Goddamn it!" He raced to the kitchen to look out back, the same view Jackson had from his room upstairs.

Almost without conscious thought, Julia made a beeline for the stairs, taking them two at a time. She scooped up her son and charged into the master bedroom at the front of the house, then slammed and locked the door behind her. She heard Jon pounding up the steps.

Julia threw open the window.

"Mama, *noooo!*" Jackson wailed, clinging to her neck.

"Please, baby, I need to get you out of here," she panted. She hoisted him over the sill and watched anxiously as the FBI agents scrambled into place beneath the window.

Jackson was scared speechless, his eyes bugging out as he looked down.

"Rosie will take care of you for a little while and then I'll come and get you." She tried to control the tremor in her voice. "I love you, sweetheart. Be strong."

Julia's heart broke as she pulled his arms from around her neck and held him out above the ground below, where the SWAT team members clustered themselves into a safety net.

Just as she let go, she heard the bedroom door crash open.

6

THE RESILIANCE of children amazed Regan. They lived in the moment, and now that Jackson Haines was safely tucked inside a police car with his babysitter, he wanted something to eat.

While they waited for an officer to return with a Happy Meal, Regan opened the back door of the car and squatted down to talk to the boy. The mental health consultant, a smug woman named Claire, came over from the negotiator area and stood next to Regan, obviously making sure Regan didn't say something that would scar the kid for life.

"It's nice to meet you, Jackson," Regan said, holding out her hand. She wondered if they called him Jack for short. That was her boyfriend's name.

He shook it. "You have dots on your face like me." He pointed to his cheeks, which were dappled with freckles.

Regan smiled. "Yep, I sure do. I think the dots make us special."

His smile showed that he liked that news. She didn't bother to inform him that, unless they faded as he got older, the dots would forever make him look like a kid. It wasn't always a good thing.

"So, Jackson, how's your mommy doing?"

"She threw me out the window!" he blurted, his face creased in a big grin.

"That's because she knew all those officers were there to catch you."

"Uh huh. They catched me."

"Jackson, can you tell me if your daddy is still holding his gun, or did he put it away?"

The boy wrinkled his brow. "Uh, I think he put it on the table by the couch. But daddy's *really* mad."

"I know, honey. He's not mad at you, though."

"He's mad at mommy. He wants her to quit her job."

"I see," said Regan. "Do you think that's why he got out his gun?" From the corner of her eye, she saw Claire straighten and cross her arms. Regan had worked with Claire before and knew her signals; this one meant *tread carefully.*

"Nope. He got mad because me and Mommy were going to go for a ride and we weren't going to take him because he was sleeping. But then he woke up. Did you know I can swim?"

The abrupt shift took a second to process. "Um, you can? Did you take swimming lessons?"

"Uh huh. Two times. I can swim underwater all the way to the other side!" He beamed.

"Really? What else do you know how to do?"

"I help Rosie put dishes in the dishwasher. And sometimes Mommy." He rocked back and laughed. "She doesn't put *Mommy* in the dishwasher, she puts dishes. I mean sometimes I help Mommy do that."

Regan smiled. "I knew what you meant, silly." She liked this kid.

And she was grateful that, so far, the events inside the house hadn't traumatized him into silent withdrawal. But if the standoff went on much longer and he couldn't see his mother, it might be a different story.

31

Regan saw an officer approaching with a McDonald's bag. "Here comes your food, Jackson. As soon as you're through eating, these nice officers will drive you and Rosie to her house, okay?"

He nodded, distracted as he dug through the red cardboard box to find his toy.

Regan motioned to Rosie to step out of the car, out of Jackson's earshot. "Mrs. Pearson, have you noticed any change in the congressman's personality recently?"

She nodded. "He's become meaner, more demanding. And sometimes he's so rude to his wife that I feel like clipping him upside the head." The middle-aged babysitter, the mother of three strapping boys, explained that such behavior would never be tolerated in her house.

"I'm afraid of what it's doing to that sweet child," she said, glancing toward Jackson and lowering her voice. "He has started wetting the bed, and I think it's because he's become afraid of his dad. Mr. Haines never plays with him anymore—he just barks at him."

Regan knew all about barking dads. Except in her case, she barked back.

"What about Julia Haines? How does she seem around her husband?"

"Dr. Haines is a beautiful woman, inside and out. She is kind and compassionate and *so* smart. If she has a fault, it's that she puts up with too much. If she was attempting to leave her husband, then I say good for her. He may be some big political hotshot now, but if you ask me, Agent Manning, he sacrificed everything important to get there."

❧

REGAN FOUND a spot in the shade and leaned back against a tree. Her thoughts drifted to what she'd been avoiding like a pit of vipers—her upcoming trip home.

Nick ambled over to her. "You're lookin' pretty intense, partner. What are you scheming?"

Regan sighed. "I'm trying to figure out how to get out of going to my mom and dad's anniversary party in a couple weeks."

"Uh oh," said Nick. "That's going to ruffle some feathers."

"I know, Nick, but I just don't feel like I can take off and fly up to Juneau right now."

"Have you told Jack?"

The knot in her stomach tightened. "No."

When she didn't continue, Nick said, "Okay, spill it, Reegs. It's not like you to clam up, especially when it comes to Jack the Power Ranger."

Regan's eyes began to prickle; tears were threatening. "Jack wanted us to announce our engagement at my parents' fortieth anniversary party."

"Hey, that's great, Regan! Congratulations. Wait … why is it that you don't want to be there for that?"

"Because I'm not sure I'm ready. But I'm afraid of losing Jack. He's been so patient with our situation, but he's getting frustrated. He thinks two years of living three thousand miles apart is long enough; at least one of us needs to make a change. I agree, but it's just …" The tears spilled over; she brushed them away with the back of her hand.

"Just that you're worried it's going to have to be you."

"Well, since Jack is a forest ranger, that pretty well eliminates DC for him. He has to be where he can continue his research on tree genetics." Jack Landis had become a national authority on the science.

"Oh man, that sucks. I know how much you love this job."

If Regan had been alone, she would have given in to the urge to bawl. But that would have to wait. In the meantime, her head felt like it was going to explode.

"I do love it, Nick, and I don't want to give it up. I also don't want to lead Jack on if marriage isn't in our future, but right now I can't make myself go up there and break it off with him. If I cancel out of the party, my dad is going to blow a gasket—just when we've finally achieved a little harmony." She touched her fingers to her throbbing head.

"What about your mom?"

"Mom won't express an opinion—mostly because she's so used to my dad expressing her opinions for her." Regan couldn't keep the bitterness from creeping into her tone. "She'll be disappointed, of course, but she's also very understanding."

"So at least *she* will buy your argument that you're too busy to get away," said Nick.

"Not really, but she won't challenge it. My dad, on the other hand, will consider it an affront to them, to their celebration, to Jack, to my whole freaking home town."

Nick chuckled. "Remind me why we thought long-distance relationships were a good idea."

Nick had met Lindsay Pryor at the same time Regan met Jack two years earlier. A dignitary protection case took them to Juneau for the Alaska Energy Summit, and Lindsay was one of the Anchorage agents who had come down to provide backup. Like Nick, Lindsay had grown up in Maine, so there was an instant connection between them.

"Because if you'll remember, Nick, we were more focused on lust than life plans. So how's it going with you guys?"

"We're just as sick of the long separations as you and Jack. That's one of the reasons Lindsay's thinking about leaving the bureau."

"Leave the bureau? Really?" Regan looked at him like he just said Lindsay had sprouted another head. "What will she do?"

"Maybe join her mother's legal defense firm in Portland. Ever since she got out of law school five or six years ago, her mom's been hounding her to come back to Maine and join the practice."

"Oh man, how great would that be? You could hop on a plane and be there in less than two hours."

"Yeah, I'd love it, but Lindsay hasn't decided for sure yet. Her mother is domineering as hell, and she's not sure she wants to subject herself to that."

Boy, I wouldn't—but maybe Lindsay isn't as easily riled by a bullying parent.

"Your dad's still chief of police up there, right? I'm guessing her mother and your father have the occasional clash."

"My dad would like to run over her with his patrol car."

Regan laughed, momentarily buoyed out of her misery. "That could make things pretty interesting for Lindsay."

"And for me if I go back," Nick said quietly.

Regan turned to look at him, a new ache pinching at her heart. "Are you thinking of doing that, Nick?"

"Don't know. Just looking at possibilities."

Both leaned back against the tree, silently retreating into their thoughts.

7

ULIA SAT facing Jon. He sagged on the couch, a pitiful expression on his face. The gun sat within arm's length on the nearby end table.

Her Mother Bear persona had won out. When Jon kicked open the bedroom door, a stunt that resulted in an injured foot, he faced the full brunt of her anger. She no longer cared if he pointed the gun at her; with Jackson out of harm's way, she refused to continue being his victim. It had gone on long enough.

Jon's tirade the night before had scared her; it was the first time he'd grabbed her with enough force to leave a bruise. She knew it was the beginning of a pattern that would only escalate as he became more obsessed with power and she resisted his demands for her to become a fulltime political wife.

She'd lain awake all night, planning her escape; as morning drew near and Jon slept soundly, she saw her chance to take Jackson and run. Now she realized what an idiot move it was. She should have been patient, should have waited until Jon was out of the house.

Subconsciously, did she *want* him to catch her?

No, but Jon's latest explosion sparked a new sense of urgency. And she never dreamed he would pull out a loaded gun.

He was right about one thing, though. She did love Peter.

"Now what, Jon?"

"I don't know, Julia. I don't know." He was in pain, and his injured foot was the least of it.

"Let's end this."

Jon's head popped up. "End what? *This* or our marriage?"

Julia hesitated, gauging his state of mind. "This standoff. Let's get it resolved so the FBI will leave. Then we can talk."

Tears began to trickle down his tortured face. "You want out."

She knew he wasn't talking about the standoff.

"You threatened to kill me, Jon. I know you were upset, that you didn't really mean it. And like I said, I'm willing to talk about that once this is over—see if there's any chance of putting things back together." The lie flowed easily from her lips.

The phone rang. Jon ignored it.

Julia sighed. "C'mon, Jon, please answer the phone."

He sat up. "Let's have something to eat."

She stared at him.

His tone became brusque. "You want to put things back together, Julia? Start by fixing me something to eat."

The cheeky demand annoyed her, but the shift in his demeanor made her heart race. She recalled how, six months ago, she had suggested to him, ever so gingerly, that he could be bipolar—and that medication might make him feel better.

He slapped her across the face.

She vowed not to make that mistake again. It was easier just to leave.

He limped behind her into the kitchen and flipped on the small flat-screen television on the counter while she frantically searched the refrigerator and cupboards for some food to throw together. What did Rosie usually fix?

"My god ..." he muttered.

She turned. He was transfixed by what appeared on the TV screen: live footage from the choppers that circled overhead, showing the swarm of officers that blanketed the neighborhood, SWAT team guns trained on their house. The screen was split between coverage of their home and the National Mall, which was overrun with hundreds of angry protestors carrying picket signs, shouting to anyone who would listen: pro-gun, anti-gun, pro-life, pro-choice, pro-women … everything from soup to nuts. And the talking heads blamed Jon for tripping the collective trigger.

Their Montclair home had somehow become the epicenter of the anxiety that gripped the nation's capitol. Julia held her breath, watching to see how Jon reacted.

He turned his gaze to her, his jaw slack. "They're going to kill me, Julia. They're going to make me a sacrificial lamb."

ॐ

"A SACRIFICIAL lamb?" said Regan. "Are you freakin' *kidding* me?"

They had gotten a court order to remotely activate the microphones on the Haines' cell phones, so they listened to the conversation inside the command post while the negotiators heard it through their headphones.

"Sounds like he's beginning to crack," said Nick.

Regan turned to Al. "We've got to find a way to keep him calm. Can we push back the perimeter, maybe get rid of some of these cops?"

"I don't know if that's a good idea," said Al. "We don't want to open up holes, just in case some of the protestors get the notion they need to hold a rally right under Haines' nose."

"Then maybe keep the cops here but just push them back," said Nick. "Right now, they aren't serving any real purpose other than holding off the press—but to Haines it looks like an army outside his house."

"Right," said Regan. "Al, we could manage the scene better with just the negotiators and the tac team."

"And if Haines escalates, it's only going to take one sniper to put him down," said Nick.

Al's look said, *Really? Tell me something I don't know, Jenesco.* As incident commander, it was his job to know everything about the situation.

"Wow, you two act like you're still part of CIRG instead of just visitors to *my* scene. And by the way, holding back the press is no small thing. Those guys are doing a helluva job."

"We appreciate your letting us be here, boss," said Regan. "And you're right, those cops are doing a great job. But if we move the media further back, their vantage point won't be as good, and I'm guessing some of them are going to peel off. They'll rely on the choppers to get the visuals."

Nick chimed in, "And the scene will look much less intense to Haines, which may calm him down."

"Okay, okay," he replied. "But if this thing goes south, *you* guys can explain it to Tate."

Regan nodded and motioned Nick away from Al. "I wonder where Winston Jennings is right now."

"I've wondered the same thing," said Nick. "I've been expecting him to ride to Haines' rescue any minute."

"Me, too; and it wouldn't surprise me if the way he goes about it is to put pressure on Garrison Tate, his favorite whipping boy. Make him think that if the bureau can't get this wrapped up immediately, he's going to start screaming about our incompetence again."

"Oh, jeez. Just what we need. What about Speaker Stallworth? Do you suppose he and Jennings are in cahoots?"

"I don't know, Nick—but if they are, this may be just the tip of the iceberg."

〜

WINSTON'S FLIGHT was scheduled to arrive in DC at four p.m. He hoped by the time he was on the ground, the hostage incident would be all over. He planned to be there to rescue Haines and squelch the hysteria.

The flight attendant in first class brought him another scotch. He took a sip, the liquor burning a trail down his throat. He was a scotch connoisseur, of sorts, but not above drinking the more common brands on occasion. Kept him humble.

For the hundredth time since that morning, he pondered what was going on with Jon. Had Winston been partially responsible for his actions? Had he pushed Jon too hard to rein in his wife?

If so, it was only because he was trying to get the boy to face reality. If Haines wanted to achieve his ambitions—including a shot at being House speaker down the road—he needed to be solidly on board with the party platform. A wife poking around with embryos in the name of science wasn't going to get it.

Maybe once this was all over, if it had indeed been blown out of proportion as Winston suspected, he would have the Haineses come out to the ranch. Betty could be pretty persuasive when she wanted to be; Julia would see that his wife had a life most women would die for.

Betty had been a third-grade teacher, and though she liked her job, she hadn't had to work a day since they were married. She labored instead at taking care of him and their three kids, now grown with children of their own. Children being raised by two loving parents, a mother and a father, the way it should be.

It incensed him that so many kids these days were brought up mostly by babysitters. Jon was troubled by it, too; he worried their boy was learning his sitter's values and habits instead of theirs, and that could be a dangerous thing.

Julia needed to be home with him. She could always get back to her career when the boy was older, and by then, stem cell research would be illegal if Winston had anything to do with it.

The plane jostled through some rough air, which displeased him; he was probably the only defense secretary in history that loathed getting on a plane. Seemed like every damn time he did, there was turbulence, as though the gods got a big kick out of reminding him there were some things he *couldn't* control.

He drained his glass and closed his eyes. Ninety minutes until landing. He wished he could sleep, but that would take a lot more booze than what would be prudent. He needed to be alert when he got to DC.

His thoughts drifted to the new defense structure that would protect the country from cyber-attack—and the critical role he would play in it. If things went according to plan, next year at this time they would break ground on a multi-million-dollar national spectrum research facility just a few miles from his Kansas home. He planned to donate the land, and he needed Jon to shepherd the legislation and make sure the contract was awarded.

But first he had to get him out of that damn house.

❧

JULIA'S VOICE broke the long stretch of silence. "Nobody wants to kill you, Jon." *Except maybe me.*

Jon held his hands against his head like he feared it would shatter into bits.

"Are you okay?" she asked.

He squinted at her. "Those negotiators outside sound different—like they're backing down. But they're not. They're just trying to lure me out of here."

Julia had wondered, too, why the agents outside suddenly started sounding like the whole thing was no big deal. Like her husband's threats and erratic behavior were somehow excusable.

But public officials like Jon didn't get a pass because of their position. Did they?

It had to be a ploy. So Julia would go along. "They're doing that because you told them to leave, Jon. We had an argument; that's all. I'm sure they're watching us, and they can see that you're a lot calmer—that you've put the gun down." It sat on the kitchen counter, several feet away from him.

He scrutinized her face, looking for signs she was playing him.

Julia kept her face neutral, her shoulders relaxed, her demeanor casual as she pulled bread from the cabinet and ham from the refrigerator. "Mayo and mustard?"

Oh god, if I pull this off I deserve an Oscar.

Jon hesitated, and then he nodded.

In a light tone, Julia said, "After lunch, let's go meet with them, explain that we had a fight and you were upset but you're okay now. *We're* okay now."

When he didn't respond, she turned to look at him. Jon stared at her, as if he was trying to read his future in her face.

"Let's just eat, Julia," he said.

8

MARLA DUNSTON lived in a doublewide trailer in a rundown part of Manassas. For several minutes after pulling up to the curb outside her house, Dan sat and took it all in, feeling pity for the woman forced to sacrifice her childhood to raise her brother. Jon had gone on to run for Congress and live like a king while she had gone on to reside in a tin box with a weedy lawn.

As he made his way to the door, Dan was struck by the gulf between the haves and the have-nots—a gulf that was getting wider by the day. He was deeply grateful for the life he had, one where he could afford to have and do most of the things he wanted; but just as deep was the empathy he felt for those less fortunate.

He knocked on the door. A window near the door was open, and he heard a child holler, "Mama! Somebody's at the door!"

The door opened a few inches and a tow-headed boy peeked out.

"Hi," Dan said tentatively. "Is your mother here?"

"Willie, I told you never to ..." The door opened wider, and Dan got his first glimpse of Marla Haines Dunston. "Yes?"

She didn't appear to recognize him, but sometimes TV celebrities looked slightly different in person. Either that or she didn't watch television, which would make her a rare bird indeed.

"Mrs. Dunston, my name is Dan Fielding, and I'm a reporter with NBC. I wondered if I could have a few minutes of your time."

"Why? What's happened?" It was hard to believe she didn't know; obviously he'd been right about her television-viewing habits.

"Uh, your brother, Congressman Haines, is involved in a hostage situation."

Her hand flew to her mouth. "Oh my god ... he's been kidnapped?"

"No, ma'am. He's the hostage taker."

"What? I don't understand. Why ..."

"Mrs. Dunston, could I just come in and talk with you for a few minutes?"

Her expression darkened. "I don't know anything. I haven't seen my brother for years. Sorry." She started to close the door.

"Please, Marla. I'm trying to help him. I don't think he ever intended for things to blow up like this, and I want to help calm it down so he and Julia can get out of there safely."

The woman paused, considering his words. Satisfied that he wasn't there to murder them, she stepped back and opened the door wider. "Okay, I guess you can come in."

"Thank you. I promise I won't take much of your time."

Dan expected the interior of the home to match the tumbledown look of the exterior, but it was clean and tidy. The furniture, though dated, still looked sturdy; an afghan in lively shades of blue and purple hung over the back of the couch and drew attention away from the worn arms. In the corner was an old cabinet-style television with rabbit ears on top, the "ears" wrapped in foil.

Boy, no wonder she doesn't watch TV.

Dan noticed a pile of library books stacked neatly on the coffee table. He was impressed to see, next to the children's books, a biography of Eleanor Roosevelt. He didn't know the first thing about Marla Dunston, but his opinion of her ticked up a couple notches.

The little boy sat back down on the living room floor next to his younger sister. They were using a deck of cards to build roadways for their little metal cars.

"Please sit down," said Marla. "I guess you already know my name—and these are my kids, Willie and Emma."

"Nice to meet you."

"Nice to meet you, too," said Willie, surprising Dan. Emma, blonde and blue-eyed like her brother, gave Dan a shy, dimpled grin before turning back to their game. Though their toys were modest and few, they were happily engaged in building an imaginary town complete with an empty-milk-carton garage.

"Beautiful children," he said. Dan found himself a little choked up; this was definitely not the way he imagined kids to be these days.

Marla smiled. Her cheekbones were prominent in a way that suggested she didn't get enough to eat, and the simple sundress she wore revealed her too-slender build. But Jon's sister was a pretty woman—in a soft, delicate way, not strikingly attractive like her sister-in-law.

"Thank you. What about my nephew, Jackson? Is he in the house, too?"

"No, he's safe. He's with his babysitter."

"Thank god," she said, still shaken from the news. "Would you like something to drink, Mr. Fielding? I have coffee, or apple juice ..."

"A glass of water would be great. And please call me Dan."

The small window air conditioner wasn't running; instead, the windows were open in a futile attempt to create a cool breeze on an unseasonably warm June day. Dan's button-down Oxford shirt quickly dampened with sweat, but the Dunston trio seemed oblivious to the suffocating heat.

Marla pulled a pitcher of water from the refrigerator and poured them both a glass. Dan moved over and sat at the kitchen table; he didn't want to disturb the kids' play with talk of their crazed uncle.

"So, Marla—by the way, is it okay if I call you that?" He was itching to roll up his sleeves and loosen his tie, but he thought it might seem rude.

She nodded.

"Marla, when was the last time you saw your brother?"

Marla's forehead wrinkled as she thought back. "Eight years, I guess. When he and Julia got married."

"So you haven't had any contact with him in all that time?"

"Well … not physical contact, but he sends me some money every month." She glanced at the kids and lowered her voice. "My husband, Ray, left a year and a half ago. Even when he was here, he used all our money to buy beer and pot, so Jon had to help me out. I don't have a job because I can't afford child care, but when the kids go to school, I'm going to go back to work."

"How old are they?"

"Willie's five and Emma's three."

So Willie is the same age as the cousin he's never met.

"I see. So your brother helps you out …"

"Yes. I get food stamps and a little bit of state assistance, and Jon helps me with the rent. He's glad Ray's gone because he never liked him. Thought he was worthless, and it turns out he was right. I should've listened."

Marla was almost *too* forthcoming; Dan felt a twinge of guilt for prying, even though he made a handsome living by meddling in people's lives.

Besides, her words weren't tinged with any kind of emotion. She was just telling it like it was.

"Can you tell me a little about your brother? For instance, what he was like as a kid?"

Marla's face softened. "Jonny had a sweet disposition. In fact, Willie reminds me a lot of my brother. Except that Jon was a lot more sensitive."

"What was his relationship with your parents like?"

"Our dad moved out when my mother was pregnant with him. Jon never knew him."

"I'm sorry. That must've been hard on all of you."

She nodded but didn't elaborate.

"So was Jon close to your mother?"

"My mom worked, and when she was home she was usually in her room. She had really bad depression. Most of the time, it was just Jonny and me, but we managed okay."

"You obviously were a big part of your brother's success. He's done well for himself."

"He has, and I'm really proud of him—though I can't say I had anything to do with it. I think when Julia came into his life, he was finally happy, and that gave him the confidence to do the things he was capable of. My brother was always really smart, but because he kept to himself and didn't have many friends—*any* friends, really—a lot of people didn't know that. Or care."

A sudden thought struck Dan. "Was Jon bullied at school?"

Marla's head dipped slightly, and when she looked back up, her eyes told him he'd struck a nerve. "It started when he was in eighth grade. Jon was small for his age, and this bunch of guys, the so-called 'popular kids,' got their kicks shoving him around and doing mean things to him. It was awful because I wasn't able to protect him."

Dan couldn't fathom being persecuted like that; he was one of the popular kids. Not that he'd ever bullied anyone.

"How long did that go on?"

"Pretty much until he graduated from high school and left for college."

The clearer the picture of Haines that emerged, the more Dan saw the emotional scars that might be driving the man to do irrational things.

"Why didn't the school authorities do anything about it?"

Marla shook her head. "Because I never told them. I begged my mom to, but she was afraid she'd lose her job if she took off work to go see them. She just told Jon to stay out of those kids' way and they'd leave him alone."

"So did that make Jon feel like it was *his* fault he was getting beat up?"

"I know my mother didn't mean it that way, but she couldn't offer much emotional support so that's what happened. I didn't know what to do except comfort him when he came home crying. Jon suffered horribly all through school. He couldn't wait to get out of here."

Dan understood why the man craved power. Payback.

"What's Jon relationship with your mother like now?"

"Nonexistent. My mother has Alzheimer's, so she doesn't know either one of us. The kids and I sometimes take a bus to the nursing home where she is, and she always brightens up when Willie and Emma are around—but she has no idea they're her grandchildren."

My god. Marla's life was like a soap opera.

"Why do you think you and Jon aren't as close as you once were?" he asked gently.

"I love my brother, and I know my brother loves me. I think it's just that I remind him of how hard his life was when he was young. Plus we went our separate ways. I went to work right after high school so I could help with the bills, and Jon went to college when he graduated three years later. I got married, and he didn't like Ray, and then he met Julia and spent most of his time with her. And then my mother moved in with us so I could take care of her, and then ... oh gosh, I'm sorry. I'm sure you didn't want to know all that." She gave him a self-deprecating grin. "I guess the simple answer is that we just lost touch."

Dan smiled back. "That's okay; it helps me understand your brother. How do you feel about your sister-in-law?"

"Oh, I'm totally in awe of her. Beautiful, and talk about smart; she's even more intelligent than my brother. She's by far the best thing that ever happened to him."

Dan had promised not to take up too much of Marla's time, and his own time was growing short. But he had one more question he needed to ask: "Marla, do you think Jon is capable of hurting Julia?"

She hesitated before answering. "I'd like to think he isn't. But to tell you the truth, I don't really know my brother very well any more. I see him on TV sometimes, and he's almost unrecognizable to me. His personality, I mean. Sometimes the way he acts—all full of himself and his opinions—it's like *he's* become some kind of bully. So I just don't know, Dan. But I hope he would never do anything to hurt Julia, because without her, I'm afraid he'd go back to being the sad, lonely person he was before—or worse."

9

A S HE climbed into his shiny new Beemer, complete with performance wheels and carbon fiber mirror caps, Dan felt shallow and materialistic.

Did he really need performance wheels to shuttle himself between home and the office or the gym? Probably not. And what the hell were carbon fiber mirror caps anyway? He suspected they did more to bolster the driver's self-importance than the car's operation. But he wanted the salesman to think he knew something about cars, so he agreed to the extra features as though only a damn fool would pass them up.

It embarrassed him to think his car cost two or three times more than Marla's house.

Dan copped to being a liberal, complete with bleeding heart, but he realized his ideology had always been more theoretical than personal. He had empathized with the less fortunate, been grateful he wasn't one of them, but he'd never felt *guilty* about his lifestyle or possessions.

Until now.

That's because he had never really encountered anyone like Marla. She hadn't had an easy life, and yet it didn't appear to define her or the way she raised her children. It struck Dan that despite all the crap life heaped on her, Marla possessed more grace than anyone he knew—certainly more than his well-heeled group of friends who thought an overcooked steak at The Palm was a crisis of epic proportions.

And she certainly had more grace than her bigwig brother. Did the scars from being bullied never really heal? Had the need for revenge been roiling around inside him all these years?

The Haines siblings had evoked emotions in Dan, and he wanted his viewers to experience a similar response—to *feel* this story, not just see and hear it. An on-camera interview with the sister would certainly add that dimension, perhaps even stir compassion for a politician who often came across as arrogant and unconcerned about the hardships many Americans faced. After all, Haines helped his sister out—even though, to Dan, that assistance seemed awfully paltry.

But who was he to judge? Maybe Marla wouldn't accept any more than that.

Was it fair of him to ask her to do an interview, and would she even be willing? Clearly this was someone who didn't seek the limelight, unlike her brother, but perhaps her desire to help him would override that.

Regardless, he couldn't call right now to ask; Marla didn't own a phone. He made a mental note to pick up a prepaid cell later, and when he returned to drop it off, he'd feel her out about the interview.

In the meantime, he had just two days to put together a compelling piece on Haines, and there were others to question —starting with House Speaker Tom Stallworth.

~

THE NEWS of the hostage incident had been a shock to Julia's colleagues in the Georgetown University Department of Neuroscience, and they were anxious for her safe release and return.

One colleague in particular. Regan interviewed him while Nick was in an adjacent lab doing talking to other scientists and lab assistants.

"So, Dr. Cordova, you and Dr. Haines work pretty closely together?"

He nodded. "We're co-principal investigators. Right now we're working on a major NIH grant that involves the use of assays for high throughput screening to discover chemical probes in the --"

Regan held up a hand. "You lost me at assays, Dr. Cordova."

"Sorry."

Peter Cordova gave a feeble smile, his handsome, olive-skinned face etched with anxiety. He crossed his arms, then uncrossed them.

Regan said, "Forgive me, but I have to ask. Is your relationship with Dr. Haines anything other than a professional one?"

"No," said Cordova. He shoved his hands in the pockets of his lab coat, averting his gaze.

"Are you married?" He wasn't wearing a ring.

He glanced at his feet before looking at her. "I'm going through a divorce, Agent Manning, but I'm not sure how that's relevant."

"We're trying to understand why Jon Haines has taken his wife and son hostage, Dr. Cordova. If he thinks you and Julia are involved ..."

He started to fiddle with the knob on a microscope. "We're not. It's just that we're under a tight deadline on a new grant proposal, and we're at a critical stage in our current project. We've been burning the midnight oil."

"Has she mentioned her husband having any problems with her research?"

"Problems?"

"Resentment over her long hours, discomfort with her work on stem cells ... that sort of thing."

A cloud darkened his expression for a brief moment and then evaporated. "Not that I know of. She doesn't really talk about her husband."

It was painfully obvious he was hiding something. Or obvious he was painfully hiding something.

Regan didn't bother to mask her impatience. "Dr. Cordova, if you have information that could help us get Julia released, now is the time to share it."

His dark eyes welled up. "Agent Manning, I care a great deal about Julia. She is my research partner and friend. If I knew anything that could help get her out of that house, believe me, I would tell you." His lower lip quivered; he was barely holding it together.

His raw pain struck a nerve in Regan. She looked away.

This man could try to hide it all he wanted, but he was head over heels for Julia Haines. Regan wondered if the feelings were mutual; in a way, she hoped they were.

"Try not to worry, Dr. Cordova," she said. But she knew it was like telling the man not to breathe.

&

AS MUCH as she loathed the bombastic talk show host, Regan tuned the car radio to his program to see how badly he was going to stir things up.

"We're finally getting some pushback against the liberals," Baxter Boone gleefully declared. In his daily rants, the commentator referred to moderates as "spineless pussys" and regularly accused them of not having the guts to stand up and prevent their "bleeding-heart liberal brethren" from turning the country into one giant welfare state.

"Folks, I don't know if Congressman Haines is acting out some convoluted political scheme, and frankly I don't care," said Boone. "Either way, it's the boot in the behind that conservatives have needed. We've been sitting on our thumbs, letting the lefties subvert the American way of life for way too long. Pretty soon we'll have as many gay couples running around our neighborhoods as we do normal couples. We'll have kids whose parents are complete strangers because they never see them. We'll have so many foreigners on our shores that nobody understands what the hell anyone's saying. We'll be at the mercy of the Chinese because we've borrowed too much money and we refuse to rein in our spending. We are systematically eroding our moral code and descending into chaos. Mark my words: this country is headed for extinction unless we change course *now*."

Nick turned to Regan, his face twisted into a look of mock terror. "Oh shit, the world is coming to an end."

"We better go pack," said Regan, matching his look.

Nick laughed.

Boone wasn't finished. "People, we have a job to do. And that job is to stand up and fight our way back to American values. Jon Haines may or may not have intended to lead the parade, but intentional or not, right now he's the grand marshal. He got us off our butts and moved us to action. Now it's time for us to use that momentum and band together to do what's right."

It was no surprise that Baxter Boone had seized on the hostage incident to advance his own political views—Regan would expect nothing less from the radical talk show host whose mission in life was to stir up trouble. But with the explosive environment of the last two days, it was an irresponsible and dangerous stunt.

"Too bad somebody doesn't pop that guy," said Regan. "Know any good snipers?"

10

"E HAD no idea, Win," said Stallworth, motioning his guest to the plush upholstered chairs in his office. "Haines never showed signs of anything like this."

"You sure, Tom?" Winston took a sip of Talisker, its rich, smoky flavor a mile-high cut above the airplane scotch. But the alcohol did little to calm his nerves.

"Well, I admit he seemed pretty ambitious, maybe a little too prone to go off half-cocked sometimes, but pull out a gun and hold his wife hostage? That's downright crazy."

Crazy enough to get him expelled from Congress? That action by his colleagues could cause Haines to crack all the way.

Leaving Winston exposed.

He had to make sure he got to him first, make sure his longtime, dutiful aide wasn't suddenly going to start waxing about his days as Winston's chief operations officer at Imhoff-Greyson or later as an assistant secretary at Defense. Both involved way too much sensitive information.

Winston was aware that, at times, he'd been overly supportive of Jon. The man was, as the speaker noted, very ambitious, and Winston had used that hunger to his own advantage.

"I don't think this is a hostage situation," he said. "It looks to me like a simple disagreement between a husband and wife that got blown way out of proportion. I know Jon Haines better than anyone, and believe me, he *isn't* crazy enough to do something like what they're saying."

"Well, you know how the media is, Win. They've gotta blow everything out of proportion to sell papers and draw viewers."

"That may be, but in this political climate, it's damned irresponsible. And it paints Jon in an unfair light. The liberal media would like nothing better than to run him out of office."

The speaker took a sip of his drink before responding. "You and I have been friends a long time, Win. So when you asked for my help with Haines, I was glad to do it. Any friend of yours is a friend of mine; you know that. But Haines, well, I'll do what I can but I'm just not sure I can get House Republicans to stand behind him on this thing." He leaned back in his chair and perched an ankle on the opposite knee, his raised foot twitching like he'd poked his finger into a light socket.

Win fixed his gaze on the speaker, enjoying the man's obvious discomfort. He knew the two-faced Stallworth not only wouldn't stand behind Haines, he'd lead the charge to get rid of him—as long as he wouldn't encounter blowback from Winston.

"Do what you can to assuage the anti-Haines sentiment in the House, Tom. If I have your word you'll do that, I can get this so-called hostage standoff shut down immediately."

Stallworth looked like he'd just been asked to do a press conference in his underwear. "Uh, I'm not sure I can persuade enough R's to back him, Winston. The Democrats are salivating at the prospect of expelling him—especially since he's been such a vocal critic of the president—but in all honesty, his Republican colleagues are going to get hammered at home if they simply overlook Haines' behavior and allow him to remain in Congress."

If Haines was expelled, it would reflect badly on Winston, perhaps diminish his own power at a time when he could least afford it.

Winston turned up the heat. "With the right leadership and some strategic PR, I assure you those Republicans can be persuaded. What I need from you is your commitment to be that leader."

Stallworth squirmed in his seat. "I'll do my best, but--"

"Get it done, Tom, and I'll owe you. I'll make sure you win your next race by a landslide."

"As I said, I'll do my best. You know as well as I do that getting the caucus in line these days is like herding cats. It's not like it was when you were up here, Win, when all of us stuck together. But if you can get Haines out of that house and get him to tell the press that it was all a misunderstanding, it'll help me make the case."

"Excellent," said Winston. He stood up to leave. "Thanks for the drink, Tom. I'll be in touch."

~

SEATED IN the speaker's outer office, Dan heard the door open and saw Winston Jennings depart Stallworth's inner sanctum. He stood up and said, "Hello, Mr. Secretary."

Jennings extended his hand. "Dan. How's it going?"

"Good, sir. Are you enjoying life on the ranch? Must be nice to get out of this town and back somewhere a little more sane."

Jennings barely slowed his pace. "Yes, it's nice to be back home." With that, he was out the door.

Dan smiled, amazed at Jennings' relative cordiality. The former secretary had never taken kindly to people sticking their noses into his business, which meant he despised reporters—Dan in particular because of his tendency to keep digging long after his colleagues had given up and moved on.

Good riddance, you old fart.

The receptionist said, "Mr. Fielding? The speaker will see you now. He just has a couple minutes, though."

"A couple minutes are all I need, Karen. Thank you."

She ushered him in and closed the door, leaving the two men alone.

"Dan! What can I do for you?" Stallworth came around his desk and shook Dan's hand but didn't offer him a seat. His face looked pallid.

"I'm doing a show on Congressman Haines tomorrow night, Mr. Speaker, and I wanted to—"

"Oh, well, I can't help you there, Dan." He retreated behind his desk, as though the piece of furniture would serve as a protective barrier. "It's premature for me to say anything at this point."

"I'm not asking you to predict the outcome of the hostage situation. I'm looking for color on the man himself—what kind of legislator he is, that sort of thing."

"Uh, I don't know that I can add anything you don't already know. Look, Dan, I'm pretty jammed up here ..." His forehead was dappled with perspiration.

"Mr. Speaker," Dan said in a firmer tone, "Jon Haines has obviously become a key member of your party. You've regularly included him in a select group that appears with you on pressers. Was there any indication that the congressman was suffering from acute mental anguish?"

"We're *all* suffering from acute mental anguish up here, Dan," the speaker snapped. "This place is a constant war zone these days." He pointed a finger at the reporter. "And don't quote me."

"I suspect the public has already figured that out, sir."

"Well, be that as it may, I don't have any idea what's behind Haines' actions. Now if you'll excuse me ..."

Dan hated to use his trump card, but he had no choice. "You're not planning to give an exclusive to the *National Journal*, are you?"

Stallworth gave him a sharp look. "Why would I do that?"

"Well," Dan said casually, "I know Elizabeth Fenster does regular features on you, so I thought ..."

"Miss Fenster is from my home state, which gives us a special bond, I guess you could say."

A special bond indeed.

"Aw, that's nice to be able to interact regularly with one of the home folks," said Dan. "So the two of you are personal friends as well?"

Stallworth averted his gaze and sat down. "Not friends, per se; she's a colleague whose work I admire."

"And who shares your taste for Bongo burgers?"

It had been a complete fluke when the pair showed up at the same roadside diner in Silver Spring where Dan happened to be one night. What were the odds? On the way home, Dan had stopped off to buy a lottery ticket.

The well-known politician had been incognito in a Washington Nationals baseball cap and glasses, and the other Bongo's patrons didn't give him a second glance. Dan had been certain the pair would spot him and try to make some excuse, but they were too enamored with each other to pay much attention to their fellow diners. Dan couldn't believe his eyes— and his good fortune—when the speaker slid into the booth next to Elizabeth, their bodies touching. He knew it would come in handy someday.

And that day was today. Dan could see Stallworth trying to figure out what to say without incriminating himself.

"I'm not sure what you're referring to with regard to Miss Fenster, but what is it you want to know, Dan?"

"I want to know what's going on here that would cause Jon Haines to flip out."

The speaker waved him into a chair in front of his desk and dropped his voice to a whisper, just in case the walls had ears. "I believe Jon Haines suffers from some degree of mental illness, so his rather sudden rise in our party might have exposed that. The man is extremely ambitious, and he's been under a lot of pressure over his wife's work—so maybe it pushed him to the breaking point."

"But certainly he was under substantial pressure at Defense, and before that at Imhoff-Greyson. Hell, just working for Winston Jennings would be like constantly having a gun held to your head—and look how long he managed to do that."

The speaker shrugged his shoulders and nodded. "Maybe it's the cumulative effect of all that. To tell you the truth, Dan, I don't know what sent him over the edge, but ..."

Dan waited, but Stallworth didn't finish his thought. "Mr. Speaker, how will the House members respond to this?"

The speaker hesitated, staring at his hands. Finally, he looked up. "I know you try to be fair in your reporting, Dan, and I've always thought you treated me with respect ... even if you were a little rough on me sometimes." He gave a forced laugh.

Dan gave him a polite smile.

"That's why I've tried to be fair with you in return and grant you some time to talk with me when you've asked for it."

"I appreciate that, sir."

"So I'm going to tell you something here, and I'm going to trust you not to repeat it in your piece on Haines. I just think you need it for background."

Dan kept his gaze level. Stallworth was asking him to bury what might be an essential—and perhaps damning—bit of information about Haines.

"Do I have your word?"

Dan was torn. He had a duty to his viewers, but he had to walk a fine line with Stallworth, especially after the veiled accusation of an affair he'd just thrown at him.

"Okay, Mr. Speaker. You have my word."

Stallworth once again hesitated. "Jon Haines is a smart, capable man who made a very bad choice this morning. He may be able to reverse things, somehow find a way to convince the FBI he didn't mean for it to happen, had no intention of setting off a country that is mad as hell and looking for a fight … but regardless of how it comes out, I think he *will* be expelled from Congress unless Winston Jennings pulls out all the stops to save him."

"Why would Jennings do that?"

"Because he takes it personally. Cross Haines and you're crossing him."

"Why?"

"I guess because he took Haines under his wing when he first started practicing law, when he was still wet behind the ears. And Jennings has major plans for Jon's political career. It's almost like he's cloning himself."

"Do you intend to use your influence to keep Haines from expulsion?"

"No, I won't. Even though Winston will be furious and try to run me out of office, right now he can't afford to touch me.

The election is five months off, and he wants to get a new defense infrastructure in place during this Congress—just in case the Dems regain control of the House."

"How does a new defense infrastructure help Jennings? He isn't defense secretary anymore ..."

"He wants to be the linchpin between industry and government. He's already chair of the cybersecurity task force, and he's using that forum to get the policies in place that he wants—things critical to our infrastructure, including financial and information services and the defense industrial base."

"Which could mean substantial benefit to Imhoff-Greyson."

"Exactly. Billions in government contracts. And Jennings' influence expanding a lot further than it was when he was defense secretary."

Dan considered the ramifications; it boggled his mind. "Mr. Speaker, I'm sure you're aware of the rumors that some of the overseas contractors employed by Imhoff—the so-called 'enforcers'—have been used here on occasion. Like when someone opposes Mr. Jennings on something, for example. Do you know if there's any truth to it?"

Stallworth squirmed in his seat. "I don't know anything about that, Dan—frankly, I think it sounds a little paranoid. But I know someone who *does* believe it—the congressman who got his House seat yanked out from under him by Haines. He'll tell you exactly what it's like to be targeted by Winston Jennings."

11

HI, BABE," said Jack. "What's going on back there? Sounds like DC has turned into a combat zone."

"Sure seems like it," said Regan. The lump in her throat made it hard to talk.

"What's wrong, honey?"

"Nothing … well, except that Nick and I are helping out with the Haines deal and the guy won't surrender. The pressure is getting pretty intense."

"Yeah, I bet."

Regan could tell he suspected something else was up; she wasn't her usual perky self. She decided to jump right in. "Jack, I don't think I'm going to be able to make it for Mom and Dad's party." She held her breath and waited.

Jack paused before answering. "Really?"

"Our investigation is at a crucial point right now, and the next couple weeks are going to be crazy." The prickling behind her eyes started in.

"Your parents are going to have a hard time with it, Regan. They're really excited about having the whole family together. Your brother and Stacy can't wait to see you, either. Colin said the kids keep asking how long before they get to see Aunt Regan."

Jack spoke so easily about her family—as though he were already a member of it. More than she was.

Her heart felt like it was being cut to bits. "I know, Jack. Mom will be hurt, and Dad will threaten to disown me."

"That's just his way. You know that. He uses anger to cover up *his* hurt."

She loved this man so much. The tears trickled down her face; she didn't trust herself to speak.

"Regan? Is this about announcing our engagement?"

In a strangled voice, she said, "I don't know, Jack ..."

She heard him sigh. "It's okay. We can figure all that out later. But please don't disappoint your parents just because you aren't ready for us to take that step. Please, you have to come ... even if it's just for a couple days."

"I'll try," she said, barely signing off before the dam burst.

෨

JULIA WEIGHED her options.

Jon dozed on the couch, but was he sleeping soundly? She'd already made that mistake once, believing he was; but this time, she only had to make it out the front door, a mere twenty feet. And she didn't have a small child to protect.

She gazed at his face, sorrow tugging at her heart. *Oh Jon, what happened to you? What made you this way?*

It couldn't just be her career. From the time they met in college, he knew she planned to be a research scientist, that she was intent on finding a cure for Parkinson's. She had watched the disease ravage her beloved Nana and vowed to do something about it.

Jon met her grandmother before she died, and Julia remembered his comment like it was yesterday: "Boy, what I wouldn't give to have a grandma like her." Nana had liked him, too; said he was a keeper.

Now he was an abuser. And if Nana were here, she'd tell Julia to high-tail it out the door. Jon was no longer worth keeping.

But the transformation had been gradual. It was only when she stopped and looked back that Julia realized it had been a long while since her husband had exhibited anything resembling love or kindness to her and Jackson. Recently it had stepped up a notch and turned into hostile, controlling behavior that sprang from his burgeoning sense of entitlement.

The sensitive Jon was still there, beneath all the bluster, but he thought he had to disown that aspect of himself in order to achieve greatness. He hated his sensitivity, hated how easily he felt disappointed by people.

Hated that he'd grown up fatherless.

Winston Jennings had helped to fill the void. Jon saw Winston as someone who cared enough about him to become invested in his life and help him find his way. Someone who toughened him up and taught him not to be a crybaby.

Jon's devotion to Winston had always troubled Julia. In her view, Winston Jennings was a ruthless man who had an abnormal obsession with power. Heaven help anyone who got in his way.

Julia leaned forward, listening; Jon's breathing was more pronounced. He was asleep.

Her chair sat near the fireplace, which meant she had to tiptoe past him to get to the front door. She rose slowly, nearly upright when the phone rang, startling her nearly out of her wits. Jon shot up from the couch and grabbed it. "What?" he said, slightly disoriented.

He listened a moment, then broke into a wide smile. "Oh hi, Winston."

12

"JON, WHAT'S going on? I'm here at the Washington apartment watching all of this on TV, and none of it makes a damn bit of sense."

"It's not what it looks like, Win."

"Good, that's what I figured. Goddamn media; they embellish everything so nobody knows what the hell is happening."

"We're fine."

"I know you are, son, but why don't you go ahead and have Julia come out so you can get the damn FBI out of there? They're creating a spectacle."

"I told them to leave, but they refused. Said they won't go until we both come out, but we're not going to do that."

"Why not, Jon? You just need to come on out of there so everyone can settle down. Tell them you got your gun out this morning because you heard something and thought there was an intruder."

"An intruder? No, I just wanted Julia to listen to me, to stay here and be the kind of wife you said—"

"I said *nothing* about Julia."

Jon didn't respond.

"Son, I think you need to take a little time off. Go somewhere and rest, you and Julia, and then come back and see where things stand with your political career."

"I can't get away right now, Win. We've got some important votes coming up in the House in the next couple weeks, and I also need to move that legislation you wanted."

"You're going to face felony charges, Jon. I'll help you beat them, of course, and Stallworth will get the caucus to stand behind you, but we can't get anywhere until you end this thing."

Jon was quiet. Win wasn't sure what he was thinking.

After a long silence that started to feel awkward, Winston said, "Jon? Are you there?"

"I'm here."

"Will you stop this now? Go ahead and let your wife come out, then we'll have a shot at just a temporary leave of absence from Congress. Especially if Julia will say it was all a big misunderstanding, too."

Another pause on the other end of the line. It made Winston uncomfortable as hell. Jon didn't sound right—but without the benefit of seeing him, it was hard to gauge how far gone he might be.

"Jon?" he said sharply. He was becoming impatient.

"Win, I know you're trying to help us, and I *will* end this." His voice had a strange, dull quality to it.

Winston felt a chill go down his spine. "You're not planning to do anything rash, are you, Jon?"

"I've got to go, Winston."

"Jon, wait--" Winston had no idea what Jon might do, but one thing was certain: his grip on him was loosening. Always before, Jon had done anything he asked.

He needed to make sure his loyalty was still intact. "Okay, son. Maybe when this is all over, you and Julia can come out to Kansas. Bring that boy of yours and spend a little time on the ranch."

"We'll think about that, Winston."

"Good deal. Betty will be thrilled. Goodbye, Jon, and remember what I said. I'll help you with this. I'll be there, wherever they … wherever you are."

As he hung up, the thought crossed Winston's mind that the FBI could have a wiretap on the Haines' home phone. He replayed the conversation in his head and didn't recall anything too incriminating—except maybe the bit about the intruder.

Besides, with everything happening so fast, he seriously doubted the FBI had had its act together enough to go for a wiretap. But Winston, of all people, knew you could never be too careful. From now on, he'd make damn sure he was.

ॐ

THE RINGING phone woke her from a sound sleep. She glanced at the clock: it was only eight p.m.

"Hi, Nick," she said in a lilting voice, trying to sound like she'd been awake.

"Wake up, sleepyhead," said Nick. "We picked up an interesting conversation a little while ago."

Regan sat up on the couch and rubbed her eyes, still swollen from her cry earlier. Her brain was lost in a dense fog. "What? Where are you?"

"I came back to the command post."

She stretched. "Oh. What did you hear?"

"Winston Jennings called Haines. Good thing Al went for that wiretap on the home line."

"Why? What'd Jennings say?"

"Hang on." Nick put his cell phone to the recorder and played the conversation for her.

"Well, I'll be dipped. Jennings told him to lie."

"Yep. He's letting Haines think that with his help, he can still turn things around."

"Hmm, I wonder why Jennings would do that." Regan's brain slowly churned back to life.

"Maybe he thinks Haines is desperate —that he'll commit a murder-suicide or something," said Nick.

"If that were the case, I would think he'd have pushed harder to get Haines to surrender," said Regan. "Seems like he's just making sure Haines still thinks he's the man—that Jennings has the power to take care of the poor little congressman who's lost his way."

"So you think this is more about Jennings than Haines?"

"That's the way it sounds to me. If I were Jennings, I would've stayed in Kansas and kept my distance. At least waited to see how it all played out. So why is Jennings here? What's he worried about?"

"Dunno," said Nick. "But I guess we're not going to get an answer to that tonight. Go back to sleep, partner."

"Like I'll be able to now, thanks to you. I'll head back there." She yawned loudly, trying to shake off her grogginess.

"I knew you would, Reegs; you hate to miss anything."

It was true—and it would also take her mind off Jack. "See you in a few, Nick."

13

WINSTON SAT still while one young woman attached a mike to his tie and another dabbed his face with powder. He checked his watch; five minutes until air time.

The CNN Washington Bureau anchor, Jeremy Traynor, had been ecstatic when Winston called to tell him he'd do an exclusive interview on the Haines situation tonight. Now, Traynor chatted him up while they waited to go on. "How many cattle do you raise back there in Kansas, Mr. Jennings?"

"A few hundred," Winston responded. "Mostly Black Angus."

"A few *hundred*? Boy, I bet those critters keep you busy. How often do you have to feed them?"

Winston smiled patiently. He knew that Traynor, born and bred in New York City, had less-than-zero interest in the daily life of a Kansas cattleman. "This time of year they're on pasture, so they feed themselves."

"Hey, that's great. Gives you more time to play golf, eh? You do have golf courses out there, right?"

"Yes, Jeremy, along with paved roads and indoor plumbing."

"I see. That's great. So is Kansas where you grew up?"

"Yep. Little town called Randolph. It isn't there anymore."

"What, did it get wiped out by a tornado?" Traynor looked slightly amused at the prospect.

"No, it didn't." Winston didn't feel like going into the story of his hometown's demise—that it was flooded when a nearby reservoir was filled. A reservoir built for flood control.

"Isn't it completely flat there?" Traynor looked like he thought the moon would be a more inviting place to settle.

"Not completely flat ... we do have hills. It's beautiful, actually—the wide open spaces, the wheat fields, the sunsets ..."

"Oh man, give me the city any day. I'd feel too vulnerable with all that flat land. You'd never know what was going to hit you."

"I'd rather get hit by weather than by a bullet or a taxi cab," said Winston.

"Well, I guess it's all about what you're used to. So, Mr. Jennings, as soon as we're live, I'll ask you a little bit about your relationship with the congressman—how he behaved when he worked for you, that sort of thing. Then we'll talk a little about what you think is going on here. Sound good?"

Winston nodded. "Fine."

The cocky anchor drummed a couple pencils on the desk like he was Buddy Rich or some damn thing. Winston was already beginning to regret the interview with Traynor.

The cameraman began the countdown with his fingers.

"Welcome to the show," Traynor said to the camera. "I'm Jeremy Traynor, and tonight I'm pleased to have an exclusive interview with former Defense Secretary Winston Jennings. Welcome, Mr. Secretary."

"Nice to be here, Jeremy."

"As you know, the hostage incident involving Congressman Jon Haines and his wife at their suburban Virginia home is causing quite a stir all over the country. Some people think there's more going on here than meets the eye, that the incident may somehow be tied to the congressman's ultraconservative political beliefs."

Traynor paused, expecting Winston to jump in. Winston waited.

"Uh, I want to get your take on that, Mr. Jennings, but first let's talk a little bit about Jon Haines—about the man who served for many years as your chief aide, first at Imhoff-Greyson and later at the Department of Defense."

"Well, Jeremy, Jon Haines is an extremely bright man. He served me—and this country—very capably and with great loyalty. I wholeheartedly supported his run for Congress."

"Has he ever acted in a way that would make you think he might be suffering from some mental issues?"

"Absolutely not. Congressman Haines is one of the most solid, stable people I know."

"So what do you think is motivating his behavior in taking his wife and young boy hostage?" said Traynor.

"Well, Jeremy, I've spoken with the congressman, and he assures me this is all a big misunderstanding. He and his wife had a disagreement last night, and this morning she happened to leave for work a bit earlier than her usual time. Haines heard something and thought it was an intruder, so he got out his gun to investigate."

The news anchor looked like Winston just told him he believed in the Easter Bunny. "I see. So once he discovered it was his wife preparing to leave for work—with their five-year-old son—why didn't he simply let them go? Why detain them—at gunpoint, no less?"

Winston felt like reaching across the table and smacking the smug look off Traynor's face.

"Apparently the argument they had last night flared up again. I don't believe he was in any way threatening her with the gun, he just happened to have it out." It sounded lame, even to Winston's ears.

Traynor let the ludicrous statement sit there a moment. "Considering that the Haines home is surrounded with FBI agents, including snipers with a birds-eye view inside the house, it appears *they* believe, at least, that he *is* threatening her with the gun. If she's free to leave, as you imply, why doesn't she? And why doesn't Congressman Haines simply agree to come out and talk to the agents so the whole incident can be put to rest?"

"The congressman happens to believe, as do I, that there is nothing happening that requires the presence of the FBI. He doesn't feel he has to kowtow to them." Winston's tone was gruff; he fixed the anchor with his most threatening stare.

Traynor squirmed in his chair but pressed on. "With all due respect, Mr. Secretary, that seems like an odd choice. If there's nothing going on that requires their presence, he and Dr. Haines can cooperate with the FBI folks, who are just doing their jobs, and end this thing in an instant. Since Congressman Haines chooses not to, it begs the question of whether there might be more to this story—that it might be some sort of political stunt."

Winston regretted the decision to talk to this little twit. But the interview was live; if he got up and walked out, it would shift the spotlight to him and raise all sorts of questions about his own involvement in the Haines situation.

It took every ounce of self-control he possessed, but he managed to produce a smile. "Jon Haines has earned a stellar reputation during his first term in Congress, Jeremy. He has no need to resort to political stunts. In fact, I believe it's because of the prominence he's achieved that there are some who want to tarnish his reputation. If there are any political stunts going on, I would look in the direction of his Democrat opponent."

Traynor's face registered total surprise. "You're saying his *opponent* is responsible for the standoff?"

Winston had to admit how absurd that sounded; he wished he could reel the words back in.

"Of course not. You're twisting my words, Jeremy. What I'm saying is that the Haines affair is a private matter between a husband and wife. There is nothing political about it—so if there *are* political shenanigans being pulled, they are coming from somewhere else. I'm not specifically pointing the finger at Haines' opponent; I was just saying the possibility exists that someone is stirring this up, that's all."

Winston could see portions of his comments, taken totally out of context, being tweeted around the globe practically before they were out of his mouth. He despised this new world of instant everything.

But he had to admit, if there was a bad choice made by anyone, it was him. He had thought going on CNN, the most politically neutral of the three widely watched cable news stations, would help to assuage the public and calm things down. He had staked his own reputation to help Jon, to reel him back from the abyss.

Instead, he may have harmed them both. To what extent, he couldn't be sure.

"Mr. Secretary, do you believe the argument between Congressman Haines and Dr. Julia Haines, a highly respected scientist in the field of Parkinson's research, had anything to do with her work involving embryonic stem cells?"

"The congressman didn't share with me the details of their disagreement, Jeremy. For all I know, they could have been arguing about which school to send their son to. I think to assume it was based on any political issue is simply grabbing at straws."

"But you don't know for certain, isn't that right?"

Winston glanced down and noticed that his hands were formed into tight fists. He relaxed them and clasped his hands together on the table in front of him. "Of course not. But I repeat what I said earlier: Jon Haines is a bright, capable man. He has served this country well and will do so for many years to come if people will give him the benefit of the doubt. He is a dedicated public servant, and he would not throw it all away in a fit of temper. It simply doesn't jibe with who the man is."

14

JULIA SLOWLY came awake, batting at something bumping against her skull. It took a second to realize it was the barrel of a gun.

She reared back, pushing Jon's arm away as she tried to spring from the chair. He shoved her back down.

"We can't be here anymore, Julia," he said. His tone was eerily flat.

"I—I know, Jon. Let's give ourselves up." But she knew he wasn't talking about *here* as in their house.

"That's not what I mean." He moved the gun back to within an inch of her head.

She couldn't believe she'd fallen asleep; sheer exhaustion had overtaken her fear. Now, staring into Jon's crazed eyes, the fear was back, worse than before. "What *are* you saying?"

"I'm saying I can't do this anymore."

A surge of anger jolted her like an electric shock. "So you've decided *I* can't do this anymore, either. What about Jackson? Do you care about our son at all?"

He blinked, momentarily confused. "He ... he'll have my sister to take care of him."

"Really? How'd that work out for *you*?"

His arm dipped slightly. "Marla sacrificed everything for me. She gave up her own childhood to make sure mine was as good as possible under the circumstances."

"And this is the way you repay her? By murdering us so she again has to sacrifice, this time to raise *our* child?"

"No ... she won't have to sacrifice. She can live here ... and have more than she's ever had before ..."

"Marla would never want that kind of tradeoff—a fancy house and a bunch of possessions in exchange for her dead brother and sister-in-law." She stood up and faced him squarely, defiant. "If you want to shoot me, go ahead, but I'll be damned if I'm going to sit here, cowering like a cornered animal, praying you won't pull the trigger."

Tears sprang to his eyes. "Please, Julia, I can't live without you. I know you're going to leave me, and I can't—"

"You need help, Jon. Your political career is eating you up. Ever since you got elected to Congress, you've become increasingly ...unpredictable." She wanted to say *cruel and demanding,* but she had to be careful. He *was* still holding a gun, teetering on the brink of sanity.

His arm dropped to his side and his head to his chest.

Julia started to breathe again.

"Leave," he said.

"Come with me." If he didn't, Julia knew it was the last time she'd see him alive.

He shook his head.

"I'm not going to leave and let you take your life, Jon." Her eyes filled with tears. "Please ... we'll get help together."

"I—I can't ... I need to lie down, Julia." He shuffled over to the couch and stretched out on his back, closing his eyes. He held the gun loosely, propped on his midsection.

Julia stood there, torn by indecision. Stay or go? *What should I do?*

Could she get someone to come in and try to talk to him? What if he shot them? Right now, he didn't look threatening, he looked defeated. But would he suddenly escalate again?

"Jon?"

He didn't answer. She wasn't sure if he'd fallen asleep or had just checked out emotionally.

Julia sat back down, furious at him for manipulating her with the threat of suicide.

But she couldn't walk away.

15

WINSTON HAD been right. Snippets of his comments on CNN ricocheted around Twitter Land like a pinball, painting him as some kind of fool.

He didn't appreciate it—and with the help of an eager new techie they hired at Imhoff, an MIT whiz kid unfettered by any kind of conscience, Jeremy Traynor would suffer a little discomfort of his own.

"Why don't you just come home, honey?" Betty said sympathetically. "You've done enough to try to help him. Jon got himself into this mess; let him get himself out of it."

"It's just a misinterpretation, Betty. He and Julia seem to be talking things over, so I'm sure they'll get it worked out. I invited them to come out to the ranch."

Betty was quiet a moment. "But isn't he going to be in jail?"

"For a little while, maybe, but this thing has gotten blown way out of proportion. Typical media hysteria."

"I know, Win, but it just seems so odd that he would take his family *hostage*. Isn't that kidnapping? Whatever it is, it's not normal."

In an irritated voice, he said, "I *told* you, Betty. He wasn't trying to create a hostage situation, he just didn't want Julia to leave without trying to resolve their problems. She shouldn't have tried to escape like that."

"You think it's *her* fault?" Betty's voice had taken on an edge that Winston didn't like.

"I don't want to discuss it. I don't know whose fault it is, and frankly I don't care."

Betty was silent a moment. Winston wished he hadn't called.

"I just think it'd odd. Don't you? For heaven's sake, Winston, he worked for you for—"

"*Enough!*" he shouted. "Jesus, woman, you don't listen. I said I don't know what's going on with Haines. Obviously he has some issues."

"Fine," Betty said, subdued. He had hurt her feelings.

Winston softened his tone. "Listen, Betts, it'll all get settled. Things will be fine. How's Gert?"

"Moping around like she's lost her best friend. Which I guess she has. She spends most of her time lying on the veranda, watching the road for your pickup."

"Tell her I'll be back soon," he said with a chuckle. He missed that sweet old hound.

❧

REGAN FLIPPED on the TV while she ate her yogurt and prepared to leave for work. The size of the crowd on the Mall, shouting and carrying picket signs, was getting worrisome—a disorganized mob with only their anger in common.

The decision by Jon Haines to take his wife and son hostage symbolized the political divisiveness gripping the country. People on both sides felt threatened.

On the screen, a female reporter held a mike in front of a bearded man, his eyes fierce with conviction. "Jon Haines is a hero. This courageous act of his embodies the issues Americans care the most about: the right to keep and bear arms, respect for the unborn, the sanctity of marriage—between a man and a woman, by the way—and last but not least, that the government has *no right* to come in and tell us how to live our lives. It's the FBI that's the problem here, not Congressman Haines." Men on either side of him nodded their heads in agreement and clapped.

"Oh, right," Regan muttered to herself. "It's *our* fault."

"So, sir, you think the congressman is using this standoff to send a political message?"

"That's *exactly* what he's doing. Finally there's a politician who's willing to put it all on the line to help save the values this country was founded on. He's willing to *do* something, not just talk about it. We need to make Jon Haines our next president."

The group burst into a rousing cheer. One guy yelled, "Haines for president!"

Regan watched with dismay, her half-eaten yogurt all but forgotten.

When the group simmered down, the reporter asked the bearded man, "Sir, what about the former defense secretary's comment that this standoff is not about anything political?"

"All due respect to Winston Jennings—he's a great patriot and all that—but he's dead wrong here. He's just trying to calm everybody down, but now is not the time for that. Jennings knows better than anyone that Haines is deeply committed to his beliefs. We need to stand up and support the congressman, not silence him."

"Crap," said Regan as she grabbed her bag and raced out the door.

∾

THE RINGING phone went unanswered.

Julia said nothing; she knew it would be futile. Jon heard the man with the beard and saw his chance at redemption.

"We can turn this thing around," he announced triumphantly.

As she watched Jon's transformation with dismay, Julia's own feelings went from compassion to pure loathing. "So what's the plan, Jon? It's been more than twenty-four hours now. How much longer?" The fury in her voice was deliberate and unmistakable.

But she was also furious with herself. Why hadn't she left when she had the chance instead of valiantly trying to save Jon from himself?

"After the sun goes down tonight," he replied, undaunted by her tone.

Her heart sank another notch; that was a good fifteen hours away. "Why wait until then?"

"I'd rather leave in the dark."

"Why?"

"Because I want to use it to my advantage."

"I guess I don't see how the darkness does that for you."

"The spotlight will be on me ... literally. My supporters won't see all the cops and news people and all that stuff; they won't see anything but me walking out of this house, head held high, with you by my side. It's a powerful image, Julia—one they'll remember when all of this blows over." He spoke in a rush, an elated expression on his face.

She gaped at him. "Do you think there won't be harsh consequences for this, Jon?"

"Of course I know there will be some legal consequences. You may recall that I *am* a lawyer. But no one got hurt and I don't have any prior arrests. I doubt I'll even have to do any time, but if I do, it'll be in one of those minimum-security places that's more like a hotel than a prison."

It sickened Julia to think there was any chance Jon might walk away with little more than a slap on the wrist—and then come back and resume chasing his political ambitions.

If he did, it would be without her.

"Aren't you going to be expelled from Congress?"

"Winston will make sure it doesn't happen," said Jon, distracted by the images on the TV screen. "Even if it did, it wouldn't mean I'm finished. It's clear I have a lot of supporters." He gestured to the TV.

"So you're going to try to make people think this was all a political stunt?"

She could practically see his mind racing. "Yes, I am. Julia, don't you see? This turned out better than I could have planned. People see me as bold, standing up for what's right in a way that's unprecedented in its courageousness. I'll be able to use that big time."

The depth of her husband's delusion was truly stunning.

"By challenging me and my work? By acting like you're just trying to keep the little woman in her place?"

"Well, it's the truth, isn't it, Julia? I told you that this morning. I want you to give up your work and stay home for now. It's the right thing to do ... you know it is. We both want what's best for Jackson."

What's best for Jackson, she wanted to say, *is for he and I to never lay eyes on you again.*

But right now, Jon was riding on the bipolar express. She had no choice but to keep her mouth shut and put up with him for a few more hours.

She had never been more anxious to see the sun to go down.

16

REGAN AND Nick arrived back at the command post.

"He says he'll surrender at sundown," Al said wearily. He looked like he had aged ten years overnight.

"Is Director Tate going to go along with that?" asked Regan. If it meant Haines would give himself up in a fairly calm state, allowing their corruption investigation to proceed, it might be a good thing—but a lot of *bad* things could happen over the course of a day.

"Reluctantly," said Al. "The coverage on TV has gotten a lot more revved up—not only what protestors are saying but also all these so-called TV 'analysts'—and now there's a concern that we might turn Haines into a martyr if we take him out."

"For christsakes, it doesn't have to be a kill shot," Nick groused. "Why are we letting this guy run the show?"

"Because it *is* a show. The media coverage on this thing is massive, Nick. Every move we make is getting beamed all over the damn world. We can't afford a screw-up—and we're not going to make Haines a hero."

"Those snipers aren't amateurs, Al," said Nick.

"I understand that—and if it were up to me, I'd have shut the son-of-a-bitch down last night."

"I wonder where Haines is mentally right now," said Regan.

"Nuttier than a goddamn fruitcake," said Al. "I feel sorry for that poor wife of his."

Regan did, too. Would Julia Haines be able to hang on another day?

It felt incredibly risky. The negotiator in Regan scrambled for ways to coax him out sooner.

"I wonder if his sister might be able to help us," she said.

"Or his mother," said Al. "Is she still alive?"

"His mother has Alzheimer's and lives in a nursing home," said Nick. "The sister, his only sibling, lives in Manassas, but we're not sure how close the two of them are. We haven't interviewed her because we didn't want her to tip him off that we were investigating him."

"C'mon, Nick," said Regan. "Let's go get to know Marla Dunston."

ॐ

THE LATE-MODEL Beemer seemed out of place in front of the rundown trailer.

"Wow, do you suppose that's hers?" said Nick.

Regan spotted the press sticker on the windshield. "Nope. It's a reporter."

"One that's doing pretty darn well, I'd say."

They made their way to the front door and knocked. A slightly built blonde woman answered; after they identified themselves, Marla invited them in.

Dan Fielding was sitting at the kitchen table drinking coffee. He stood and introduced himself.

Nick was too star struck to speak; Regan knew he was a huge fan of the reporter and watched Fielding's show religiously.

"I'm doing a piece on the congressman this week," Fielding explained. "Mrs. Dunston has agreed to be interviewed, so we're just waiting on my camera crew."

"I see, Mr. Fielding," said Regan. "Right now, though, we need to conduct our own interview with Mrs. Dunston. If we could ask you to step outside ..."

"I don't mind if he stays, Agent Manning," said Marla. "There's nothing I would say to you that I haven't already said to him."

Regan noticed Marla's two children sitting quietly on the couch, watching the activity with rapt faces. Clearly it was a lot more excitement than they were used to.

"Hi, guys," she said. "My name's Regan. What's yours?"

"I'm Willie and this is Emma." Willie held out his hand, so Emma followed suit.

It charmed the socks off Regan. She shook each of their hands. "It's very nice to meet you both. That guy over there is my partner, Nick Jenesco."

Nick waved. "Hey, guys."

They waved back. Regan couldn't believe how polite they were—and how damn cute. Miniature replicas of their mom.

"Mama, can we watch Backyardigans?" Willie asked in a stage whisper.

"My two nieces love that show," Regan whispered back.

"You can watch it with us if you want," said Willie.

Regan felt like hugging the boy but touched his arm instead. "Thank you, Willie, but I better do my work."

Marla came over and turned on the TV and the kids sat down on the floor to watch Pablo and the gang. With only rabbit ears for reception, the picture wasn't that great, but Willie and Emma didn't seem to mind.

The young mother appeared fairly relaxed, despite having her home invaded by people asking her questions about her brother. "So, Mrs. Dunston--"

"You can call me Marla. And can I get you something to drink?"

Regan and Nick both accepted a cup of coffee and the four adults sat down at the kitchen table. Nick was quieter than usual; a couple of times, Regan looked at him to see if he had questions of his own, but he pretty much left the interview to her. She planned to tease him mercilessly when they were alone.

After Marla told them about her childhood and painted a clearer picture of Jon, including their current relationship, Regan said, "Marla, would you be willing to come with us to his place? See if he'll talk to you?"

Marla hesitated. "I don't have anyone to watch the kids ..."

"Don't worry; we'll take care of that."

"Well ... okay then," she said. "I'm not sure if he'll listen to me, but I'm willing to try."

"That's all we can ask," said Regan. "Let's go."

Perhaps his sister was the one person who could get through to him. If not, they were rapidly running out of options.

17

OUTSIDE, NICK and Dan bonded while Regan got Marla and the kids settled in the SUV.

"Wow," said Willie, his eyes wide. "This is *cool*."

"Yeah, it's a pretty fun car," said Regan. "When we get close to your uncle's, we'll run lights and sirens so you can see what that's like."

Regan caught a glimpse of Marla's face in the rearview mirror. She smiled at her son's excitement, but her eyes revealed her anxiety. It had been a long time since she'd seen or talked to her brother; doing so under these circumstances clearly wasn't the way she would have chosen.

Regan rolled down her window. "C'mon, Nick!"

Nick waved at Dan and moved toward the car. When he got in, Regan said, "I hate to pull you away from you new BFF, but we have work to do, remember?"

"I *was* working," Nick said defensively. "We were talking about what he's putting together for his show."

"Ah, I see. I'm surprised he didn't ask you to be on it to give the FBI angle."

"He did, actually. I declined."

Regan broke into a big smile. "Dang, Special Agent Nicholas Jenesco gives up his shot at fame. Oh well, since that's the case, could you put in a call to Rosie Pearson? Ask her if she'd mind watching Jackson's cousins for a little while."

Nick made the call and reported that Rosie was more than happy to have them. Thought it would be really good for Jackson, too.

Marla said, "Guys, remember your cousin I told you about?"

Willie nodded; Emma looked puzzled but nodded along with her brother.

"You get to meet Jackson. He's your age, Willie."

"Oh, boy!" Willie clapped his hands.

The kids and their mother were quiet for the rest of the ride to Rosie's house. They went inside, and after a minute or two of shyness between them, the kids dashed off to play in the back yard.

"I hope they won't be any trouble, Mrs. Pearson," said Marla.

Rosie took hold of her hands. "They're lovely children, Mrs. Dunston. We're happy to have them as long as you need us to. I just pray your brother will listen to you."

ﺮ

"HAINES SAYS he'll surrender at sundown," Stallworth told Winston. "I don't like waiting that long, but Tate thinks under the circumstances it'll be best. I just hope someone down on the Mall doesn't get shot before then; those gun protests are getting tense. People are riled up like I've never seen before, Win."

"I'll see if I can put a lid on this thing. The sooner we can get the media backed off, the better off we'll all be."

Stallworth grinned. "Yeah, I saw how you got chewed up on CNN last night. Traynor was trying to come across as this big hard-hitting journalist, and--"

"Traynor's a clown. I shouldn't have agreed to the interview. But we've all been there, right?" It was a gentle poke to remind the speaker that he was getting chewed up daily.

"Yeah, ain't that the truth. The decent interviews are more the exception than the rule these days." He gave a humorless laugh.

"By the way, I saw Dan Fielding waiting to talk to you yesterday. Better watch your back, Tom; that guy's a shark."

~

MARLA'S UNEXPECTED departure threw off Dan's schedule for the day. He would have to try to tape their interview near the scene of the hostage standoff rather than make another trip to Manassas.

He was concerned about her vulnerability. She was willing to do just about anything to help her brother, and he was worried Jon might rebuke her if she tried to talk him out of the house.

If Jon did treat her badly, it would break Marla's heart—perhaps even damage their relationship beyond repair. And the poor woman had too few relationships as it was.

As Dan sped along behind the black SUV on the way to Montclair, he made a call to his producer to discuss the taping of the news package. Then he called a couple other sources, hoping to tease out more information about what might have led to Haines' bizarre actions.

None of his political contacts wanted to comment. Not even the D's.

Speaker Stallworth may think the rumors about the former defense secretary and his clandestine team of enforcers were nothing but paranoia, but others believed it enough not to test the theory.

One thing was obvious: Winston Jennings still had the power to open doors and close mouths.

18

I T HAD been a long night with little sleep, but Jon seemed back on solid ground. Those vocal supporters on TV had done wonders for his morale.

They sat in the kitchen, sipping their coffee in silence. Finally, he met her eyes. "Have I made you afraid of me? I mean, not just these last two days, but before that. Have I?"

Julia felt the tears welling up in her eyes. She nodded. "You're just so driven, Jon. It's like your political ambition has clouded everything else—things that used to matter so much to you."

"Like you and Jackson."

"Not only who we are as a family, but who I am as a scientist. You're asking me to give up something I love—something I'm good at and that I'm passionate about."

Jon leaned forward. "That's the way I feel about my political career, Julia. I'm passionate about doing things to help make this country better."

"But the difference is that I'm not asking you to give up anything to support me in *my* efforts to make the country better. You're asking me to put my work aside and be part of *your* career."

She saw him stiffen. "That's because your work is at odds with the party platform. If you continue, it kills my chances of getting anywhere politically. I just think if you really cared about me--"

Julia stared at him, anger rising in her chest. "What do you mean, *if I cared about you?* That's not only manipulative, it's offensive, Jon. And I don't understand why it is that you and your pals believe a man's career is more important than a woman's."

Jon's voice took on an edge. "Because women have traditionally taken care of the home and family. And I believe it's that break with tradition that has caused the majority of the problems in our country."

"You sound just like Winston Jennings."

"That's because he's right."

Julia jumped up and began pacing. "So you believe if we just go back to watching 'Father Knows Best' and mothers stay home with the kids all day, we'll return America to greatness?" Her voice dripped with sarcasm.

"I do, Julia," he said, his tone pleading. "I know that sounds sexist. I understand that. But women are simply better at taking care of children and handling all the things that keep families functioning properly. Men are lousy at multi-tasking, whereas women not only see that the kids do their homework and have lunch money and go to the dentist when they're supposed to, but they also nurture them so they grow up with the confidence they need to be successful."

"Oh, so the boys can become leaders and the girls can become mothers, right? Am I understanding correctly?"

"No, Julia, you're not. What I'm saying is that you do both things well—family *and* career. I'm just asking that you don't do them at the same time. You can go back to your career when Jackson—and any other kids we have—are in school fulltime."

Any other kids we have? Is he delusional?

Yes, he is, she reminded herself. *Otherwise, our house wouldn't be surrounded by cops pointing guns at us.*

Their marriage was over. No amount of discussion was going to change that.

"I just don't think we're going to be able to get past this, Jon." She wrapped her arms around her middle and stared at the floor.

Jon jumped up and rushed over to her. "This standoff? I told you I was sorry ..."

"No, Jon, I mean the way we want to live our lives. I love you, but I love my work, too."

"You love me but you're willing to give me up, unlike your job," he said bitterly.

"My job isn't asking me to choose."

"And your job includes Peter. Admit it, Julia, he's the one you really love."

"I love *working* with Peter. We share a commitment to our research."

"And *we* share a commitment to our child."

Julia gazed at her husband. "I'm sorry, Jon. Please let me go."

Jon grabbed her arms. "No! Julia, please ..."

Julia winced.

Jon looked down at the purple bruises that had blossomed on her upper arm from the day before. He released his grip and stepped back, a stunned expression on his face. "Did I do that?"

Julia nodded.

"I won't lay a finger on you again, Julia. I *swear*. Please don't leave me ... I need you!"

"I'm holding you back, Jon. Without me, there will be no stopping you. I'm a hindrance, not a help. You have to see that."

Jon stared at her for a long moment, then turned and left the kitchen.

Julia followed him to the living room, unsure what to do. Should she sit down? Make a run for the door?

Jon sat down on the couch and turned on the television, staring at the images on the screen. The standoff still dominated the networks with split-screen visuals; the usual programming was suspended while they all tried to dissect what was happening in Montclair.

Julia looked for the gun; she spotted it on the end table. Easily within Jon's reach.

"I'm going to take a shower," she announced. She gave Jon a once-over, sending a clear message that he might want to do the same before his dramatic exit. Otherwise, he would look more like a skid-row bum than the future president he hoped to be.

Pathetic, she thought as she trudged toward the stairs. She spotted her cell phone on the table in the foyer. The battery was dead; she picked it up to take it upstairs and plug it in while she showered.

"Leave it," Jon snapped.

"I was just going to recharge the battery," she snapped back. "Did you think I was going to call the cavalry to come and rescue me? Well, look outside—they're already here."

"I don't like your tone, Julia."

"Tough shit, Jon." She marched up the stairs.

Jon stood and followed her up.

"What, you're going to guard me while I take a shower?" She stared at him with contempt.

"I'm just going to rest on the bed."

"Why, Jon, are you afraid I'm going to fling myself out the window?"

He gave her a smoldering look but said nothing.

"Oh, for god's sake." She stomped into the master bathroom and slammed the door.

Actually, she *might* have flung herself out the window if he hadn't followed her. She'd had enough. All she wanted was to get back to Jackson, back to her work, back to Peter. Away from Jon.

She knew how frantic Peter had to be. His feelings for her were so obvious, had been for a long time, so why hadn't she told him she felt the same way?

Because she didn't want to break up his marriage. It broke up anyway, and now hers was over, too.

The thought that they might be together soothed her. For the remaining hours until this nightmare was over, Julia would cling to those images.

She was about to step into the shower when she heard the home phone line ring. She bristled as Jon let it go to the answering machine. Then she heard the negotiator's voice: "Congressman, your sister is here. She wants to talk to you. Would you please pick up?"

Julia threw on her robe and opened the door. Jon lay on the bed, a strange expression on his face.

"Jon? Marla is out there. She wants to help you."

His eyes became moist. "I can't believe she'd do this," he muttered. "She's the only one I trusted."

19

MARLA GLANCED over at Regan. "I'm not surprised he won't pick up. Jon retreats into a shell when he's upset. Mind if I try using the bullhorn?"

Regan turned to the negotiator. "Okay with you, Tess?"

"Yes, of course," she replied. She handed the device to Marla and showed her which button to push.

"Jon? It's Marla. I came here to help you. I won't let anybody hurt you, I promise. Please talk to me."

Regan, watching the house through binoculars, saw Jon peering out the same upstairs window where Julia had tossed Jackson to the SWAT team below. Haines was trying to spot his sister, but she was out of sight behind a stand of trees and rose bushes.

"He's looking out the window, Marla. Tell him you're going to call him so you can talk privately." She put on headphones so she could hear both sides of the conversation if he answered.

Jon picked up on the third ring. "Why are you doing this, Marla? They're just using you to get to me. Those agents don't care about you *or* me."

"*I* care about you, Jonny. I can't stand to see you acting like this. This isn't who you are."

For a moment, he was silent. "You don't know me anymore, Marla."

"Yes, I do. People don't lose their basic goodness. I know how hard things have been for you sometimes, but you've overcome them. I mean, just look at you! You're a member of Congress. And you have a beautiful family. Don't let those things slip away."

"I won't. I just have to make Julia go along with--"

"No, Jon. It's not your place to make Julia do anything. Besides, this isn't about Julia. It's about our parents. You felt neglected. *We* felt neglected. But we're okay, aren't we? We survived."

"I don't want my boy to grow up the way we did," he whined. "He needs his mother to be there, just the way you're there for your kids. You've *always* been there, Marla."

"You're confusing things, Jon. The situation isn't the same at all. Julia has so much to give the world—she can do that and still be a great mom."

"See? I knew they'd brainwash you, make you--"

"Stop it," Marla snapped. "Stop your ridiculous little pity party."

Her sudden sharp tone was like a cracking whip. Regan glanced at Nick and Al; they were as astonished as she was. This wisp of a woman was a hell of a lot stronger than she looked.

"It's time to end this," Marla said firmly, forestalling any argument. "You and Julia need to come out now. It's gone on long enough, and it's upsetting people. Jackson needs you guys."

Haines didn't respond. Regan had a sinking feeling; was Marla pushing him *too* hard, given his mental state? Had it been a mistake to bring her in?

"Marla," she whispered, "what if he--"

Marla held the phone against her hip for a moment. "It's okay, Regan. Really. This is what he does."

"I understand that, but he's not a kid anymore. This is a *hostage* situation, and we don't know how unstable he might be right now."

"I know, but I still think he'll listen to me." Marla put the phone back to her ear and waited.

After another minute that felt like an hour, he said, "Okay."

Regan gaped at Marla.

The woman nodded. "Good, Jonny. I'm proud of you. And like I said, I'll make sure nobody hurts you. C'mon out."

❧

J ON HUNG up the phone and looked at her. "Marla begged me to end this. I said I would."

Julia smiled for the first time in two days. "Thank you, Jon." She stepped out of her robe and slipped her clothes back on. She could bathe at the townhouse as soon as this was over and Jon had been taken away.

"I'm going to get cleaned up first," he said, moving toward the master bathroom.

Julia felt a surge of impatience, and then it dawned on her: she could escape while he was in the shower. She gave a quick nod.

He stepped back out of the bathroom and touched her arm gently. "Will you wait for me, Julia? Can we walk out together? I know I probably don't have the right to ask you that, but I want us to be able to resolve our issues on our own, away from the media glare. If we leave together and we look perfectly normal, there won't be much for them to talk about. This will all go away much quicker."

Julia gave it some thought; she was as eager to avoid drama as he was, ready to put it all behind her and get back to her work. There would be a divorce either way—and he was going to be arrested either way, too.

"You promise this is it, Jon? You *will* surrender?"

"I promise. I just don't want to leave looking like this. Give me ten minutes, okay? Then I'll be ready."

Julia stared at his face, looked into his eyes. He held her gaze; he *did* seem ready. Or at least resigned to his fate.

She nodded and sat down on the end of the bed. When she heard the water start to run, she got up and looked out the window. A sea of FBI agents surrounded the house, and in the distance, police officers of every stripe waited. It was a daunting sight.

How would they all react when the two of them stepped out the door? Would they slam Jon to the ground and cuff him? Or would the fact that he was dressed as if he were heading off to the halls of Congress forestall that?

And what about her? Would she be whisked off someplace for questioning?

She sat back down on the bed. All she cared about was seeing Jackson. She would submit to a lengthy interview if necessary, as long as she could have a little time with her son first.

Julia wondered what Jon was thinking as he stood in the shower, water raining down on his head. This wasn't exactly the exit he envisioned; what if he reneged?

A sudden knot gripped her stomach. *Go. Run.*

She got up just as the bathroom door opened. Jon stood there with a towel wrapped around his waist, curly wisps of wet hair plastered against his forehead, arms hanging at his sides. He looked like a lost little boy.

It took her back to the first time she saw him in the library at UVa; he was sitting at a long table by himself, a pile of books in front of him, surreptitiously watching her as she strolled by. She made eye contact and smiled, which seemed to catch him off guard. A few minutes later, she left her friends at another table and went over to sit with him. Something about Jon drew her— beyond the fact that he was a really cute boy. She felt his utter aloneness, sensed his hunger for connection. So she connected.

The memory filled her with deep sadness.

"Is my gray suit back from the cleaners?" he asked.

It was his favorite; he wanted to look his best. "I'll check," she said.

Julia moved over to the walk-in closet. She spotted the suit, draped in clear plastic, and reached up to get it. Just as she did, she felt a crushing blow to the back of her head, pitching her forward into darkness.

20

REGAN HAD a sinking feeling. "What's taking so long? It's been fifteen minutes."

Al spoke into his mouthpiece. "Tess? Make another call. See what the holdup is."

"Maybe he's just getting himself pulled together first," said Marla. "My brother's really particular about the way he looks."

Perhaps she was right. Maybe Jon wanted to exit the house looking as well-groomed as possible so the footage that was beamed all over the planet wouldn't portray him as the unhinged nutbag he truly was.

She heard Tess through her headphones. "No answer, boss."

Al said, "Sierra One, do you have a visual?"

"Negative," was the reply.

"Sierra Two?"

"Negative."

"Shit," said Al. He stomped over to the negotiation area and grabbed the bullhorn. "This is Agent Al Rinehart, head of the Crisis Negotiation Unit. Congressman, you need to exit the house *now*." He waited a few moments, then hit the broadcast button again. "You have sixty seconds to come outside with your hands where we can see them. Otherwise, the tactical team will enter the house and remove you by force."

"Should I talk to him again?" said Marla, her eyes riddled with angst. "Please, Agent Manning, let me try again."

Regan turned and put her hands on the woman's shoulders. "You did a great job, Marla. But it looks like he changed his mind about coming out. I know you're concerned about your brother, but we need to move you back for your own safety."

Marla started to weep. "I can't leave him to—"

"Marla, please." Regan motioned to one of the other agents in the command post. "Nate, could you escort Mrs. Dunston to the police officers on the outer perimeter? Thanks." She turned back to Marla. "You can wait in one of the police cars over there and I'll come and find you as soon as this is over."

Marla paused, then she nodded and moved off with the agent.

Regan went over to Nick, whose eyes were riveted on the house. "Bet you wish you had your sniper rifle about now, huh?"

"Yep," said Nick. "The second he stepped into view, *blam*. Not enough to kill him, just enough to convince him we're through fuckin' around."

"Wonder why they haven't tossed a flashbang in there to get him moving."

"Because somebody up top told Al he had to play nice. Stallworth has Tate scared shitless that we're going to screw up and it'll be broadcast all the way to Timbuktu."

Al's terse voice came through their headphones. "SWAT, move in. Repeat, move in."

They watched, holding their breath as the tactical team converged on the house like a swarm of bats.

Seconds later, they stared in shock as the back side of the house erupted in flames.

BY THE time the firetruck on scene started pumping water on the burning house, the fire had spread to the surrounding woods. From there it would be just a short hop to the seventeen-thousand-acre Prince William Forest Park. The unusually hot summer and lack of rain meant there would be an abundance of dry timber to feed the flames.

Regan watched Al scramble to control the chaos that had suddenly exploded in front of their eyes. "Call the park superintendent and tell them to evacuate," he screamed at one of the CIRG agents before rushing over to see how many of the tac team members were down. A half dozen of them remained poised with weapons drawn in case Haines ran out of the burning house.

"My god, Nick, what happened?" said Regan.

"I don't know; did *we* do that?"

Al came over to them, his face grave. "Two of our guys were hit with debris; they're in bad shape. Several more have injuries that don't appear to be critical."

"Damn," said Nick. "Do we know the source of the explosion?"

"We know it was triggered from inside the house."

"A bomb?"

"Don't know yet, Nick."

"If he had a bomb in there, he was never going to give himself up," said Regan. "He planned a murder-suicide all along. So maybe the fact that he found Julia leaving yesterday morning wasn't really the trigger—he had already decided to do something drastic."

It was a subtle difference, but it went to Jon Haines' level of insanity.

"Do we know if either of them survived?" said Nick.

Al shook his head. "Not yet ... oh wait, they're bringing somebody out." They ran over to where firemen carted a limp body out the front door.

It was the congressman. "He's still alive," shouted one of the paramedics. Other emergency workers ran over with a stretcher.

Regan waited, scarcely breathing. *What about Julia?* She watched, both horrified and mesmerized, as the massive flames devoured the house, crackling and popping as they chewed the wooden structure like a ravenous beast.

She looked up and saw firefighters pull Julia's motionless body through an upstairs window, the same one she had used to toss her son to safety. The men carefully descended the ladder, then laid her on the ground. Paramedics rushed over and placed an oxygen mask over her face.

Regan ran over, too. "Is she alive?"

"Barely," said one of the paramedics. "Her pulse is weak." He turned and shouted, "Get a board over here!"

A Medevac chopper landed on the lawn, and Julia was quickly loaded inside, along with the SWAT team member who had suffered the most critical injuries. A minute later, the helicopter lifted off, bound for a DC hospital.

The paramedics had summoned another one for Jon, who was awake and responsive. He was loaded on the second chopper, the onboard Medevac team joined by two police officers and a CIRG agent. A third chopper was on its way to pick up the other two injured SWAT guys.

More firetrucks arrived to douse the flames, but the house was a total loss. One crew continued to spray water on the hot spots while the other crews raced off to contain the forest fire.

Regan felt dazed. One minute, everything was hushed while they watched and waited for Jon to come out like he promised, and the next, it had burst into a wild cacophony of sound—thunderous explosion and roar of fire, piercing sirens, choppers circling overhead, and everywhere, people shouting. Cops and emergency personnel doing what they do to somehow try and get things under control and prevent loss of life.

Al looked equally stunned at how quickly everything had gone so horribly wrong. Regan knew he would be questioning his own actions for a long time to come.

"It's not your fault, Al," she said softly.

"I should've sent SWAT in sooner. I gave him too much time. He was never going to come out of there …"

"There was no way to know that. He played us."

Al shook his head and looked at his feet.

Regan put a hand on his arm. "I'm sorry about our guys who were injured. And if any of them don't make it, it's on Jon Haines, not you. And he's going to pay."

She looked around for Nick. He was over talking to one of the firefighters.

"We'll find out which hospitals they've all been taken to and see what we can learn out about their conditions. I'll let you know, okay?"

He nodded. They both knew he would be tied up for some time explaining the course of events to his boss, the head of the Critical Incident Response Group, as well as others on up the food chain. And if there were deaths, they would need a body count as soon as possible.

Regan prayed Julia wouldn't be included in that number.

21

WINSTON WATCHED in horror as Jon's house burst into flames in front of millions of TV and online viewers all over the globe. Though he couldn't be absolutely certain, he doubted the FBI was behind the explosion; Tate and his minions were trying *not* to blow the lid off the situation. So it had most likely come from inside. An intentional fire.

Why, Jon, why? We could've fixed this.

He leaned forward, arms perched on his knees, head in his hands; it felt like someone had hollowed out his insides with a soup spoon.

Jon was throwing his life away. And for what? There was nothing that couldn't be overcome with some careful planning and execution—he'd always told him that.

The boy had been born with superior intelligence, but he had never acquired an ounce of mental toughness. That's why Winston had always been there to provide it for him.

And he should've seen this coming.

For the past year, Jon had grown increasingly erratic. Winston could easily deal with the young man's self-worth issues—he had for years, and in fact exploited them a little—but when Jon began to alternate low self-esteem with displays of inflated self-importance, that's when Winston stepped back. Decided to observe his behavior for awhile, then work on correcting it.

But he never got to that last part. And now it had spun out of control.

He'd invested too many years in Jon to simply give up and walk away. If he and Julia had survived—and early press reports indicated they did—there had to be a way to reverse the damage. A way to feed an explanation to the public that sounded defensible.

All it would take was a little careful planning and execution.

౭

DAN FELT like he was trying to drink water from a fire hose. His piece on Haines would air in three days, and the explosion sparked a whole new dimension that had to be woven in.

The networks and cable news were going berserk, reporting things that hadn't been adequately fact-checked so they wouldn't fall behind the breaking news. Dan's show was technically entertainment rather than news, so he had the luxury of a little more time. He intended to inject a measure of professional calm, to be the grownup reporting the story. *Fielding Questions* would present a more thoughtful picture of the congressman and contemplate what led him to take the bizarre actions he had over the last two days.

That meant Dan needed a psychological angle. He opened his electronic file of contacts and scanned it, trying to decide which one might be the best fit.

Wait … what about the psychologist who's usually on scene with CIRG negotiators? She'd been there; she'd be perfect.

Dan put in a call to his new buddy, Nick. Maybe he could get not only the woman's name but also some inside info on the investigation. He knew Jenesco was a little dazzled by him.

As he waited for the agent to pick up, his thoughts shifted to Marla. How was she handling all of this? She had to be completely traumatized. Not that she wasn't used to shit happening, but this was big. He would go see her, try to offer a little comfort and support.

Would she still be willing to talk on camera? *Maybe I can get an exclusive.* With that, he could hit this thing out of the park.

Dan left Nick a message, asking him to call back ASAP. Then he ran to corral his cameraman and set off for George Washington University Hospital.

22

REGAN SAT with Peter Cordova in the hospital waiting room at Georgetown University, where he and Julia worked. Fear and grief wafted from him like cheap cologne.

"It's my fault," he said. "She was afraid of him, and I should've been more insistent that she leave."

"So the two of you do have a relationship that extends beyond your work together," Regan said softly.

"Never formally stated, but certainly felt and subtly acknowledged by both of us. It was only a matter of time. Now, I don't know if ..."

Regan squeezed his hand. "She's alive, Dr. Cordova. And it's your colleagues here that are treating her. You know she's getting the best care possible."

He nodded, brushing a hand across his eyes.

"What about Julia's family?" said Regan. "Do you know where they are?"

"Her mother lives in Palo Alto. Julia's dad died last year, which devastated her. He was a neuroscientist at Stanford, and they were extremely close. She doesn't have any siblings."

"Has her mother been notified?"

"I knew she'd see it on TV, so I called her. Told her Julia was being treated and I'd let her know when we knew something."

"Is she planning to come?"

Peter shook his head. "She just had knee surgery, so she can't travel. Might be just as well, though; Julia and her mother have always had kind of a strained relationship."

A doctor walked into the waiting room. Peter jumped up and rushed over to him. "Mac? How is she?"

The doctor glanced at Regan; she pulled out her credentials. "Special Agent Regan Manning from the Washington Field Office."

His brow wrinkled but he refrained from the usual *You look too young to be an agent* and instead held out his hand. "Dr. Sean Mackenzie, Agent Manning." With the introduction out of the way, he said, "I'm afraid Julia's not out of the woods yet."

The doctor fixed his gaze on his friend. "She's in bad shape, Peter. She's suffering from smoke inhalation, and she also sustained a severe contusion to her skull. We opened her up."

"She's having *brain* surgery?" said Regan.

Peter looked over at her. "Mac's saying she has a brain hemorrhage. They're doing surgery to stop the bleeding and relieve the swelling."

"How did she get the contusion? Did something fall on her?"

"I can't tell for sure," said the doctor. Something in his face told Regan he had questions about the way she might've sustained the head trauma.

"We'll see if the fire investigators might be able to shed any light on that," she said. "What about burns?"

"Fortunately, there aren't any."

She'd been at the front of the house, away from the initial explosion. *So what hit her head?*

"Guys, I need to get back ..."

"I'm staying here, Mac. Let me know as soon as she comes out, will you?"

Dr. Mackenzie nodded. "I know how much you care about her, Peter. You'll be the first to know." He scurried back down the hall.

Regan wasn't sure if the doctor was aware of Julia and Peter's romantic feelings for each other or whether he was simply alluding to their close working relationship. Often when a pair of colleagues tried to keep their romance on the down low, especially if one or both were cheating on a spouse, they weren't really fooling anybody but themselves.

Regan had some personal experience with that, back when she was a cop. She quickly brushed the memory aside before the familiar guilt had a chance to take hold.

Nick came into the waiting room. "What did the doctor say?"

She pointed to the hallway. "Let's step out here." She filled him in while Peter went to sit back down and contemplate the news he'd just heard. He leaned forward in his chair, hands on his face; Regan could see he was barely holding it together. She suspected it was because he had an in-depth knowledge of what an injury like that could mean to future quality of life—not only Julia's, but his, too.

"So what did you find out about the congressman?" she asked.

"He's had some smoke inhalation, but he should be recovered enough to leave the hospital in a few days."

"Good. That means we can nail his ass to the wall sooner rather than later. What about his sister? Is she over there?"

Nick nodded. "I feel sorry for the poor woman. She acts like it's her fault."

"Let's go see her."

Regan walked back over to Peter. "We need to leave for awhile, but call me if Julia gets out of surgery before I get back, okay?" She handed him her card and he nodded. The angst written all over his face was even more pronounced than the day before, when she'd blithely told him, "Try not to worry, Dr. Cordova."

Turns out, he'd had every right to.

≈

THEY entered the waiting room at the other hospital and saw Dan sitting next to Marla, leaning close as if to shield her from the painful blows that kept coming her way.

Marla saw them and stood up.

Dan got to his feet, too. "Hey, guys. How's Julia?"

"Don't know yet," said Regan. "She's still in surgery." She looked at Marla. "How are you doing?"

"I'm okay. Your partner probably told you that my brother's going to make it." She looked almost apologetic.

"I'm glad, Marla. Have you been able to see him?"

She shook her head. "The police officers won't let me."

Dan turned to Nick. "I'm not sure if you got my message, but—"

"I got it," said Nick. "Just haven't had a chance to get back to you."

"Hey, I hear ya. It's not like you guys don't have your hands full right now. I just wanted to get the name of that psychologist who's usually at hostage scenes with the CIRG negotiators."

"Claire Campbell."

Regan watched Nick's face to see if his expression changed. Claire used to have a giant crush on him, even though he never showed the slightest interest. Everyone knew he was off the dating circuit because of his girlfriend in Alaska, but Nick the

Chick Magnet was too nice of a guy to tell Claire to beat it. It wasn't until he transferred to the WFO that she finally gave up the dream of Nick being the father of her babies.

Regan winked at him, but he pretended not to see her.

"Think she'd talk to me?" said Dan.

"About what?" said Nick.

"About what might have led to the congressman's behavior. I'd like to have that psychological perspective for my show tonight."

"I doubt she knows, but you can ask; if she doesn't want to, she'll say so. Hang on a second." Nick called CIRG headquarters and got Claire's number. He gave it to Dan.

"Okay if I use your name? Might give me a better shot."

Regan muttered, "I can practically guarantee it."

"Excuse me?" said Dan, glancing at Regan.

"Nothing, Mr. Fielding ... I was just talking to myself. Marla, come with me ... I might be able to get you in to see your brother for a couple minutes."

Regan wasn't entirely motivated by compassion, although she did believe Marla needed some contact with him in order to move on. Regan wanted to help re-establish lines of communication between Haines and his sister in case it could assist the FBI down the road. Marla would be a stabilizing influence for him, and God knew he needed that.

The congressman's room was under heavy guard. Regan knew a couple of the agents, one of whom was a major jerk named Ted.

"Hey guys, I'd like to give Mrs. Dunston a minute with her brother." She hoped her tone sounded firm enough to discourage argument but collegial enough not to inspire a pissing contest.

Ted said, "We're under orders. No visitors."

Regan smiled with as much charm as she could muster.

"I get that, Ted, but we have kind of a special circumstance here. Mrs. Dunston was on scene at the hostage standoff, and she—"

"Take it up with my boss," said Ted, unmoved.

"I'll take it up with *my* boss," said Regan, pulling out her phone. Roland had seniority over Ted's boss at the WFO.

He glared at her, aware he was about to lose. "All right, Manning, she has one minute. And you go in with her."

"Thanks, Ted," she said sweetly. *Asshole.*

They entered Jon's room and saw him in the bed, oxygen mask over his nose and mouth. He lay staring at the ceiling.

"Jon?" Marla's voice sounded feeble and uncertain.

He shifted his gaze to them.

Marla moved to the bedside and took his hand in hers. She began to cry.

With his other hand, he lifted the mask off his face so he could speak. "Marla," he said in a raspy voice. His eyes revealed the deep affection he had for his sister.

She leaned over and hugged him. "I'm glad you're going to be okay."

Jon looked over at Regan. She stepped closer and identified herself.

"Do you know how my wife is?" he asked.

"She's in critical condition," said Regan.

He wiped tears from his eyes. "It was an accident. We were coming out when something exploded." He began to cough. He reached up and pulled the oxygen mask back down and breathed deeply.

Regan was dying to ask him more questions, but right now he'd have difficulty talking. And this was technically Marla's visit, not hers.

"I'm going to help you get better, Jonny."

He looked at his sister and nodded, but Regan could see the skepticism on his face.

"We better go, Marla. He needs to rest."

But I'll be seeing you sooner than you know, Mr. Congressman.

Marla leaned over and kissed his forehead. She started to move away.

"Wait," he gasped, grabbing her arm. "Get Jackson. I want him with you, Marla."

23

CLAIRE AGREED to meet Dan for coffee later that afternoon. "I'm sure it's because I said you gave me her number," he told Nick. "As soon as I mentioned your name, her tone changed completely."

"I've known Claire a long time," said Nick. "She knows her stuff. Sometimes she's a little too know-it-all for Regan's taste, but she means well."

"Speaking of your partner, she's cute as hell." He shook his head in wonder.

"Feisty as hell, too."

"I just think it would be tough to work so closely with a sexy woman like Regan Manning and not be distracted. She's got those green eyes and that husky voice ... oh man."

Nick laughed. "It was distracting at first, but now she's like a sister to me. Closer than a sister, in fact. She's my best friend."

Dan gave him a sidelong glance. "Really? I've never actually thought a man and a woman could be best friends, because the guy, at least, would always be picturing them romping around in the sack."

"I think men with respect for their female friends and a reasonable amount of self-control can get past that pretty quickly. You should try it."

"Touché. I sound like a horny teenager. So let's get back to the story. What do you know about Haines' mentor, Winston Jennings?"

"I know he scares the shit out of people," Nick replied.

"Right! That's what I'm finding out, too. But why? He isn't as powerful as he used to be. Or that most people are aware of, anyway."

"It's just his persona," said Nick. "He makes people believe he can do something to them if they don't cooperate. Whether he really can or not, who knows?"

"I had a hell of a time getting anybody to talk about Haines *or* Jennings," said Dan. He was dying to tell Nick about his conversation with the speaker, but he had given his word that he'd keep it under wraps.

Not that the FBI would blab. And maybe Dan could use the information as leverage … tit for tat.

"So, Nick, I had an interesting conversation with Speaker Stallworth yesterday. Told me some stuff that might be useful to you."

"I see. Are you going to share it?"

"Well, I thought maybe we could help each other out. You know, I give you information, you give me information."

"Nah. Regan and I will go meet with him and get it straight from the horse's mouth."

Dan detected a lessening of his star power with Nick. He regretted his immature remarks about Regan; it made him come across as a clueless fop.

It struck him that he'd been trying to impress the agent. Buddy up to him.

"Listen, Nick, I apologize for what I said before. If either my mother or my sister heard that, they'd drown me in the bathtub."

"Hey, don't worry about it."

"I sounded like a jerk. And don't worry, when I'm around your partner, I'll behave like a gentleman, not some drooling hound dog."

Nick laughed. "Regan is more than a little used to drooling hound dogs, Dan. She's perfectly capable of handling men. And here she comes."

She and Marla came back into the waiting room where the two men sat.

Regan looked at her partner. "We need to go pick up Marla's kids and take them all home. I can do that while you—"

"I'll do it," said Dan. "I have some time before I meet with Claire." He was careful to keep his tone professional, without the slightest hint of flirtiness.

"Oh, she agreed to meet with you," said Regan. She glanced at Nick and smiled. "Well yeah, that'd be great if you have time to run Marla home. If that works for her."

Marla nodded. "I appreciate it. I know all of you are busy."

"No problem," said Dan. "Let's go." It would give him another chance to talk to her privately, find out how her conversation with her brother had gone.

Not only that, he truly liked Marla Dunston.

&

THIRTY-FIVE miles outside Washington, fire continued to ravage Prince William Park while anxious area residents watched in horror. It had eaten up precious time to get all of the campers and hikers out of the park before a full-scale fire relief effort could be launched, but even that was limited somewhat by the park's proximity to a heavily populated city like DC.

"Man, look at all that smoke in the air," said Regan. She and Nick were on their way to meet with Adam Mohr.

"Pretty damn sad," said Nick. "Didn't have to happen."

"At least we should be able to add arson to the list of charges."

"Small comfort."

"Yeah, I know; that park is a refuge for a lot of nature lovers. It's going to be a terrible loss if they don't get the fire out soon." She knew Jack would be heartsick if he saw all those trees being burned.

They entered the building on Constitution Avenue that housed the Justice Department's Criminal Division and made their way to Adam's office. As chief litigator in the Fraud Section, he was a busy man, but he shifted his appointments to meet with them. After all, the Haines case was his hottest ticket, especially after the events of the past two days.

"Hey guys," he said in a spirited tone as he welcomed the agents into his office. After they were settled with coffee, he said, "Boy, things with Haines have literally exploded, haven't they?" His eyes lingered on Regan.

"Yes, I think it's safe to say that," she replied.

"So he's facing a mix of federal and state charges, which means we'll be coordinating with the Commonwealth's Attorney of Prince William County. The county authorities can go ahead and arrest him on the abduction charges so he'll be in custody while we assemble our bribery case against Imhoff-Greyson. So let's talk about the bribery charges. How many counts are we looking at?"

"We have three in China that our informant attested to, but we know there are more that were arranged by other so-called consultants," said Regan. "We've identified seven people in other countries that entered into BCAs with Imhoff-Greyson, where Haines was the principal contact." BCAs, or business consultant agreements, were routine territory for the Fraud Section.

"Which means those three counts against Haines in China are just the tip of the iceberg," Nick added.

They spent twenty more minutes discussing possible scenarios for other charges of corruption to be revealed and affidavits obtained.

"You guys have your work cut out for you," said Adam. "I'm going to get with the U.S. Attorney and talk about the initial charges we'll file to get the grand jury process rolling. Let me know what you find out about the arson and the extent of Dr. Haines injuries."

"Okay," said Regan. "We're heading back out to Montclair to see what the fire investigators have found." She and Nick stood up and prepared to leave.

"Regan?" said Adam. "Could I have a word?"

"Sure." She turned to Nick. "I'll meet you in the outer office in a couple minutes."

Once Nick left them alone, Adam said, "This doesn't have to do with the case. I, uh … I just wondered where things are with you and your boyfriend these days."

Good question, thought Regan. She wasn't exactly surprised that Adam had asked it; he'd made it clear for months that he was interested in her.

"The distance is hard on us, but we're hanging in there."

"Well, I just thought maybe we could get a drink sometime. I'm not trying to get in the way of anything, but I just, you know, thought …"

Regan smiled. "Now's not a great time, Adam. But thanks."

24

NICK DIDN'T say anything until he had started the car and they were on their way to Montclair. "Adam asked you out, didn't he?"

"Why do you say that?" said Regan.

"Jesus, Regan, it's obvious as hell. He's got the hots for you."

"I think that might be overstating it a little. He asked if I'd like to get a drink sometime, that's all. He's just a friend." But she *did* like Adam a lot. And he lived in the same town.

"What did you say?"

"I said that now isn't a great time."

"But you left the door open."

"Not really ... I guess I just didn't feel like I needed to say, 'Thanks, Adam, but there's no way in hell that's ever going to happen.' Besides, when Claire kept throwing herself at you, I didn't jump down *your* throat."

"That's because I didn't encourage Claire at all. Trust me, in Adam's mind you left the door open."

"Well, I can't help what Adam thinks," she said irritably. But so what if she *had* left the door open?

"Regan, I'm no Ann Landers, but let me just say one thing: don't give up on Jack. Believe me, I know what you're going through—but I also know you two are made for each other. I've never seen you happier than you are when you're around him.

123

You'll get this figured out. Maybe there's some alternative you guys haven't thought of."

"Like what, Nick? I've been over it in my head a million times. Every scenario involves one or both of us leaving a job we love. And they're not just *jobs* ... what we do is who we are."

"As I recall, you were willing to leave the bureau two years ago and take that JPD job in Juneau so you guys could be together."

"I do remember. And I also remember how Jack knew it wouldn't be right for me, even if it did mean we could be together. That's how perceptive he is." *How unselfish.*

The prickly eye thing started in again. It was getting to be a nasty habit.

"See? That's what I'm talking about. You two understand each other—and how important your work is to both of you. Do you honestly think Jack would ask you to sacrifice what you're doing and go live somewhere close to the woods for his sake?"

"No, I don't think he would. Which means he'll sacrifice what he's doing and come and live in the city for *my* sake. And I'll feel like a selfish bitch. The relationship will suffer anyway."

"So you think it's better to cut to the chase and kill it."

Regan didn't answer. Nick knew much of her history—about the affair with her married partner when she was at JPD, about the time she coaxed a few of her high school buddies into exploring an abandoned gold mine and watched her best friend suffer a leg injury so debilitating that the two girls would never again be a double threat on the basketball court. Or friends, either, for that matter.

Regan sometimes did things that were selfish and hurt others. She would carry the guilt and shame forever.

"I know what you're thinking," said Nick. "But people make their own choices. It's not your fault if things don't always turn out right. You're not God, you know."

She broke down then, mentally cursing Nick as the sadness and confusion poured from her in a giant torrent.

"I'm sorry, Regan. I didn't mean to upset you. I just think you need to give Jack a chance."

It dawned on Regan that Nick was talking as much about his own situation as he was hers. But it wasn't the same at all.

She turned to him, wiping the tears from her face. "I'm happy for you that Lindsay is willing to give up her career with the bureau and move back to Portland. And that you're thinking about chucking yours to go sell lobsters on the beach or some damn thing. That's great—the two of you will get to be together. But I'm not Lindsay, and I'm not you, Nick. I'm *not* willing to give up this career for Jack or anybody else. I worked hard to get this assignment, and I'm good at it. And even though I love him—I truly do—I can't give up being who I am. I have no goddamn idea who I'd be without this. If that's selfish, then so be it—but this time I won't try to drag anybody else along with me."

He stared at her, his face registering total surprise. "I'm just saying, Regan, that I think you'll regret it if you choose Adam over Jack, simply because he's in close proximity."

"Well, thanks for the pep talk, Nick, but stay out of my love life. If I choose to go out with Adam, it's none of your business."

He had gotten one thing right, though: she did need to do something about the situation with Jack. As her dad always said, *It's time to fish or cut bait.*

25

WINSTON GOT ready to throw his weight around. A punk agent named Ted was refusing to let him see Jon.

"I believe Garrison Tate will change your mind about that," he said, index finger poised and ready to punch in the FBI director's phone number.

It did the trick. "Fine, I can let you see him for just a couple minutes, sir. But I'll need to come in with you."

"I appreciate the couple minutes, Agent--"

"Swanson."

"Yes, Agent Swanson. But I'll talk to him alone."

Swanson looked flustered. "Sir, I'm just trying to follow the orders I've been given. I'm sure you understand ..."

"I do, son. And if anyone attempts to punish you for letting me in to see the congressman—by myself—then you send them to me."

Swanson slowly nodded, his whole demeanor registering defeat. He extended a hand toward Jon's room, inviting Winston to enter.

Jon's eyes were closed, and he wore an oxygen mask over his nose and mouth. Winston moved to the side of the bed. "Jon?"

His eyes popped open. Behind the mask, Winston saw Jon smile.

"How are you, son?"

Jon pulled the mask away from his face. "I'm okay, I guess."

Winston turned around and glanced at the door to be sure Swanson hadn't followed him into the room. He lowered his voice and said, "Jon, I need you to tell me exactly what happened so I can help you put this thing to rest. And trust me, we *will* put it to rest."

"Is Julia going to make it?"

"As far as I know she is. What happened?"

Jon's eyes filled with tears. "Everything fell apart ... from the minute I found her in the garage, getting ready to leave me."

"So you tried to reason with her to stay."

"Well, I was extremely angry, and I—"

"No, you were just trying to reason with her. That's understandable."

Jon stared at him a moment, then nodded. "I think she's been seeing this guy she works with. I was trying to get her to admit it."

"Might have been the best thing just to let her leave, Jon. Her job is getting in the way of yours. But ... that's water under the bridge. We need to go forward from here. So what about the fire?"

"After I talked to my sister—"

The door opened and Swanson stuck his head in. "Sir? I'm going to have to ask you to leave now."

"In a minute, Swanson," Winston barked. "Shut the door."

When it was closed, Jon said, "I was in the shower, and I knew that even though I had talked Julia into staying and walking out of the house with me, she was going to leave me anyway. I couldn't let that happen, Win. Julia means everything to me. Without her, I'm nothing."

Winston swallowed the sound of disgust he was about to make. "So what did you do?"

The tears overflowed Jon's eyes and trickled down his cheeks. "I—I grabbed a wooden statue that was on the dresser and hit her with it. She never saw it coming." His sob turned into a cough; he took another hit from the oxygen mask.

"Then what?"

Jon's raspy voice dropped to a whisper; Winston had to strain to hear him. "I wanted us to perish together—but I couldn't risk just setting something in the house on fire and having the blaze put out before it engulfed the house. I think there was already a fire truck standing by out there." He had shifted his gaze away from Winston.

Winston was sickened by Jon's suicidal confession. "How did you cause the explosion?"

"Pulled the gas line from the water heater and let the furnace room fill up with gas. I lit a candle I found in the kitchen and waited a couple minutes, then I opened the door to the furnace room and tossed it in." He started to cough again; another hit of oxygen.

"What about the statue you hit Julia with? What did you do with it?"

He stared at the ceiling while he thought back. "I carried it downstairs with me. I think I set it down in the utility room."

I sure hope you're right. Winston paused, visualizing the explosion. "I'm surprised you weren't killed instantly, Jon."

"I should've been, but I panicked and ran. Like a goddamn coward. I made it almost to the front door before the explosion happened."

"So you decided you didn't want to die after all."

Jon closed his eyes and gave a tiny nod.

"That's the good news in all of this," said Winston.

Jon opened his eyes and stared at him.

"You want to live, son. That's the important thing. And we're going to find a way to get things back on track."

☙

IT WAS late afternoon by the time they reached the burned-out house, and Regan was starting to feel the effects of their stressful day. Her emotional breakdown in the car only added to the fatigue —and produced a strained silence between her and Nick.

They made their way over to the fire investigators. "Agents Manning and Jenesco, FBI," said Regan. "We'd like a word with the team leader."

One of the men came over to them. "That would be me. Bill Knight." He extended his hand and they each shook it.

"Have you found the source of the explosion, Bill?" said Regan.

"Yep, it came from an area that contained the furnace and water heater, probably a utility room. Both of those appliances combusted, and we haven't determined yet which one was the source of the ignition."

Regan noticed he addressed his comments to Nick, even though she was the one who had asked the question. Some men were just uncomfortable talking to women; others acted like she must be too young to actually be a *real* agent, despite the fact that she was about to turn thirty-five and had a dozen years of law enforcement under her belt, the last seven with the bureau. A year longer than her partner.

"Is there a chance it could've been an accident?" said Nick.

Knight shrugged. "It's possible. We'll know more when we've had a chance to examine things closer."

129

"I'd like to take a look at the master bedroom area," said Regan. That corner of the house was the only part that still bore any resemblance to a residential structure.

"The floor is going to be extremely unstable," said Knight. "I wouldn't advise walking on it, but you could take a look at the room from the ladder." He led them over to the ladder that was perched against the window sill of the second-floor bedroom.

Regan had climbed several rungs when her phone rang. It was Peter.

"Julia's out of surgery. She's going to make it." The relief in his voice was palpable.

"That's wonderful news, Dr. Cordova. Is she awake?"

"No, they're keeping her in a medically induced coma for right now. If the swelling on her brain is significantly reduced by tomorrow morning, they'll start to bring her out of it."

She had to admit she was glad they couldn't interview Julia right away; Regan didn't think she had it in her to do anything but go home and crash after they were finished here.

"Thanks for letting us know. We'll see you at the hospital in the morning."

She gave Nick the update, delivered in a cool tone, then proceeded up the ladder while he went off to have his own look around. When she got to the top, she stepped through the window and sat down on the sill. That way, she could move a couple of feet inside the room and still grab for the window opening if anything gave way.

Regan sat for a moment and scanned the area. The opposite side of the spacious room, near the doorway, was badly charred, but the rest of the bedroom was amazingly intact.

She stood and pulled on latex gloves, then slowly took a step forward. The floor seemed sturdy enough to carry her weight. She crept toward the middle of the room to get a better vantage point, and from there, turned slowly in a circle, surveying the space for clues. In particular, for blood.

She saw something sticking out from under the bed near one of the night stands. She moved over and bent down for a closer look; it was a handgun, still loaded. She engaged the safety and deposited the gun in an evidence bag, then slid it toward the window to pick up on her way back down.

Regan looked in the master bathroom but saw nothing interesting. She made her way to the walk-in closet, which was situated closer to the burned section of the room. As she got close, she heard a loud creak underfoot. She stopped and waited, holding her breath.

"Regan?" Nick's voice came from outside the window; he was on the ground below.

She tiptoed back to the open window. "What?"

"I just wondered where you were. You're not walking around up there, are you?"

"Just right near the window. It's fine."

"See anything?"

"I found Jon's gun." She picked it up from the floor and leaned out the window to hand it to Nick. He climbed up the ladder.

When he got to the top, Regan stepped back. "Look at this room ... it survived mostly intact except for that far wall."

"I wouldn't trust that floor, though," said Nick. "Some of the supporting beams under it were burned pretty bad."

"Then it's a good thing I'm as light as a feather," she replied breezily, inching her way back across the floor.

"C'mon, Regan, you heard what Bill said."

"I know ... I just want to take a quick peek at that closet."

"Jesus," Nick mumbled. He'd learned long ago there was no point in arguing with her once she was determined to do something.

The closer Regan got to the walk-in closet, the less stable the floor felt under her feet. She moved closer to the wall and kept one hand on it for support. She heard a loud crack; Nick heard it, too.

"Goddamn it, Regan, get the hell out of the room."

She ignored him and leaned around the entrance to the closet. She was startled to see the back half of it was missing, illuminated by daylight.

But she could also see a patch of blood on the carpet in the middle of the closet.

"This is where he hit her, Nick." She turned around and looked at him.

His face showed real fear.

"Okay, okay," she said, dashing back across the room. Another loud crack; the floor suddenly tilted downward, away from the window. The furniture began to slide, adding enough weight to the disintegrating section of floor to make it collapse into the living room below.

Regan crab-walked the rest of the way to the window and grabbed her partner's outstretched hand. He lifted her over the sill and onto the ladder.

"Hey!" It was Bill Knight's voice, coming from the foot of the ladder. "Were you walking around up there? I warned you not to."

"We needed to retrieve the handgun," said Nick. He held up the evidence bag.

"And *we* have an unfinished fire investigation," Bill retorted. He shook his head and stalked off.

Regan put her arms around her partner's neck and gave him a hug. "Nick, I'm sorry for acting stupid."

"That's okay—I'm glad you're safe." He glanced at the caved-in floor and smiled. "But you may want to rethink the whole light-as-a-feather thing."

26

WINSTON WAS back in Stallworth's office. "It's not what it looks like, Tom."

The speaker gave him a skeptical look. "Didn't he attempt to blow up the house with him and Julia in it?"

"No, he didn't. The water heater exploded—it was an accident."

"The timing of that is a little suspect, don't you think?"

"Well, you know what they say, the truth is stranger than fiction. And the truth is, Jon and Julia simply had a disagreement. They resolved it and were coming out of the house when the explosion occurred."

Winston knew that once Julia recovered enough to tell her story to the FBI, a day or two from now, she would claim otherwise, but by then, he would have killed the vote to expel Haines from Congress—if he moved quickly enough. They would likely censure him instead, but at least that wouldn't be fatal to his political career.

And just for good measure, he'd have a chat with the FBI director and find a way to discredit Julia.

"That's the story Jon told you?" said Stallworth.

"Yes, it is. And I know the man well enough to tell if it wasn't legitimate."

Stallworth shook his head. "I don't know, Win, this whole thing has become so sensationalized that the media is on it like stink on shit. I doubt they're going to buy that the explosion was just an unfortunate accident at precisely the moment the standoff was about to end."

Winston felt his temper start to burn. "Jesus, Tom, since when does the media determine our course of action?"

"I told you before, things have changed since you were up here, Winston. Political blogs are now a fact of life—people devour them and tweet their opinions all over the damn place. And all the traditional media outlets—the Washington standard bearers—believe me, they do play a major role in our course of action. We ignore that fact at our peril."

"I'm not saying we should *ignore* the media, I'm saying we should force them to report the news accurately and objectively."

Stallworth gave a derisive snort. "Good luck with that."

"Cut the bullshit, Tom. I'm not going to stand by and allow Jon Haines to be eviscerated by the press. He doesn't deserve it. And I need you to step up and do your fucking job."

The speaker's jaw became rigid. "So you expect me to put pressure on the Republican caucus to support Haines."

"That's exactly what I expect. And I'll also talk to the key members myself to explain the situation in more detail—get them to commit to *not* voting for expulsion."

Stallworth crossed his arms and remained silent.

Winston knew he was risking the speaker's future cooperation on the cybersecurity policy structure, but he had no choice. Once Jon's seat in the House was no longer in jeopardy, he'd ply Stallworth with a truckload of campaign cash to get back in his good graces. "I need you to start working the phone, Tom. Get the other members of leadership to help you. I promise, I'll make it worth your while."

≈

HE'D BEEN forced to make a lot of promises, but Winston desperately needed the votes to keep Haines in Congress, as much to do his bidding as to preserve both of their reputations. An expulsion would cause the media—led by that bloodsucker, Dan Fielding—to take a closer look at their longstanding association. Winston felt confident he couldn't be implicated in anything, but Fielding and his cohorts would raise questions and, at the very least, make his life damned uncomfortable.

He was putting a lot on the line, but Winston was confident he could get Jon straightened out. The hostage thing and house fire were setbacks, to be sure, and it was unfortunate that they had happened at a time when Winston needed to marshal support for prioritizing cybersecurity in the federal budget— including, of course, the national research facility in his own back yard and his leadership in establishing spectrum policy.

It wasn't the first time Winston had a hand in creating security policy, but this would be the most far-reaching effort he'd ever undertaken. Yes, it would mean billions in profit for Imhoff-Greyson, but it also meant a safer country. It was a win-win.

First he had to save Jon.

He glanced at his watch. It was getting late and he still had a half-dozen reps to talk to before the expected motion for expulsion was made the next day.

He stepped up his pace, but Winston felt like he was slogging through mud, fatigue nipping at his heels.

Maybe it was time to bid goodbye to Washington once and for all. Lord knew he had an enviable life waiting for him in Kansas if he'd just settle down and allow himself to enjoy it.

Soon, he thought. *When I've finished what I need to do.*

27

DAN TEXTED Nick the next morning to see if he could stop by the Washington Field Office.

"Our man Jennings has been a busy boy," he reported when he arrived.

"How so?" said Nick. He pointed to a chair near his and Regan's desks.

Dan sat. "I have a source in the Capitol who told me Jennings is running around lining up votes against Haines' expulsion."

"Interesting," said Regan. "Why is he so intent on saving Haines?"

"That's what I'm going to find out," said Dan. "What's the latest on the congressman? Anything you can share on that front?"

"When Marla and I went to see him, it was obvious he's upset about Julia divorcing him," said Regan. "He seems to be holding out hope that she won't, despite his foray into whackoland."

"Could you use that?" said Dan. "Maybe get Julia to lie and say she won't divorce him if he'll agree to help you build your corruption case against Jennings?"

Regan gazed at him warily. "What makes you think we're building a case against Winston Jennings?"

Dan smiled. "They don't call me Digger Dan for nothing."

Regan wasn't amused. One glance at her partner told her Nick wasn't quite as enamored with the journalist anymore, either.

"C'mon, guys, it's not rocket science," said Dan. "You're on the task force for the Foreign Corrupt Practices Act. I figured you wouldn't have been on scene at the hostage standoff if you didn't have a vested interest—i.e., an active investigation into Imhoff's—and therefore Haines'—possible violations of the FCPA. From there, it wasn't a huge mental leap to figure out Jennings is the one you're really after since he's the head of the company. There's no way in hell Haines would have bribed anybody on his own; he's been Winston's water boy for fifteen years."

Regan didn't know whether to be impressed or annoyed. "No comment," she said.

"Okay, I get that you don't want to give me the specifics. Not yet, anyway. But I can help you."

Nick leaned back and clasped his hands behind his head. "How?"

"I have contacts all over the place. Longstanding relationships built on mutual trust. They'll tell me things they might not tell you."

"I thought you said people had been tight-lipped about Jennings," said Nick.

Dan nodded. "They have. But if I can tell them Jennings is under FBI scrutiny and it looks like he might go down, I think that would loosen their lips. Jennings may be widely feared, but he's also widely despised."

"Do you have a contact at Imhoff-Greyson?" said Regan.

"No," said Dan. "But I used to date a woman who is legal counsel at one of its competitors. If Imhoff used bribes to win contracts, you can bet they know about it—or at least suspect it. And they'd be over the moon if Imhoff got caught."

"If she's a lawyer, it's unlikely she's going to share any suspicions they may have," said Regan. "Not to mention with an old boyfriend."

Dan displayed a cocky grin. "I'm pretty sure I can get her to talk to me."

Regan almost laughed out loud. The reporter wasn't all that good-looking, but she had to admit he was loaded with charisma. Obviously he was used to using it.

"Unless her own company has resorted to bribes," said Nick. The problem was pervasive among companies that operated in countries with corrupt government officials; they saw it as a necessary evil if they wanted to compete.

"True," said Dan. "But it's worth a try to see if it might help us connect the dots leading to Jennings."

It seemed like a flimsy plan at best. Still, it couldn't hurt to let him talk to his old flame to see if she offered anything up. They needed everything they could get.

"Okay," said Regan.

Nick looked a little startled. "Okay?" he asked.

Dan looked a little startled, too. "So you want me to go see my friend?"

Regan nodded. "Take Nick with you. It'll give credibility to your story that the FBI has painted a target on Jennings' back." The fact that her partner was a hottie didn't hurt, either.

"What about you?" said Nick. "What's your next move?"

"First, I'm going to go update our boss on everything. After that, I'm going to go see Julia."

28

ROLAND HAD spoken with the director that morning. "He's anxious, Regan. He wants answers on the hostage situation and explosion before we move forward with the bribery case. Since it's likely that Winston Jennings was also involved in the payoff scheme, we need to exercise an abundance of caution. Jennings has for years been telling anybody who would listen that we're inept when it comes to national security, so we need to make sure this thing doesn't blow up in our face."

"I understand, ma'am. We'll make sure our ducks are in a row before Jennings has any inkling we're looking at him."

It wasn't Regan's first time going after a powerful government official. Two years earlier, it was her sheer determination that brought down the vice president of the United States. She knew if you weren't sufficiently prepared, it was like poking at a sleeping bear without your running shoes on.

"Will you be able to secure enough evidence without the need for Haines to provide testimony against his former boss? Given his mental state, he isn't exactly a reliable witness."

"We're working on it, but I have to admit that Haines' cooperation is pretty crucial. He's been Jennings' right-hand man for a long time—probably the only one Jennings really trusts. The Imhoff accountant, Mason Weir, can produce the paper trail to Haines, but it gets a lot murkier after that—even though we know Jennings had to have approved the payoffs. Their so-called 'bribery budget' was too massive for him not to have known about it—especially given what a control freak Jennings is."

Roland nodded, but she didn't look entirely convinced. Regan debated whether to tell her about Dan Fielding's corporate attorney friend; she decided to keep it to herself for now. Wait to see if it yielded anything.

"I'm planning to go see Julia Haines when we're through here," said Regan. "I hope to be able to get a sense of where she is emotionally with regard to Jon. It's possible she could have a huge effect on his level of cooperation going forward."

"I don't doubt that. Have you had an update from your contact in the Fraud Section at Justice?" asked Roland.

A twinge zipped through Regan's gut at the thought of Adam. Was it awkwardness or anticipation?

"Uh, not since we met with him yesterday, but I'll get in touch with him after I have a chance to talk to Julia."

"Okay, good. Make sure we're in lockstep with them and we're clear on the timing and scope of charges against Haines. It needs to be absolutely solid. And Regan?"

"Ma'am?"

"Don't make a move toward Jennings until you've cleared it with me."

&

THE VOTE to expel Haines failed. Instead, the House passed a resolution to censure the congressman. He would be allowed to keep his seat, at least until the voters in his district had the chance to decide in five months.

Winston was flooded with relief. Though it was problematic that Haines lost his committee assignments, especially the one on Homeland Security, it was only temporary. Stallworth insisted he had had no choice.

No backbone is more like it, Winston grumbled to himself.

Jon had been released from the hospital after Winston assured his medical team that he would get in-home nursing care for his breathing treatments. He was immediately placed under arrest for kidnapping and taken to the Prince William County Adult Detention Center in Manassas.

It took less than two hours for Winston to get him released. The Commonwealth's Attorney had argued for denial of bail, given the possible addition of several more serious charges, but the judge set bail at two hundred and fifty thousand.

For now, Jon was a guest at Winston's apartment. "I'm going to go lie down," he announced. He looked like a withered version of himself.

"I think it might be better if you're up and moving around, Jon. You'll get your energy back faster."

Jon gave him a bleak stare. "I can't, Winston." He shuffled off to the guest room.

Winston watched helplessly. He knew Jon was spiraling downward into depression, and he couldn't let that happen.

He had an idea. He picked up the phone and made a call, then went to pack a bag.

An hour later, he opened the door to Jon's room. "Get up; we're going to Kansas."

Jon looked at him like he was speaking in tongues. He didn't move.

"Jon, get up. Let's go."

"I'm not supposed to leave town, remember? And I prefer to stay here anyway, Win."

"Can't let you do that, son. You've suffered a major blow and I know you're feeling pretty down right now, so a little time on the ranch—and eating some of Betty's cooking—will be just the ticket. You'll be feeling like yourself again in no time."

"You go. I'll be okay here."

"You *won't* be okay because you'll be trapped inside the apartment in order to keep the media from eating you alive. You won't have to worry about that at the ranch; you'll be able to get lots of rest and fresh air."

Jon just stared as though he didn't have enough strength left to argue.

"C'mon, let's go. I've got a charter plane waiting for us at Dulles."

Jon slowly got up and trudged off to the bathroom.

Winston put in a call to Betty. "We're going to have company, Betts."

"Who?" said Betty. After forty-two years of marriage, she was used to accommodating her husband's sometimes-sudden demands.

"Jon." He gave her a brief update, talking softly so Jon wouldn't hear.

"I'll get the guest room ready," she said. "And I'll tell Gert that Papa's coming home."

29

JULIA LOOKED fragile but grateful to be alive.

Peter was her watchdog, keeping visitors at bay. But he allowed Regan into her room for a few minutes.

"This is the agent I was telling you about, sweetheart," he told Julia.

The term of endearment was likely a new thing, as was the two of them holding hands. It was clear Peter didn't want to waste another minute pretending they didn't love each other.

"Hi, Agent Manning," Julia whispered.

Regan moved close to the bed. "Hi, Dr. Haines. I'm so glad to hear you'll make a full recovery."

She smiled. "Thank you."

"Do you feel up to telling me a bit about the hostage situation? Or would you rather I come back later?"

"No, I need to talk about it. I still can't believe Jon tried to kill me."

"Do you remember the blow to the head?"

She nodded. "I went into the closet to get his suit, and he came up behind me and hit me with something."

"Possibly the butt of his gun?"

"No, it was something bigger and heavier than that."

Regan hadn't seen anything that looked like a weapon when she surveyed the bedroom, but maybe the object had been destroyed when the fire reached part of the closet.

"Do you have any idea what precipitated the attack?"

"No—and it still shocks me. After Jon talked to his sister, he agreed to surrender, but he wanted to take a shower and put on a suit first. He told me that if we looked as normal as possible when we came out, we'd have a better chance of addressing our marital issues out of the media spotlight. He seemed so sincere that I believed him."

Still, Regan couldn't imagine why she didn't escape while he was in the shower.

"I know it sounds crazy, but—" Julia trailed off and closed her eyes.

Peter turned to Regan. "I think you better go now, Agent Manning. Julia needs to rest."

"It's okay, Peter," she said softly. "I want to talk about it. It was the second time during the standoff that I could've escaped and I didn't. The first time, the night before, I knew Jon would shoot himself as soon as I left. Then yesterday, when he went to take a shower, he begged me to stay and leave the house with him. He looked so … so defenseless. It's stupid, I know, but Jon has always been able to manipulate me like that."

"Has he exhibited mental,uh, lack of stability before?"

"Ever since I first met him," she replied. "But it's gotten a lot worse. He has undiagnosed bipolar disorder, and his highs and lows have become much more extreme."

"Do you have any idea what caused the explosion? Had you seen any kind of incendiary device?"

"No." Julia's voice had become more strained; Regan could see she was getting fatigued. The worried look on Peter's face told her he could see it, too.

Regan said, "I appreciate you talking to me, Dr. Haines; I need to let you rest now. We'll talk more when you're feeling up to it, okay?"

Julia nodded. "I'll have Peter call you when I'm feeling a little stronger. I want to help, Agent Manning; we can't let Jon get away with what he did."

৯

DESPITE THE excess of charm surrounding her, Dan's old flame had refused to dish.

"I think she knows something, but she's not saying," said Nick.

"Kinda makes you wonder about her company's own practices, doesn't it?" said Regan.

"It certainly does. May have to put them on our to-do list."

"How was Dan?" Regan asked. The reporter had dropped Nick back at the office and headed to the Hill so he could talk to House members about the censure.

Nick smiled. "I think he was a little embarrassed that she wasn't the putty in his hands he thought she'd be. In fact, she was downright hostile to him."

"Well, you know what they say, hell hath no fury ..."

"And after Dan told me the story about their breakup, she *was* a woman scorned. I can't imagine why he thought she'd be eager to hear from him again."

"A little something called ego, which our buddy Dan has in spades," said Regan. "I thought he might be able to help us a little bit, but I think that might be too dicey. We better not let him think he's part of our investigation."

"He already does think that—but I agree," said Nick. "We don't need a reporter tagging along. His interests won't always align with ours."

"And Roland tells me the director is nervous enough as it is. We need to keep a tight lid on things until we're absolutely sure of our next move. One leak could set off a firestorm."

"Or add fuel to the one that's already raging."

"Speaking of raging fires, they apparently have the Prince William Park fire under control," said Regan. "And it's supposed to rain this afternoon, too."

"Finally," said Nick. "Some *good* news."

☙

JON LOOKED better already. They lounged on the veranda and watched the sun go down, bellies full of Betty's special chicken casserole and homemade cherry pie.

"What did I tell you?" Winston said, absently scratching Gert's head as the animal leaned against his chair, her face the picture of doggy bliss. "Soothes the soul, doesn't it?" He puffed on an expensive cigar; Jon, of course, declined. His lungs were impaired enough.

"Yes, it does. It's beautiful here." He sighed, lazily nudging the porch swing back and forth. "I just wish Julia and I had a place like this—far away from Washington. Maybe if we did, I wouldn't have ..."

"Jon, you can't look back. You can't change what's already happened. The best thing now is for you to get healthy and get back to work. You have a lot to accomplish."

"Win, I'm not sure I have it in me anymore."

"Nonsense. I've known you for fifteen years and you're one of the sharpest and most ambitious men I know. Things just got a little off-course, that's all. You were under a lot of added pressure because of all the recent news about Julia's work, but you no longer have to worry about it. I'm telling you, son, the sky's the limit!"

Jon didn't reply; he kept his gaze on the prairie vista in front of them. Winston could feel himself losing patience, but then he checked it; the rah-rah speech was simply too much too soon. Jon had only been here a few hours, and he was still in a weakened state.

Let him rest a couple more days, Winston thought. *He'll come around.*

30

KANSAS?" said Dan.

Marla nodded. "He called me from there this morning. Mr. Jennings insisted Jon needed to go out to his ranch to recover and get away from the media. They left yesterday, just a couple hours after Jon was released from jail."

Dan wondered how the judge would feel about it—and if his FBI friends had heard the news.

But he was discovering there wasn't much that got in Jennings' way. Dan had had a conversation with Nolan Hall, the thirty-year veteran of Congress who had suffered the fallout from mysteriously planted allegations, despite having been enormously popular in his district for more than twenty years. He swore the rumors were completely false, but he went down like the Hindenburg and Jennings' protégé took over his seat.

Dan knew he should probably hurry and report Jon's Kansas trip to the agents, just in case they didn't know, but he was reluctant to leave just yet. He liked the way he felt around Marla. He could relax and just be himself, not the famous broadcast journalist, and she was perfectly okay with that.

"More coffee?" she said. A blonde wisp had escaped the bun holding the hair off her neck; she looked sexy as hell.

"I should get going, but ... okay, half a cup." He waited until it was poured, then said, "How are *you* doing, Marla?"

"Me? I'm fine. Why?" She tucked the wisp behind her ear.

149

"I don't know ... I just wondered. I'm sure all the media focus on your brother hasn't been easy for you." He reached over tentatively and touched her hand.

Marla's cheeks colored. "I've gotten pretty good at taking things in stride, Dan."

"I know you have. But you deserve better."

He couldn't tell for sure, but he thought she teared up a little. "Things are okay. Really." She glanced over at Willie and Emma, both flopped on the couch with their noses in library books.

"Would you go out with me?" he blurted.

Marla looked startled. "Go out where?"

He smiled. "On a date."

"Oh! Well, I don't have anybody to watch the kids, and ..."

"They can come, too." Dan noticed his voice had taken on a pleading tone.

"Dan, I know you're just trying to be nice, but--"

"I'm *not* trying to be nice, Marla. I truly like you. I want to spend time with you."

"I'm not exactly in your league," she said quietly.

Dan reached over and grabbed both of her hands. "You know what? Neither am I. We'll make our own league."

Dan's impassioned voice caught the kids' attention. Both stared at them with curiosity.

"And we'll include Willie and Emma," Dan said with a wide grin. "Starting tonight. I'll pick you guys up at six and we'll go get pizza."

"Okay," said Marla. "They'd like that. *We'd* like that." She looked over at her children, an unmistakable new glow in her eyes. "Guess what, guys? Dan's taking us out tonight."

෨

REGAN CALLED Adam. "Guess where Haines is?"

"No idea. I let my bureau friends worry about that. And it sounds like you *are* worried about that."

"Yep—he's gone out to Winston Jennings' ranch in Kansas."

"*What?*" said Adam. "Does the judge know?"

"No idea. I let my attorney friends worry about that."

"I'll put in a call to the Commonwealth's Attorney. They'll have his bail revoked."

"I have a better idea," said Regan.

"What would that be, Agent Manning?" His voice dripped with seduction.

"We get his sister to come up with some excuse that will coax him back here. I saw the way he looked at her in the hospital; he has a lot of affection for Marla. If she could get him back here without the courts or law enforcement becoming involved, it'll give us a chance to talk to him when he's not behind bars—see if he's open to any type of plea agreement on the bribery charges. And if it's just that Marla needs him for some reason, we might be able to keep Jennings from coming back here with him."

"Do you think Marla would go along with something like that?"

"I think she might if it means that ultimately her brother has a shot at a shorter prison sentence—which he might if we can get him away from Jennings long enough to turn him."

"I guess it's worth a try."

"Great. I'll let you know what happens."

"I look forward to your call," said Adam. "Or better yet, stop by."

31

TOWARD EVENING, Peter called Regan. "Julia's feeling much more rested. She asked me to call you and invite you to come back for another visit."

Regan arrived at the hospital a half hour later. Peter still hovered near Julia's bedside; Regan wondered if he'd left the hospital at all.

"I can see you feel a lot better, Dr. Haines," said Regan.

"Please call me Julia. And yes I do. I'm finally starting to feel a little more like myself."

"You feel up to talking about the events of the last few days? And by the way, I'm Regan."

"I do feel like talking about them, Regan." She reached over to touch Peter's hand. "Would you mind leaving us alone for a little while?"

His face showed his reluctance to leave, but he didn't argue. "I'll run home to shower and change clothes."

"Take your time ... I'm fine, Peter. Really."

He nodded and left the room.

Regan smiled at Julia. "So ... you and Peter ..."

"I'm sure you've guessed that we're more than just friends."

"I knew it within two minutes of meeting Peter the first time. His feelings for you were very obvious. As are yours for him. I'm happy for you both."

Julia put her hands to her cheeks as if to dim the radiance. "Thank you—but we still have to keep our relationship under wraps. We can't risk giving Jon a reason to fight my petition for sole custody of Jackson. I'm sure he's already going to contest the divorce."

"What can you tell me about those two days being held captive?"

Julia recounted the terror of the standoff, explaining Jon's wild mood swings, the continuous loop from homicidal to remorseful to suicidal. And how when he finally said he would give himself up, she believed him.

"You mentioned before that Jon has always been able to manipulate you," said Regan.

"Yes, from the minute I first saw him in the library at the University of Virginia, I've been hyper-aware of how sensitive and vulnerable he is. After I got to know him, I learned what a sad childhood he had—his father left the family and his mother sank into a deep depression and never recovered. Poor Marla had to become the caretaker at a very young age."

"So if he wanted you to do something, he'd pull the pity card."

"Right. I have a compassionate nature—too much sometimes. He knew that and exploited it. But the past two years, ever since he was elected to Congress, it moved up the scale from exploitation to abuse. I know it sounds odd that I permitted it that long, but--"

"I don't find it odd at all, Julia. I know that when behavior changes gradually over time, sometime it's hard to recognize how bad it's become. You're not to blame for any of this."

"I do blame myself because of the effect it's had on Jackson. That sweet boy became afraid of his dad—and while I might be able to justify Jon's behavior to myself, Jackson doesn't have the capacity to do that. He simply reacted to his dad's hostility."

"Speaking of your son, did you know that Jon asked Marla to take him for right now?"

Julia nodded. "Rosie told me. Her family was willing to keep him, and I said I preferred that—but not because I have any problem with Marla. I think Jon's sister is an absolute saint. I just didn't want to put Jackson through too many changes at once, and he's used to being at Rosie's. Her boys spoil him rotten, and he needs a little of that right now." She smiled. "Rosie's bringing him to see me tonight—I can't wait."

"Julia, there are some things I need to tell you about Jon."

Julia gave her a curious look. "Sounds serious."

"It is." Regan told her about the pending corruption charges against Imhoff-Greyson, including her husband as chief operations officer—and that they hoped to use him to snag Jennings.

Julia stared in disbelief. "No wonder he was always so vague about his work at Imhoff."

"I'm sure he didn't want you to find out about the illegal activities he was involved in," said Regan. She paused, choosing her words carefully. "And there's something I'd like you to just think about ... you don't have to say yes or no right now."

"Okay."

"I wondered if you might consider holding off on filing for divorce, just for awhile. Let Jon think there might be a chance of preventing it—make him believe that, once again, he's been able to play on your compassion. Then we make him choose between you and Jennings."

"You mean double-cross Jon? Lie and say I'll stay with him when I have no intention of it?"

Regan nodded, afraid she was about to witness some of that compassion firsthand.

"Nothing would satisfy me more, Regan. Anything I can do to get both Jon and that tyrannical mentor of his locked up, count me in."

32

D AN WATCHED Emma take another bite of pizza. When she caught his gaze, she smiled. "Yum," she said.

He thought his heart might burst. As he looked at the blonde trio sharing the table with him, he couldn't remember a time when he ever felt so content. So at *ease*. It was a welcome departure from his demanding, deadline-filled world.

Not that he didn't love his work as an investigative reporter; he did. He doubted that his assertive, inquisitive nature would let him do anything else. But right now he wanted to savor this moment. After dinner, he would return to the office, back to his normal life. Things on the Haines story were heating up.

"How's your salad?" he asked Marla.

"Delicious. Thank you for this, Dan."

"It's my pleasure, believe me."

His cell phone vibrated in his shirt pocket. He pulled it out to look at it; it was Nick.

"I'm sorry, Marla; I better take this."

"Sure. Go ahead."

Dan moved out of earshot. "Hey, Nick. What's up?"

"I have a favor to ask. A favor of Marla, actually." Dan had told Nick earlier that he was taking the Dunstons to dinner.

"Okay ... what do you need?" He felt instantly protective.

"We need her to help us get her brother back here—without Winston, if possible."

"How?"

"I don't know … can she make up some kind of story?"

"I'll talk to her and see what she thinks. What's going on?"

"Julia has agreed to do what you suggested. She's going to make Haines think she'll reconsider the divorce if he'll give up Jennings."

"Really?" Dan kept his voice low. "Man, that's great."

"Yep, and we want to keep Jennings in Kansas until we're ready to move on him. He's a bigger threat if he's here."

Dan had an uneasy feeling. He glanced over at Marla; she was smiling at whatever Willie was saying. "Nick, the only problem for Marla might be going along with letting Julia lie to Jon and make him think he'll get her back. I mean, Marla's natural instinct is going to be to protect her brother, and she might think that's cruel."

"That's why we need you to convince her it will help her brother in the long run," said Nick. "He's not going to get Julia back either way, but he'll be looking at a lot less prison time if he helps us get Jennings."

"Right, I know." He hated to spoil their evening; Marla so rarely got to do something fun. Asking that favor would be like throwing a bucket of cold water on her.

Nick must have sensed his reluctance. "I'm sorry to have to do this, Dan. I know you care about her."

"I'll talk to her after we're through with dinner and let you know."

&

EARLY THE next morning, Regan and Nick checked in with their informant, Mason Weir, Imhoff's senior accountant. This time, like before, they met with him in the park, safely away from the eyes and ears at the company compound.

"I've changed my mind about testifying against Haines," he announced in a trembling voice.

It felt like a stab to Regan's chest. "Oh, Mason, no. Why would you do that?"

"Because I don't think there's sufficient evidence," he replied, his eyes revealing the depth of his anguish.

"When the charges against Jon Haines are brought, the U.S. Attorney can compel you to testify. Remember, you showed us the paper trail of the payoffs he made, and as we told you before, you're culpable, too."

"Then arrest me," said Weir. "But I don't know anything about a paper trail."

Nick leaned toward Weir. "I hope, for your sake, that you did not destroy evidence. Because if you did, you won't be getting any kind of deal. You'll be locked up in prison along with Haines. Hell, maybe the two of you will even bunk together."

The accountant briefly shifted his gaze to Nick, then back to the sidewalk in front of the bench where he sat. Not that he was actually seeing it; he was blinded by fear.

Jennings was still chairman of the board at Imhoff, even though he had handed off the CEO reins when he became defense secretary. The company would be Jennings' baby as long as he drew breath.

Or went to prison.

If that was going to happen, they needed help building a water-tight case against him. Their exhaustive investigation over the past nine months made it clear the accountant and Haines were their best—if not their *only*—shot at Jennings.

"Why is it that you were willing to cooperate until Mr. Jennings made a visit to Imhoff headquarters a couple days ago?" said Regan. "Did he say something to you?"

"Of course not—other than to say hello and ask how things were going. That hardly constitutes a threat." He stood up. "If you two will excuse me, I've got to get back to work."

"Not so fast, money man," said Nick. "While he was at the office, did Mr. Jennings say anything about the situation with Haines?"

Weir sat back down. "Just that he expected us all to remain loyal to him—that what was reported on the news was inaccurate and there was no hostage situation."

"What about the explosion?" said Nick. "Or are you actually naïve enough to think Haines didn't cause that?"

"I have no idea … I just don't want to be involved in any of this."

"You already are, Mason. We know how imposing a man Winston Jennings is—but he can't be allowed to operate outside the law. He encouraged illegal payments to foreign officials in exchange for preferential treatment on government contracts. *You* know that and *we* know that. He approved the annual 'bribery budget' that you were asked to oversee. But the paper trail, as you know better than anyone, points directly to Jon Haines and stops there. He is key to getting Jennings, and you are key to getting Haines."

Weir's eyes welled up. "What if you fail? What if you try to make a case against Haines and he's exonerated? Or he won't agree to expose Jennings?" He spoke in a low voice, as though Winston might be hiding behind a nearby tree.

"We think he will," said Nick.

"You *think* he will, but you don't know for sure. If I testify and you don't get Jennings, he will come after me. Wherever I go—even if it's into witness protection—he and those security people of his will find me. Do you know what that would do to my family, if we had to go on the run?" He shook his head. "I can't live like that, always looking over my shoulder, and I won't ask my wife and kids to, either."

Regan hated to admit it, but the man was right. Jennings had made a career out of controlling everything around him—*everyone* around him—and he would not go down without a fight.

They had just one shot. They had to make it count.

≈

NICK WAS right. Adam was not the least bit daunted by Regan's refusal of his invitation to go for a drink.

His attention was still focused mainly on her, just like before. "So Marla will play along with our little scheme to get Haines back here?"

"She was a little reluctant at first, but she said she would."

"Good. What about Julia Haines—is she willing to say she'll reconsider the divorce in exchange for his testimony against Jennings?"

"Yep," said Nick, his tone sharper than necessary. "She won't, of course, but if he *thinks* she will, it's our best chance at getting him to cooperate."

"She was pretty shocked at the depth of his involvement in the overseas bribes," said Regan.

Adam's gaze flickered toward Nick and then back to her. "She didn't know anything?"

"She said there were times when he acted secretive and she suspected he was up to something, but she never confronted him because he'd developed such a nasty temper. He was becoming more and more abusive."

"Why didn't she leave when that first started? My god, she's way more accomplished than *he* is—it's not like she needed his support."

"She stayed because she still thought she could help him," said Regan. "He had a tough childhood. Julia became his anchor—the protector of his feelings—so she was afraid of what would happen to him if she left. She ignored a lot of the verbal abuse; told herself it wasn't that big a deal, that he was just stressed and didn't really mean it. But it stepped up after he went to Congress."

"And then it became physical?"

Regan nodded. "Just in the last few months."

"Boy, this guy's a real prince."

"He is," said Nick. "And we're hoping the prince can deliver us the king." He grinned in spite of himself.

Regan rolled her eyes. Adam smiled and shook his head.

"Okay," Adam said, grabbing a yellow tablet from his desk drawer. "Let's talk strategy—the charges we're going to file and the timeline. How will Julia deliver her ultimatum to Jon?"

"Through her attorney," said Regan.

"She doesn't want to see him face-to-face?"

"No, she doesn't. Julia is completely fed up with Jon and doesn't want to see him, but mostly she just wants to get all of this behind her and get on with her life."

"That's why we can't let it drag out too long," said Nick. "We've got to put the deal on the table and force Haines to choose between Julia and Jennings before something unforeseen happens."

"We'll go ahead and ask for an expedited grand jury hearing to up the pressure. You guys will need to bring Weir in, along with his evidence, so we can determine the number of counts and figure out his plea deal. Ideally, Julia's attorney should plan to meet with Haines right after we get our indictment."

They got up to leave. Adam said, "Hey, Regan, you like baseball? I've got tickets to the Washington Nationals game on Sunday if you'd like to go."

Stop asking me out, Adam, she said with her eyes. She didn't need to look at Nick to know he'd have a dour look on his face.

Adam must have noticed it, though. "You can come, too, Nick. I'm sure we can scare up another ticket."

"No, thanks," said Nick. "We've got too much work to do. You may recall we have a grand jury hearing to prepare for."

This time, Regan did look at him, and *her* expression was dour. "Apparently my partner speaks for both of us."

"Actually, he's right," said Adam. "We do need to make sure we're well prepared. We can take in a game another time."

"I'd like that," said Regan.

33

JON WAS becoming a little *too* comfortable at the ranch. Winston began to worry he'd never get him to leave.

"I don't get it, Win," Jon said as the men drove through the pasture, Gert perched on the seat between them. "Why would you still spend time in DC when you have all this?"

"The call to duty," said Winston. "I have expertise that will make this country safer, and I have the ability to lead others. You have a lot to contribute, too, Jon."

"Maybe I'd rather contribute from a different platform. Getting out of Washington has made me see how toxic it is there, how we're all primed for battle all the time. I'm beginning to see there are more important things in life."

"Such as?"

"Family."

Winston sighed. "You still thinking you can get Julia back?"

"I don't know, Win, but I'm going to try."

"And then what? Give up your seat in Congress and move somewhere like this? Do you think she'll just drop everything and leave Georgetown?" He couldn't believe Jon could be so damn naïve.

"Georgetown isn't the only place Julia can do her research. She's a leader in her field. She can go anywhere."

Winston stopped in front of a gate and got out of the pickup to open it. Walking back, he studied Jon's face as the younger man gazed out at the hilly landscape dotted with cattle. It had only been twenty-four hours, and though he still had a nasty cough, he looked utterly transformed.

Betty had invited their kids and grandkids over for dinner, and suddenly Winston worried his brood might be another pulling factor for Jon. They were a lively bunch who made guests feel right at home.

Could he uninvite them?

No, Betty would have a fit. The roast was in the oven and the homemade rolls were rising. If he pulled a stunt like that— getting in the way of her family and her culinary offerings, both of which were a source of great pride—it might be the last good meal he ever saw.

Better to go ahead and let Jon enjoy his stay, get himself put back together mentally. In a couple days, it would be time to return to Washington.

By force if necessary.

ॐ

JON WAS in the middle of hearing about the Jennings grandkids' 4-H projects when he got a call on his cell phone. He looked over at Winston and said, "It's my sister."

"Hey, Marla," he said, moving toward the front door so he could step outside.

Winston had an uneasy feeling, though he couldn't pinpoint why. Marla was likely just calling to see if Jon was feeling better.

"He seems nice, Dad," said his daughter Kate. "Like a normal person. It's hard to believe he did what he did."

"What did he do?" asked her eight-year-old boy.

"Nothing. Go play." The kids drifted off to the family room to play a Wii game.

Betty got up and started clearing dishes from the table. She'd been cordial to Jon since he arrived, and had certainly fed him well, but Winston could tell from the set of her jaw that she had serious reservations about their guest. In bed the night before, she started to say something, but Winston cut her off. As far as he was concerned, there was no point discussing it.

"He *is* a normal person, Kate. That was all a misunderstanding."

"What's going to happen to him?" said Kate's brother Rob.

Winston glanced over at the window; he could see Jon pacing back and forth on the veranda. "We're hoping to get the kidnapping charge dropped. Depends on what his wife is willing to do."

"I don't care what the reason is," said Kate. "If Steve pointed a gun at me like that, not only would he find himself without a wife, he'd be looking at the inside of a jail cell."

Kate's husband smiled. He never raised his voice, much less a gun, so the whole notion was absurd.

Betty looked over at her daughter. "I agree, Kate. A little jail time might help the congressman curb his temper toward his wife — if she's crazy enough to stick around after this."

"Damn it, Betty, I *told* you …"

"Mom's entitled to her opinion, Dad," Kate said brusquely.

"I didn't say she wasn't. But if it was up to your mother, they'd lock him up and throw away the key."

"I did not say any such thing," Betty said heatedly, buoyed by her daughter's support.

Winston waved dismissively and got up from the table just as Jon was coming back in the house.

"Everything okay, Jon?"

"I need to head home tomorrow. Marla needs my help."

"With what?" He was relieved he wasn't going to have to hog-tie Jon to go back, but the situation seemed a little suspect.

Jon moved close to Winston and lowered his voice so the others wouldn't hear. "My nephew, Willie, is acting out, and she's upset. Said he lit a match and threatened to burn his little sister. Marla thinks he's doing it because their father left them, and she knows I can help him deal with that."

"It's that urgent?"

"No, she said I didn't have to rush back, but I could tell she was scared. I want to be there for her—I owe her that. I'm going to call and see if I can get on an early flight tomorrow."

"I'll get us a charter."

"No need for that, Winston. Stay here and enjoy your family for awhile."

"I'd rather be there to help you sort things out, Jon. We'll leave first thing in the morning."

❧

IT WAS after eleven, and Jon had gone to bed. Winston sat in his office, watching the news with a sense of foreboding that hung over him like storm clouds.

"Looks like they're all wondering what's going to happen to him, too." Betty's sudden appearance in the doorway made him jump.

"Jesus, Betty, give me some damn warning. You startled me."

"Sorry. Do you want me to bang on a frying pan when I'm coming down the hallway?"

Winston was even more startled by her sarcasm than her sudden appearance. Obviously her patience was starting to wear thin.

"No, of course not. I'm sorry to be such a bear. Come and sit down, Betts." He pointed to the hunter green plaid sofa near his recliner.

Now it was Betty's turn to look surprised. He *never* invited her into his office except to vacuum; it was his private kingdom.

She took a seat next to Gertie on the sofa. "Are you all right, Win?"

"I'm fine, honey. I'm just concerned about Jon is all. None of this business makes any sense to me. He has a sterling political career in front of him, and he seems intent on throwing it away."

"But it's *his* career, Winston, not yours."

"I'm aware of that, Betty. I just worry that he's having a mental breakdown and needs help."

"It's obvious he is. I think you should let him go back to Washington alone. His sister will help him."

Gertie sighed loudly.

That's the way I feel, too, Gert, thought Winston. *She has no clue what's at stake here.*

Betty always saw things in black or white, right or wrong, not all that complicated. But most of the time, things *were* complicated.

"I'm afraid his sister won't be able to handle him. She thinks she can, but she's had very little contact with him during the last fifteen years. He's not the same person he used to be."

Now Betty sighed loudly. Gertie popped her head up and looked at her.

"Winston, stop trying to play God. You know I never tell you what to do—because it wouldn't do any good—but this time I'm going to try. Stay here and let things play out however they're going to. Jon is no longer your worry."

Oh, Betty, Winston thought sadly, *if only that were true.*

34

THE SOUND of his voice was like a cozy blanket.

"I'm glad you changed your mind, Regan. I'm glad you're coming."

"Me, too. We need to talk."

"I know we do." He paused. "Do you still feel the same, Regan? I mean, do you still … love me?"

She felt a twinge of guilt about Adam. "I do, Jack."

He gave a sigh of relief. "Then I promise we'll come up with something—even if it's marriage-by-Skype."

She giggled. "What if we want kids?"

"Then Skype might not be our best option. I'll keep thinking."

"You do that. How's your research coming, babe?"

Jack gave her an update, his voice buzzing with excitement. In the two years since she'd known him, she'd learned a ton about trees. There was a lot going on behind that bark.

"How about your investigation? How's that coming?"

"We're close—in the final, critical stage. This is where it all comes together or it all falls apart."

"Yikes."

"I know. If it falls apart, we may have our solution. I might be unemployed."

"I'd love to have a solution, but not like that. Besides, your instincts are too sharp for things to fall apart. Your gut, Agent Manning, is second to none."

"Why, thank you, sir. I didn't realize you loved me for my gut."

"I love you for a whole lot more than that. And I can't wait to see you."

≈

DAN SUGGESTED that Speaker Stallworth might be more forthcoming if he came along for the meeting, but Regan figured it was just Dan's ego talking again. Two FBI agents were enough without adding a reporter to the mix.

Since it was Saturday, it was quieter than usual in the Capitol. They made their way to the speaker's office, where he personally escorted them in and closed the door.

"What can I help you with?" he asked. He seemed a little amped up by their visit.

"Mr. Speaker, we're hoping to have a candid conversation with you about Winston Jennings," said Regan. "It would remain completely confidential, of course, but it's critical to our current investigation into Congressman Haines."

Stallworth relaxed slightly, striking a philosophical tone. "There was a time when I truly respected Winston Jennings. Even wished I had the kind of presence he does. It took me awhile, but I finally figured out that, for all his rhetoric about love of country and about his duty to serve it, the man only cares about serving Imhoff-Greyson—and himself."

"So with the president being a Democrat and not an ally of his, Jennings is trying to use *your* leverage to get the new defense structure in place," said Regan.

"That's right. The Republicans are the minority party in the Senate, so right now I'm his only avenue."

"He's stuck with you, like it or not," said Regan.

Stallworth smiled. "Correct. And I'm sure he *doesn't* like it, even though he acts like we're old pals. But he needs me to help him get that national research facility in Kansas—and keep the House reps he wants on his cybersecurity task force. He can't afford to make an enemy of me because I can negatively affect both of those things."

"How do you feel about his grand scheme, Mr. Speaker?" said Nick.

Stallworth hesitated, clearly weighing how much of his true opinion to express. "You know, at one point I supported it. The U.S. needs a stronger defense structure to protect us from cyber attacks. I'm sure I don't have to tell you guys how damaging they are to this country economically—your bureau plays a key role on the cybersecurity task force. Jennings knows better than anybody how the architecture can all fit together seamlessly—so I downplayed in my mind how self-serving and manipulative he can be."

"And now?" said Regan.

"Now I see that if Jennings is able to carry out his plan, he will get away with circumventing the competitive bid process on even more government contracts. He'll continue to build his empire at Imhoff-Greyson, adding spin-off divisions so it's harder to track. He'll do what he's always done, but on a much grander scale."

"And he'll accrue enormous wealth in the process," said Nick.

Stallworth held up his hands. "Don't get me wrong—I don't have a problem with wealth. No self-respecting Republican would." He gave a hollow laugh. "But I do have a problem with bending the rules to achieve it."

"Not only bending the rules but breaking the law," said Regan. "It sounds like this wouldn't be the first time Jennings has been able to skirt the bid process and steer contracts to his company."

"It's not the first time, but technically he isn't breaking the law," said the speaker. "Let me give you a little background. Before Jon Haines went to work at Imhoff-Greyson, he was with one of the big Washington law firms—and his area of expertise was contract law."

They already knew that, but Regan wanted to hear what Stallworth had to say.

"The firm's biggest clients were companies bidding on government contracts, and they needed lawyers who were intimately familiar with the complexities of the Federal Acquisition Regulation. Even though he was a young associate, Haines was their best guy, and he became something of a thorn in Winston's side because of that talent. Imhoff got beat out on some major contracts. So Jennings decided to hire Haines, and ever since he joined Imhoff, the company has never lost another contract bid."

They didn't know *that*.

"Which means Haines became indispensible to Jennings," said Nick.

"Right. And since the Defense Department is one of the agencies that administers the law, Haines was the perfect fit to oversee the Federal Acquisition Regulation when Jennings became defense secretary. Haines wrote a supplement to the regulation while he was in that job—one that was particularly beneficial to Imhoff because it added required provisions pertaining to security that only Imhoff could meet."

Click. The dots were connected. And what the picture showed was the astounding depth of Winston Jennings' power and greed.

"Wow," was all she could say.

"What about antitrust laws?" said Nick. "Isn't Imhoff's monopoly on these contracts a violation of those?"

"Not if there aren't any competitors. Many people are fully aware that the FAR supplement Haines wrote is, in essence, an antitrust violation because it effectively favored a single company. But he framed it around security, which is a growing concern and arguably one that needed to be included more fully in government contracts."

"So if Jennings succeeds at getting the defense architecture in place that he wants," said Regan, "Imhoff will almost be like another government agency."

"Bingo. But without the constraints of a government agency—and without congressional oversight."

It struck Regan that, from Jennings' perspective, it probably had as much to do with successfully pulling off such a feat as the wealth he'd accrue in the process. It would allow his legacy to live on long after he moseyed off to Kansas to manage a cow herd.

But to do it, Jennings needed Haines more than ever. And so did they.

35

THE IMHOFF headquarters looked more like a military installation than a privately owned business. A large sign at the entrance to the property instructed all visitors to check in at the main building, a one-story concrete affair that squatted like a sentry in front of a cluster of larger structures that housed about twenty thousand of Imhoff's employees, including its CEO when he was in town. A training facility of some kind was partially visible in back of the buildings.

"Jeez, look at that place," said Nick. "I wonder if anybody informed Jennings he's no longer with the U.S. government."

"I guess global security begins at home," said Regan.

Nick parked the SUV across the highway from the entrance while she placed a call to Weir. They were there to pick him up but didn't want to arouse suspicion. Earlier he had described the fortress-like interior of the main building, complete with armed guards.

"I guess he must have stepped out," his assistant informed her.

"Could you have him call me as soon as he steps back in?" said Regan. She gave the woman her name and number.

They settled in to wait. Regan said, "I'm still reeling from what Stallworth said."

"Me, too," said Nick. "You certainly got your question answered."

"Which question is that?"

"Why Winston Jennings is afraid to let Haines out of his sight," said Nick. "He's afraid the man's gonna crack and all those secrets are going to spill out."

"We're going to have to figure out how to get the secrets out of him *without* letting him crack. And Julia is still our best bet."

"At least until he figures out she has no intention of staying with him—and that he's lost them both."

"I hope Marla can help us convince Jon that putting Jennings away is the best thing for his own preservation," said Regan. "Jennings ratchets up the pressure on him a little more every year, which is probably what finally made him pop his cork."

"If we do our job right, Jennings will spend the rest of his life behind bars," said Nick. "Haines will serve a shorter sentence, and once he's out, he can start over. If we explain that to Marla, maybe she'll help us put Jennings away."

"Maybe, but I think we need to move slowly and feel her out. Otherwise, it could blow up in our faces."

"I agree, but we're running out of time."

"I know." She sighed and looked at her watch. "Speaking of which, we've been waiting quite awhile. I'm going to call again."

Mason still wasn't in. "Let me check to see if anyone has seen him since lunchtime," said his assistant. A couple minutes later, she came back on the line. "Nobody has seen him for a couple of hours at least."

Had Jennings shown up and freaked him out again?

"Do you happen to know if Mr. Jennings has been in the office today?"

"Hang on."

The voice that came back on the line belonged to a man. "May I ask who this is?"

"This is Special Agent Regan Manning. And who are you?"

"Name is Boyd. I'm head of security here."

"Well, Mr. Boyd, we--"

"Just Boyd."

"Okay, Just Boyd, we wish to speak with Mason Weir."

"Regarding?"

"A confidential matter."

Silence on the other end. Finally, he said, "Mr. Weir isn't available."

"Can you tell me if he's left for the day?"

"I don't have that information, Agent Manning. You might try back tomorrow." He hung up.

"Thank you, Just Boyd," Regan said to the disconnected line. "We appreciate your gracious assistance. Have a good day."

Nick gaped at her. "I can't believe that asshole hung up on us."

"I can't believe that asshole monitors Imhoff calls like that."

"Now what?"

"I hope I'm wrong, Nick, but I have the sinking feeling that Mason Weir has gone to ground."

&

ANITA WEIR'S distress was genuine. She clearly didn't know why her husband had gone into hiding—just that he had.

"He sounded strange ... said he had to leave for awhile and he'd call me when it was safe." She brushed the back of her hand across her damp cheeks. "I don't understand. He's an accountant. Why wouldn't he be safe?"

"We're investigating some potential improprieties at Imhoff-Greyson," said Regan.

Her eyes widened. "Did Mason do something wrong?"

Regan remained noncommittal. "Not necessarily. We're simply looking into things at this point."

Anita's hand flew to her mouth. "That's why he's been saying he wanted to leave there—kept saying the company had changed a lot. But he's been there for more than twenty years, and they've always paid him extremely well. I told him he wouldn't be able to find a better job anywhere else."

It wasn't loyalty, or his wife's advice, that made him stay. It was fear of Winston Jennings. Mason simply knew too much.

"Is it Jon Haines?" asked Anita. "Did he do something illegal? Or ... or ... *Mr. Jennings*?"

It was amazing how quickly she nailed it.

"What makes you say that?" said Nick.

She shrugged. "Mason has never liked Jon Haines. Thought he was devious and mean. But Haines also seemed to have a closer relationship with Mr. Jennings than anyone else at the company."

"Did your husband ever tell you he suspected them of acting illegally?" said Regan.

"No. Did he tell *you* that? If he did, maybe he's afraid they found out."

Regan chose her words carefully. "We believe your husband has special knowledge of the processes at Imhoff—and that by talking to us, he's put himself at risk."

"Are we in danger? Not just Mason, but the kids and me, too?"

"Mrs. Weir, if Mason fully commits to helping us, we'll make sure all of you are protected," said Nick. "Right now he *is* extremely vulnerable."

She shook her head and struggled to keep a lid on her composure. "Tell me, how did you get Mason to cooperate in the first place? I would like to think he'd automatically do what's right, but I know my husband. He would rather stick his head in the sand and hope it all goes away. He hates confrontation more than anyone I've ever known. So why was he cooperating?"

The woman was more than a little astute. "Because we intercepted some emails with his name on them," said Regan. "We made contact, and he acknowledged that he knew the company had made questionable payments to foreign officials."

From the look on her face, it was confirmation she was hoping not to hear.

Nick said, "We promised him a light sentence—maybe even probation—if he testifies."

"I see," Anita said in a trembling voice.

"We need your help," said Regan. "We need you to get him to come in."

"How?"

"Next time he calls, tell him we're looking for him and we *will* find him," said Nick. "But things will go a lot better for him if he comes back on his own."

36

JULIA SAT on the edge of the bed, resting after her slow trudge down the hall and back. She hugged Peter as tightly as she could without hurting herself. "See you in the morning, sweetheart," she murmured. "Get a good night's sleep. I'm going to be fine."

"I hate to leave you here alone," Peter said sullenly. "Why don't I just stay here and sleep in the chair again? I don't mind at all. I'd rather--"

"I'm not alone, Peter. I'm surrounded by a lot of our friends and colleagues here. Now go." She gave him a mock-stern look and pointed at the door.

"Okay, okay. I'm going." He started to leave the room, then turned and came back over to her. "I love you, Julia." He kissed her forehead.

Though she had known it for a long time, it was the first time he had spoken the words out loud.

She wrapped her arms around his waist, her cheek against his chest, joy coursing through her. She could feel his heart beating. "I love you, too, Peter."

"Knock, knock."

They both turned and saw Dr. Mackenzie. How long had he been standing in the doorway?

They would soon be together for all the world to see, but not yet. Not until Jon couldn't do anything to hurt them.

"How's the patient this evening?"

"Much better," said Julia.

Peter said, "I'll get going. See you in the morning, Julia." His tone was almost business-like after the tender words he'd spoken a moment before.

After he left, Julia said, "I'm not sure how long you were standing out there before you came in, or what you heard, Mac, but Peter and I are--"

"It's okay, Julia. We've all suspected for a long time that your feelings for each other went way beyond your mutual excitement over discovering a new drug compound." He grinned.

"Okay, yes, you're right ... but we never acted on it. Now, after all that's happened, it's hard to keep our feelings locked inside. But I need to resolve things with Jon first."

"I understand. You don't want to give him any ammunition to use against you."

"Exactly."

"We're your family here, Julia. Nobody will do anything that could possibly compromise you—least of all, me. I couldn't be happier for you and Peter."

"Thanks, Mac. That means a lot."

"Let's take a look at that head wound, see how it's coming along." He unwrapped the bandage from her head and inspected the gash, then quizzed her about how she felt when she was up walking around.

"A little dizzy, but not too bad."

"What about your lungs? Are you coughing a lot?" He placed his stethoscope on her back.

She shook her head. "Only a little."

He asked a few more questions, then said, "Okay, let me grab a nurse and we'll get you bandaged up again."

"How much longer will I be here, Mac?"

"Let's give it a couple more days. That head wound was pretty severe, so I'd like to keep an eye on it—make sure you don't have a recurrence of the swelling. When I'm sure you're past the danger point, I'll go ahead and spring you and you can continue your recovery at home. But I'd plan on some in-home care for awhile."

Peter would be first in line to volunteer, but she would hire a nurse so he could get back to the lab. Back to their work.

After the doctor left, Julia got into bed and closed her eyes, exhausted but euphoric. She and Peter would have an amazing life together—and Jackson would have a stable, loving stepfather.

The phone beside her bed rang, making her jump. "Hello?"

"Julia?"

Her heart began to race. "What do you want, Jon?"

"I just want to talk. To tell you I'm sorry. I know I don't deserve your forgiveness, but I'm asking for it anyway." His tone was contrite. The way it always was after he'd gone too far.

She felt her anger flare. "You tried to kill me—after I agreed to stay and walk out of the house with you. So we could look like a normal couple, as if that was even possible after you held a gun on me for two days. I could've left while you were in the shower, but I didn't. I stayed because you asked me to. And then you bludgeon me with God-knows-what and try to bash my skull. And burn the house down. You're ... you're a very sick man, Jon."

"I—I know that, Julia. And I'm going to get help. But I did all of that because I love you too much to let you go. I've always loved you too much."

"That's not love, it's fear. It's obsession. It's manipulation. And it's *over*."

She flashed on the promise she'd made to Regan about letting him think there was a chance at reconciliation, but holding in the hurt and anger right now was like holding back the tide.

"I swear I'll change, Julia. I'll do whatever you want me to. If that means leaving Congress, if it means going to therapy every single day—whatever you want, I'll do. I just want to salvage some kind of relationship with you."

"Do you have any idea how much trouble you're in, Jon?"

He was silent a moment. "It was all an accident."

"Really? How was slamming a heavy object into the back of my head an accident?"

"That ... that was temporary insanity. Brought on by the stress of having all those FBI agents and cops surrounding our house for two days. I just lost it ... I wanted both of us to die. And I'm sorry. I will never, ever hurt you again, Julia. I promise."

A nurse came in the room and checked Julia's monitor. The concerned look on the nurse's face told Julia that her blood pressure and heart rate had spiked.

"I've got to go. And don't call me again."

"I still love you, Julia, and I always will."

"Goodbye, Jon."

❧

WINSTON WAS more than a little perturbed. He had asked Jon to draft policy language, along with the documents they would need once the cybersecurity policy was adopted by Congress and signed into law in just a matter of weeks. Nobody understood the intricacies of it better than Jon, and right now he could use the distraction.

But Jon was too busy whining over Julia. He could barely put one foot in front of the other, much less draft complex materials for Imhoff.

Like it or not, Winston needed a backup plan. He needed someone else that could at least get them started until Jon had his shit together.

That someone was the head accountant, Mason Weir. True, there was no love lost between Weir and Haines, but that wasn't Winston's problem. Weir was smart, if a little too twitchy for his taste. He hadn't wanted to be involved in the movement of funds overseas, but in the end he'd gone along. That fact, along with his ability to grasp complexities in general, made him the obvious choice.

He might be on edge about it, but his allegiance was guaranteed.

Still, just to sweeten the deal, Winston would give him a nice little bump in salary. He planned to stop by the office and visit with Weir in the morning.

He glanced at his watch; it was just after nine p.m. He thought about calling Betty to say goodnight, but when he called after he had landed in Washington, she'd been frosty. He knew it was because he hadn't taken her advice and stayed home—but he had no intention of letting his wife tell him what to do. Never had, never would.

Winston tried to get Jon to come back to his apartment to stay, but he insisted on sleeping on his sister's couch so he could help straighten out his nephew. Winston could only hope Marla was keeping a close eye on him.

He flipped on the TV and sat down to watch Jeremy Traynor's special report on identify theft. Sadly, Traynor himself had become the victim of identity thieves just this week.

Winston smiled.

37

JULIA PHONED Regan the next morning.

"Jon called me last night," she told the agent. "I think I may have messed up our plan."

"What happened? Did he threaten you?"

"No, he just wanted to talk to me. To tell me that everything that happened was an accident — and it was because he loves me too much."

"Oh, lord."

"I know ... he loved me too much to let me live." Julia recounted his promise to do whatever it took to have some kind of relationship with her — and her angry response. "I'm sorry, Regan. I couldn't help it. All that fury just came pouring out."

"He put you through hell, Julia. No one expects you to simply brush that off."

Julia felt a rush of gratitude. "Thank you for understanding."

"Of course. So how were things left?"

"I told him not to call me again."

"I think we're still okay with our plan. Once the grand jury hands down the indictment — and we're confident they will — Jon could be convinced you had a change of heart after he was carted off to jail again. It would be that familiar compassion he's always gotten from you."

"Okay, yes," said Julia. "I think you're right. He's delusional enough to think that could still happen."

"You have the leverage, Julia. He needs you, not only because of his twisted love for you but also because he wants to play down the whole hostage standoff."

"I just want all of this to be over. I want to finish my recovery and get back to my life—with Jackson and Peter. *Without* Jon."

"I know this is hard, Julia, and it's going to get a little harder before it's over. But Jon is going to pay for his mistakes. We just need you to hang in there a little longer."

Julia sighed. "I will. I promise." And unlike Jon, she *kept* her promises.

~

ON MONDAY morning, Winston pulled into the underground garage at Imhoff-Greyson. His cell phone rang; the caller ID said it was his longtime attorney, Howard Perkins, whom he had assigned to Jon's case.

"Good morning, Howard."

"I have some bad news, Win. I just got word that a grand jury is being convened tomorrow to hear charges of bribery against the company. Violations of the Foreign Corrupt Practices Act."

The news knocked the wind out of him. "Do you know what kind of evidence they have?"

"No," said Howard. "But these federal charges will be bumped to the front of the line. The state has already charged Haines on two counts of abduction, and it's likely they'll add attempted murder and arson if we don't find a way to knock those down. We need to discuss our defense strategy."

Winston felt his nerves start to jangle. He'd been scheming ways to fight the state charges, but the federal charges of corruption took things to a whole different level—one that would of course involve him. "Okay, go get Jon at his sister's and let's meet in my office in ninety minutes."

"Do you have reason to believe there's any truth to the bribery charges, Win?"

One-point-six billion reasons, he wanted to tell the attorney. But not yet. He wanted to see how much the feds knew before he had that conversation.

"See what you can find out, Howard. We need to know exactly what they have."

He signed off and took the elevator up to the top floor. He deposited his brief case in his office and headed down to three, where Mason Weir's office was located. He needed to find out from the accountant if any agents had been sniffing around lately.

"He left just after lunch on Friday and hasn't been back," said Weir's assistant.

Winston's apprehension kicked into overdrive. "Did anyone call his house?"

"We called both his cell and his home line, but there was no answer. I even left a message, but he hasn't called back."

Okay, what the hell is going on?

Whatever it was, Winston didn't like it. He went to see Boyd.

"Mason Weir has mysteriously disappeared."

"I know," said Boyd. "Two FBI agents called on Friday looking for him, and he'd already been gone for … I don't know, a couple hours I guess."

"And you didn't think to alert me?"

Boyd looked remorseful. "I thought he went home sick and would be back in today, Mr. Jennings. I didn't see anything suspicious about the situation."

"It didn't strike you as odd that two FBI agents were trying to reach him?"

"Kind of, but I figured it was something personal. Why? Has he done something to compromise the company?"

Winston pointed a finger at his security chief. "That's what I pay *you* to know."

"Okay, sir," Boyd said, leaping out of his chair. "I'll get on it."

෨

"WHERE'S WEIR?" said Adam. "He's key to this thing; we need his testimony along with Lee's." He was more businesslike today, perhaps aware he'd been causing tension between Regan and Nick. He looked over at her. "Any idea where he might be?"

"Nick's coordinating the search." She turned to her partner and waited for him to update Adam.

"We've got a car on the house and we've put out a BOLO on his vehicle," said Nick. "Our techs are pinging his phone, so if he hasn't dumped it, they should come up with a location."

"Okay, I'll get to work on a subpoena for Weir's computer and physical files," said Adam. "Once we have those we should be able to add to the number of counts against Haines."

"At a minimum, there will be at least a dozen more," said Nick.

"Enough to keep Imhoff from ever bidding on another government contract," said Regan. She shuddered to think of Jennings' reaction to the news that his company was about to be knocked out from under him.

"That's good; I just wish that damn accountant would show up. His disappearance is making me nervous." He stood up from where he'd been sitting on the edge of his desk.

"I want to go pay another visit to Anita Weir," said Nick. "Ready, Regan?"

"You go ahead. I'm going to walk back to the office."

"It's almost two miles from here, Regan. C'mon, I'll drop you off."

"I need to clear my head, Nick. Think about where we are. Go ahead and go."

Nick looked back and forth between her and Adam, as though he suspected they were up to something. Finally, he turned around and stomped out.

"What's his deal?" said Adam. "He acts like it's his job to protect you."

"Actually, he's protecting Jack. Nick's worried I'm going to forget I have a boyfriend in Alaska."

Adam inched closer to her. "Do you *want* to forget you have a boyfriend in Alaska? I'd be glad to help you with that, you know."

She gave a nervous laugh. "I think you've made that pretty clear, Adam. I'm a little conflicted about my relationship with Jack right now, but I need to resolve things with him one way or the other. It wouldn't be fair--"

Adam leaned over and kissed her, cutting her off.

38

REGAN WALLOWED in guilt all the way back to the office. She'd all but given Adam the green light. But she had to admit the kiss was titillating, and that left her feeling more troubled than ever.

What the hell am I doing?

She was behaving as though her relationship with Jack was already over. As though having a new one under way when she saw him in a few days would insulate her from chucking her career and moving back to Alaska to be with him.

It was a shameful act of callousness, using Adam like that. She could tell he'd developed some pretty intense feelings for her; it was selfish to encourage him while she was in her current state of confusion.

She would call and apologize to him when she got back to the office. Tell him it wouldn't happen again.

Regan couldn't afford to be distracted right now anyway. She was dealing with Winston Jennings, and she needed to be firing on all cylinders.

She had just arrived back at her desk when Dan called to say he'd been trying to reach Nick without success.

"He's tied up at the moment, Dan. Is there something I can help you with?"

"Just wanted to report what Marla told me. Jon's staying with her to help with Willie, but she came clean and told him it was only a ruse to get him back here. Five minutes around that sweet kid and he'd have figured it out anyway. She told him she was scared that he would get into a lot of trouble for leaving town—and make things worse than they already are."

"How did he react?"

"I guess he got a little mad at first, but then he thanked her. Said he was sorry for putting her through all of this."

"Did she ask him why he changed his mind about coming out of the house after he promised her he would?"

"She said they haven't talked too much about it. I think they both see this as the calm before the storm. They just want to spend a little time getting to know each other again before he goes off to jail. He needs Marla, and she's eager to help him— he'll always be her baby brother, no matter what."

"Thanks, Dan. I appreciate the info. Have you gone over there to try to talk to him yourself?"

"No, Marla asked me to give them some space. I'm hoping I get the chance later on. My show Friday night ended up to be little more than a puff piece, so I'm going to take another run at it this week."

Regan had missed it. "Was Claire able to help you with the psychological stuff?"

"Not really. Seems like she mostly wanted to talk about Nick. Does she have some big thing for him?"

"Yep, she keeps hoping he'll dump his girlfriend so she can have a shot. What she doesn't know is that, even if he and Lindsay split up—which is highly unlikely—he wouldn't date her anyway. Claire's not his type."

"Well, a girl can always dream, I suppose. I noticed she was awfully tight-lipped about you. I nudged her a couple times to get her to dish, but she wouldn't." He chuckled.

"Dr. Campbell is a little too fond of her own opinion for my taste, and I'm sure her three degrees in psychology have allowed her to detect that. Now that we're no longer at CIRG, Nick and I don't have to see her—so it works out nicely. I better get back to work; do you want Nick to call you?"

"I left him a message, so he will if he wants to. Let me know if anything juicy pops up."

"You'll be the first one we call, Dan."

 ∂ゃ

NICK SPENT the rest of the day working with the surveillance teams to locate the missing accountant. He called Regan around midnight.

"We found Weir."

From his dull tone, Regan could tell it wasn't good news. "And?"

"His car was in the Potomac, and he was inside it."

Regan let out a sigh, disappointment and sorrow washing over her. "Oh, *no*. Does it look like foul play or suicide?" No way in hell it was an accident.

"Don't know yet. I just got here."

"What about Anita? Has she been told?"

"The surveillance team we've had outside her house is informing her right now."

Regan had had the task of death notifications before and knew how awful it felt to deliver such a crushing blow to loved ones. Her heart went out to Anita Weir and her children.

"What's your location, Nick?"

He described exactly where the car had gone into the river.

"Okay, I'm on my way."

By the time she got there, questions were pounding her brain. Did Jennings kill Weir to silence him? And without Weir, how could they possibly explain—or even comprehend—the convoluted trail that pointed to Jennings?

39

A ROUND FIVE a.m., Regan called Adam. "We need to push back the grand jury hearing a couple more days."

"Why?" He sounded awake and alert; Regan wondered what time he usually got up.

"Weir's body was pulled out of the Potomac a few hours ago."

"Oh my god," Adam muttered. "Was he murdered?"

"We aren't sure yet if it was a murder or suicide."

"Where's Haines?"

"At his sister's in Manassas," said Regan. "I think you should go ahead and get the judge to revoke his bail for leaving town and have the locals pick him up. We need him in custody for his own protection."

"Okay. I'll make the calls."

&

THE CALL went to Nick's voicemail. "Hey, man, could you call me?" said Dan. "I just heard about that Imhoff accountant's car being found in the Potomac. Call me as soon as you get this."

Dan wasn't confident his FBI buddy would comply, but it was worth a shot. It felt like they were freezing him out; he told himself it was only because there was so much happening in their investigation that keeping him informed was hardly a priority.

He had to find a way to get into their good graces so he'd have access to the investigation. But first he had to deal with Marla. When Jon was taken into custody a couple hours ago, she seemed to hit a breaking point.

"You didn't need to come," she said when she opened the door.

The kids were playing on the living room floor. "Hi, Dan," they called in unison, seemingly oblivious to her turmoil.

"Hey guys," he said, following Marla into the kitchen. "I wanted to come, Marla. I want to help you through this." He pulled her into his arms and held her.

"I'm just so scared for Jon," she said in a wobbly voice, clinging to him. "He's starting to spiral, just the way my mother did. We both knew he'd be going to jail, but now that it's happened, I'm worried it might push him so far down he'll never be able to climb back out."

"Maybe they won't be able to prove their case against him," said Dan. "And in the meantime, if Jon is suffering from severe depression, the authorities will see that he gets help."

If for no other reason than to make sure he's sane enough to stand trial.

Marla stepped back and looked at him. "Dan, I'd like your help with something—if you're willing."

"Of course. Name it."

"I want you to help me find my father."

Whoa. He hadn't seen that coming. "Why, Marla? What good will that do?"

"Maybe he can help us."

"But Jon doesn't even know him," Dan said gently.

"I know, and that's always been the hardest thing for him to accept. It seems like ever since he became a father himself, he's gotten more resentful and confused about why our dad left us.

Maybe if Jon could just meet him, he'd find out our parents' divorce had nothing to do with him. They might even be able to build some kind of relationship."

It seemed to Dan that it would only complicate things— maybe even make them worse. "I'm not sure that's a likely scenario, Marla. Your father has had ample opportunity to come forward, and he hasn't. I mean, I'm sure he's seen all the news coverage ..."

"Maybe he feels too guilty, like some of this is his fault."

Dan didn't believe that for a minute, but looking at Marla's tear-streaked face, he could hardly say so.

"Okay, I'll try to see if I can locate him."

Sometimes it wasn't so much fun being Digger Dan.

40

NICK CALLED from the FBI garage where Weir's car had been towed. "At this point, it looks like a suicide. Weir didn't attempt to apply the brakes as he went down the embankment."

"Maybe he was unconscious," said Regan.

"Maybe, but the ME found no trace of drugs in his system and no abrasions on his scalp. It's possible he was outrunning somebody, but there are no skid marks or other evidence to suggest that. The cause of death appears to be drowning."

"Damn," said Regan.

"I know. If Jennings had something to do with Weir's death, we're going to have a tough time proving it."

"Would we expect anything less? Remember, we're dealing with Jennings and his shadowy band of merry men."

"Speaking of which, I'm going to see if I can run down any leads on who they are, starting with Just Boyd," said Nick. "Maybe if Jennings has his attention on helping his boy out of a jam, we'll be able to peel off an associate or two and shake something loose."

"I'm sure if you stop by Imhoff headquarters those nice soldiers in the main building will be glad to help you."

Nick chuckled, then his tone became serious, like he just remembered his duty to protect her from that lecherous lawyer at Justice. "What about you? What are you working on?"

"I thought I'd go visit Anita. Express our condolences and see if there's anything we can do to help the family."

"Good idea."

"Let me know if you come up with anything, Nick—I'll do the same."

A half-hour later, Regan pulled up in front of the house. Anita opened the door and let her in, her expression stony. Her two children—a teenage boy, a pre-teen girl—sat on the couch, pain and bewilderment clouding their faces at the recent news of their fatherlessness.

"We were just leaving to go to the funeral home, Agent Manning."

"I won't keep you, Mrs. Weir; I just wanted to stop by to tell you how sorry I am for your loss." The sentiment was genuine.

Anita gestured toward the kitchen; Regan followed her.

"I know it doesn't do me any good to blame the FBI, Agent Manning, but I can't help feeling like you all were responsible for Mason's death."

Regan looked into the woman's ravaged eyes, searching for the right words. "Your husband was put in a situation at Imhoff that was extremely troubling for him. He carried the burden of it for a very long time, and I believe he wanted to expose the wrongdoing once and for all—regardless of the personal price he had to pay."

Anita began to weep softly. "Then why would he take his own life before he had a chance to do that?"

Regan wished she had the answer. "I can only speculate that he felt like he was somehow protecting you and your kids."

Anita sat down at the kitchen table and put her face in her hands. "I feel so guilty," she said.

"Why?" Regan sat down beside her and gently touched her arm. "You have no reason to feel that way."

"He wanted so badly to leave Imhoff and I kept telling him to stay there."

"Mom?"

Anita and Regan both jumped at the sound of the girl's voice. She stood in the doorway, a worried expression on her face.

Anita wiped the tears from her face. "What, honey?"

"Are you okay?"

Anita nodded. "I will be, baby … I'm still in shock, that's all."

"They're saying on Twitter that Dad might have been murdered." She held an iPhone in her hand.

Regan jumped up. "Who's saying that? Can you show me?"

The girl showed her the Twitter feed that stemmed from a blog by none other than Dan Fielding.

Regan felt her temper flare. She turned to the girl and said softly, "Your father's death is tied to a larger case involving his employer, so there's going to be a lot of speculation and rumors flying around. I think you might want to avoid reading that stuff because I'm afraid it'll make you more upset than you already are."

"She's right, Caroline," said Anita, coming over to wrap an arm around her daughter's shoulders. "Don't look at that stuff."

"I know Dad was involved in something," Caroline said solemnly.

"Why do you think that, honey?" said Anita.

"Because he hides stuff. Out in the garage. He didn't know I saw him."

"Where is it?" said Regan, her heart pounding.

"I'll show you."

They followed the girl out to the garage. Her brother, Clayton, got up and tagged along, his dazed expression replaced by curiosity.

Caroline climbed up on a workbench that had a pegboard at the back adorned with tools of all sorts. Above the workbench was a built-in shelf lined with boxes. She pulled down one of the boxes and handed it to her brother.

"In there?" said Regan.

"No," said Caroline. She used a screwdriver to pry open a little door cut into the wall behind the box. "In here."

41

ON HER way back to the office, Regan put in a call to Dan.

"Fielding."

"Hello, Dan. It's Regan." Her voice sounded like a growl, even to her own ears.

If he noticed, he pretended not to. "Oh hi, Regan, what's up?"

"You can tell me what the hell you were thinking by posting that blog. You're sticking your nose into the middle of an active investigation just to see what you can stir up. You have nothing to support your provocative little theory that Mason Weir was murdered, so all you're doing is trying to make people think you know more than you do in order to beef up your fan base. Thanks to you, Twitter is lighting up with all kinds of wild speculation."

"I'm guessing I know as much about the true cause of Weir's death as you do," he said calmly. "I've been dealing with Winston Jennings for years and I know what he's capable of — including the possibility that he or his henchmen could have killed Weir and made it look like a suicide. He certainly has a motive to do so."

He was right, which incensed her even more.

"I get that you're a big shot investigative reporter, Dan, but it makes our job a lot harder if you start throwing things like that out to the public with little to back it up. We end up chasing down a bunch of worthless leads from people who just want to be part of the action. And you know better than anybody what's at stake—we're dealing with a very troubled, very unpredictable man. Time is critical if we're going to get any help from him."

"I understand that, Regan, and you'll recall I offered to work with you and Nick to put the pieces together. Instead, you chose to freeze me out, not return my calls. So I'll do my own investigating while you do yours."

"Freeze you *out*? Where did you get the idea you were part of our investigation?"

"When you asked me to speak to my friend at one of Imhoff's competitors, I thought--"

"Why you thought that offer, which as you'll recall produced a big fat zip, would entitle you to an inside track on our case, is beyond me."

"Because I have the inside track on Jon Haines, through his sister—who, by the way, I'm quite fond of, not just using for information."

"Oh, so you're not planning to dump her the way you did that friend of yours at Imhoff's competitor?"

"Ouch."

"Sorry, Dan. I shouldn't have said that. Your love life is none of my business."

"No, it isn't, but for the record, Marla is more likely to dump me than the other way around. So, Regan, do you actually believe Weir committed suicide?"

"I, um … "

"I don't, either. I thought if I raised speculation that he was murdered, Jennings might think you're going to start looking closer at him. I thought we could just see how he reacts.

Jennings hates my guts, but he keeps an eye on what I'm saying because he knows I do my homework."

Maybe Dan *could* be helpful after all. Regan decided to climb down off her high horse and find out.

"Okay, maybe you have a point. Maybe we can tag team on Jennings."

"Exactly. If time is critical, then use me."

"Fine. See what you can learn about those so-called henchmen of Jennings'. I want to know who has his back. We need names."

"What do I get in return?"

"The inside track. As long as you promise not to print anything until we say so."

"Deal."

☙

REGAN EMPTIED Weir's file folders and spread the papers out on the conference room table, arranging them chronologically. She moved down the line, scrutinizing each one, looking for some sort of pattern.

Nine months before, their investigation had begun when bank officials in Switzerland contacted U.S. authorities over millions of dollars of suspicious Imhoff payments flowing to offshore bank accounts. Regan and Nick flew to Switzerland to meet with them and scour records for possible illegal activity; they got it confirmed when a trustee confessed to setting up front companies to conceal money trails from Imhoff to bank accounts in Dubai and the British Virgin Islands.

It was the first layer in a massive web of transactions— bribes of corrupt government officials in nine countries, money flowing to and from offshore bank accounts in five others. It eventually led them to Imhoff's Washington headquarters—and to Jon Haines, chief operations officer, and Mason Weir, head money man for the company.

Up until being elected to Congress two years ago, Haines had made frequent treks to the nine countries, meeting with Imhoff managers, assembling the company's intricate pattern of corruption. But the FBI didn't have actual proof of the dirt on Haines' hands. Now it was right here on the table in front of Regan.

As she read, a pattern began to emerge. Each time a new business consultant agreement was established, Haines sent a coded email to Weir. A string of numbers and letters told the accountant which country, which business consultant agreement, the amount of money to be transferred, and the offshore account it should be transferred to.

Regan studied the BCAs and learned that bribes typically ranged from five to six percent of a contract's value but jumped as high as forty percent in the countries that were particularly corrupt. What it meant was that a lot of money was changing hands—and with more than three thousand of the agreements, it took a genius to keep it all straight.

That genius was Mason Weir, now lying on a slab in the morgue.

Regan thought of Anita, completely unaware of the key role her husband played in the global conspiracy. How was it possible to spend your life with someone, lie next to them in bed every night, and have no idea they were involved in something like that?

Regan wasn't naïve; she knew it happened all the time. But it never ceased to amaze her.

She couldn't imagine Jack keeping such secrets from her. But no doubt Anita thought the same thing about her mate.

Even when Mason said he wanted to leave Imhoff, she still didn't have a clue something like this could be the reason.

"Hey, partner," said Nick, startling her out of her thoughts as he blew into the conference room. "Did you get it all figured out?"

"Pretty close. There's enough solid proof here to put Haines away for a long time. Unfortunately there's no solid proof pointing to Jennings, so we still need Haines to give it to us."

"Do you think our ploy with Julia will do the trick?"

"I sure hope so ... but I also think we need to distract Jennings. Give Haines some room to breathe."

42

REGAN PAINTED the picture for Nick, Adam, and Brad Culpepper, the assistant U.S. Attorney assigned to the case. "Imhoff's company managers and sales staff overseas used the funds to pay off government officials who were known to be open to bribes," she explained.

"And Haines managed the managers?" said Adam.

"Correct. From what I can tell reading Weir's notes and emails, Haines gave them strict orders to use the so-called business consultants. He wanted to keep that layer between Imhoff and the corrupt government officials."

"To muddy the waters and make Imhoff's involvement less discernible," said Nick.

Brad said, "Regan, why don't you take us step-by-step through the process?"

It took her another hour to lay it all out for them. When she was finished, they sat for a moment in stunned silence.

"So," said Nick, "all totaled, Imhoff spent roughly $1.6 billion on bribes between 2006 and 2011."

"Yep," said Regan. "And the biggest problem is that Weir's documentation doesn't show any direct link to Winston Jennings. Only an implied one."

"I guarantee you he knew about every dollar used for those bribes," said Adam. "From what I understand, nothing at Imhoff gets by him."

"What about the rest of the board?" said Brad. "How much do you think they knew?"

"Unless Jennings and Haines found a way to explain it away in the budget every year, those people gave their approval to the bribes, too," said Nick.

"That's an awful lot of money to hide," said Brad. "Almost two hundred and seventy million a year, if my math is correct. What was the line item in the budget documents called?"

"Research and development—but it was split between divisions, so it didn't show up as a two-hundred-and-seventy-million-dollar chunk," said Regan. "Still, it's a huge amount of money, so you'd think the board questioned it unless they were complicit."

Adam, who sat on Regan's right, swiveled his chair toward her, his knee touching her thigh. "So you guys will need to interview the board members to see if you can get a sense of how much they knew."

"Yes, we were planning to," she replied, pretending not to notice the physical contact—or the tiny buzz it stirred in her body. "It's a question of timing, though. If we're lucky, we'll be able to have Haines provide the last piece of the puzzle and get us some evidence pointing to Jennings. We arrest him, and *then* we talk to the board members."

"Right," Nick agreed. He sat on the other side of Regan, and she saw his gaze flicker to Adam's errant knee. "If we try to talk to them first, they're going to clam up until they get their marching orders from Jennings."

"That might already be happening," said Adam. "Even just the state charges against Haines ought to be enough to cause Jennings to start battening down the hatches."

"Yes, Adam, we're aware of that." Nick's tone was curt.

Regan gave him a piercing stare.

"What are the chances Haines is still sane enough to be persuaded to flip?" said Brad, oblivious to the tension at the table.

Regan shifted away from Adam. "Don't know yet, Brad. I get the sense he might—Julia's attorney will meet with him in a couple days, which might give him a whole new sense of purpose."

43

WINSTON WOKE up feeling paranoid. His head ached and his chest was tight, as though his body suspected everything was about to blow wide open.

No, he told himself. He was just tired, hadn't slept well. Too worried about whether Jon would ever be able to find his way back to normal.

But shouldn't he be prepared, just in case the company's bribery scheme was exposed? *Offense is the best defense* had always been his mantra; in fact, his staff used to say he should be called Offense Secretary, not Defense Secretary. Ha ha.

But hell yes. He needed to get out in front of this thing. Stop tiptoeing around, waiting for his life to implode.

Winston pulled out the phone book and put in a call to an attorney friend at a firm that competed with Howard's. It was time for Jon to have separate counsel.

And it was time for Winston to come clean with Howard.

&

REGAN STARED at her computer screen, not seeing it. She kept thinking about how to turn Haines against his mighty mentor.

They would find out tomorrow, after Julia's attorney talked to Jon, whether he could be duped into cooperating. But even if he *was* desperate to please Julia, would it be enough?

She felt frustrated, but right now there was too much tension between her and her partner to talk it out with him. She tossed her pen on the desk and stood up. "I'm leaving for awhile."

Nick looked at her curiously. "Where are you going?"

"I don't know. I just need to get out of here for awhile."

His expression became suspicious. "Planning a little rendezvous over at Justice, are we?"

Regan slammed both hands on her desk and leaned toward Nick. "*Stop* it, Nick. I told you to stay out of my affairs. You're being a jerk, and I'm sick of it."

She stomped out.

When she got to her car, she felt her phone vibrate. It was a text from Nick.

You're right. I'm sorry. Won't happen again.

It only made her feel pissier.

Her tires screeched as she pulled out of the garage and headed off toward Manassas. Regan would go see Marla, driving the back roads so she could take in a little scenery along the way. Maybe it would settle her down and help her gain some needed perspective.

She knew she shouldn't be encouraging Adam; she loved Jack. She did. But it was complicated—three thousand miles' worth of complicated.

And she liked Adam. He was smart and sexy and … close.

She sighed, knowing that if Jack were here, he would relish the scenery, too. He would see things she didn't. She loved how he engaged with nature in such an integral way. He was good with people, but he was most relaxed—most himself—when he was outdoors, communing with trees, careening over the waves in his boat, or watching wildlife in their natural brilliance.

Regan would never ask him to give all that up and settle down among the traffic and concrete and mobs of people in DC. It would kill his soul.

Her heart ached for him, but she had to face reality. It was time to tell him goodbye.

꙳

MARLA'S HAIR was pulled into a messy ponytail, and her porcelain skin looked pasty. It appeared she'd lost weight in the two weeks since they'd met, something Marla's too-thin body could ill afford.

"Are you doing okay?" Regan asked.

Marla nodded. "I'm just worried about my brother, that's all."

"What can I do to help, Marla?"

"Can you make Jon see a psychiatrist?" She gave Regan a rueful smile.

"Actually, my boss spoke with the Commonwealth's Attorney to suggest that. I believe he's being evaluated this afternoon, and hopefully he'll be put on meds that will make him feel better."

"Oh, good," she said, looking a bit more encouraged. "But I know he still has a lot of hard things to face."

"Yes, he does. I'm glad he has you, Marla."

"He'll always have me. I just wish there was more I could do to help him. But there is one thing that might ..."

Regan gave her an inquisitive look.

"I asked Dan to help me find my father."

The news shocked Regan. "Really? Have you had any contact with him since he left?"

"No."

"What about Jon? Did he ever try to find him?"

Marla shook her head, her eyes sad. "No, and it broke his heart that he never knew our dad. At least I have some memory of him, that he was this big bear of a man who was really kind. I remember his smile. I just think if he could come around, maybe go talk to Jon, explain things, it would help my brother get better."

All at once, Regan understood why it was taking such a toll on Marla. She'd had an up-close-and-personal view of the way depression, and then dementia, had snuffed out her mother's life, and she was afraid that's what was happening to her brother. No wonder she was frantic; one by one, she was losing her family.

Regan reached over and squeezed Marla's hand. "I hope Dan is able to find him, Marla. How wonderful it would be if he came back into your lives."

The kids popped in the back door. "Mom? Can we get in the pool?" said Willie.

"Sure, honey." Marla turned back to Regan. "And think how wonderful it would be for them to have a grandpa. Mind if we sit outside so I can keep an eye on the kids?"

"Sure," said Regan. "Need any help?" Not that she had a lot of experience with kids, other than the fact that she used to be one—and many people thought she still was.

"That'd be great, Regan. I'll get them into their swimsuits and you can spray them with sunscreen."

Both kids giggled and jumped around when she sprayed the cold sunscreen on their bodies. It made her laugh, too.

Regan had never spent much time thinking about having children, but she hadn't ruled it out, either. Just in the past week, she'd met three kids that made it an inviting prospect.

At thirty-four, she needed to decide soon whether it was in the cards. And Jack would be a perfect dad. *Would have been.*

She sighed, her heart heavy as she found a spot in the shade to watch Marla fill the kiddie pool. Once Willie and Emma had hopped in, Marla sat down next to Regan.

"They love to play in the water," she said with a smile. "I'm thankful they're so easily entertained."

"They're really great kids, Marla," said Regan. "Hey, can I ask you something?"

"Of course."

"I was just wondering how you feel about Dan."

Marla's face colored slightly. "I like him. Why? Did he do something wrong?"

"No, of course not. I get the feeling he likes you, too."

"Did he say something to you about me?"

No matter how old we were, all of us were back in junior high when it came to wanting details like that when a romance was blossoming.

Regan laughed. "No, not really. It's just that … he seems, I don't know …"

"Out of my league? I know; that's what I told him."

"I wouldn't say he's out of your league—more like he has a different set of sensibilities than you do."

Marla looked confused. "What do you mean?"

What *did* she mean? Regan wished she hadn't brought it up. In fact, she wasn't sure why she had. Maybe she was trying to warn Marla away from him.

"I mean you're a gentle soul, Marla, and Dan is used to being around people who aren't like you. If you guys decide to have a relationship, I hope he'll always appreciate that about you. Believe me, you're a rare find."

She smiled. "You're kind to say that, Regan. But I suspect that Dan is just momentarily interested in me because I *am* different than the people he's used to being around. And also because I'm Jon's sister, which means I'm a source of information. Believe me, once my brother's case is resolved, Dan will realize how boring I am and move on."

It was clear Marla kept her expectations low. Life had taught her that.

"Then he's a fool, Marla."

44

HOW THE hell did you get Roland to approve that?" said Nick.

"Well, for obvious reasons, she understands women's intuition," said Regan. "I told her I have a gut feeling Betty Jennings might be key to this in some way, and she got it. I'll jump on a military transport and go out and back today."

"Want me to tag along, or is this a girls-only party?"

"I think she'll be more forthcoming if it's just me, Nick. Besides, I'd rather you stay here and keep an eye on Jennings. Now that we're tightening the screws, it'll be interesting to see how he reacts."

"Okay. I'm off to meet Dan the Man. He's come up with some information about Winston's enforcers. Apparently they're former Navy SEALs whose job descriptions at Imhoff are a little fuzzy."

"Who's his source?"

"He wouldn't say—and he didn't want to talk about it over the phone."

"I hope they're solid leads. I really want to get this thing wrapped up before I leave for Juneau next week."

Nick looked at her. "I'm glad you're going, Regan. It'll mean a lot to your parents."

"And it'll give Jack and me a chance to talk."

"Hope that all works out the way you want it to."

She smiled at him. "No more pleading Jack's case for him?"

"I wouldn't touch that topic with a ten-foot pole."

ɹ

THE MILITARY jet landed at Forbes Field in Topeka. A little over an hour later, Regan pulled her rental car off Interstate 70 and found the road leading to Jennings' place.

Once she saw the lavish homestead, Regan wondered why on earth Winston still hung around Washington. She parked the car in the circle drive, and a yellow Lab sprinted over to greet her, tail literally wagging the dog.

Betty Jennings stepped out onto the veranda to see who her visitor was. Regan pulled out her bureau identification. "Mrs. Jennings, I'm Special Agent Regan Manning with the FBI's Washington Field Office."

A look of alarm darkened her expression; she put a hand over her mouth.

"Oh no, everything's fine. I just wanted to ask you a few questions."

"I see. Please come in, Agent Manning. Get back, Gertie. Sorry … she gets excited when we have visitors."

Regan leaned over to pet the Lab. "She's okay; I love dogs."

"So does Winston. Especially this one. The two of them sit out here together every night and watch the sun go down—weather permitting, of course."

They made small talk about Kansas weather while Betty fixed them something to drink. Once they were seated in the living room, sipping on the best iced tea Regan had ever tasted, Mrs. Jennings said, "My husband is in Washington, Agent Manning. But I suspect you already know that."

"Yes, I do. I wanted to talk to you, Mrs. Jennings."

"About?"

"About your husband's relationship with Jon Haines."

"You came all the way out to Kansas to ask me about that?"

"Among other things, yes."

"Well, I'm sure you know Winston was Jon's boss for many years. I think he particularly valued Jon's work, and I know he's always placed a high level of trust in him." It sounded almost rehearsed, as though she'd been telling herself that for a long time.

"Mr. Jennings appears to be quite protective of the congressman."

Betty's eyes became red-rimmed and glassy; she touched a finger to her lips. Regan could see the woman's spousal loyalty doing battle with her own questioning. Finally, she met Regan's gaze. "I just don't think it's normal."

No kidding, thought Regan. "What makes you say that?"

"Winston is obsessed with protecting him. And I don't understand why." Her voice was raspy with emotion.

"Do you think he sees himself as some sort of father figure to him?"

She shrugged. "I've always wondered if there was some of that in their relationship, but even more so lately with everything that's happened. He acts far more concerned about Jon than his own three kids."

"Maybe that's because his own three kids don't have the issues Jon has."

"Yes, that poor man is a lost soul. When he was here a few days ago, you could tell he was hesitant to go back home. It was like he just wanted to stay here and be part of our family, forget all the problems he's caused."

"I guess I can understand that," said Regan. "It's so peaceful here. Jon's life in DC is anything but."

"But why does Winston have to keep putting himself in the middle of all that? I pleaded with him to stay here and let things run their course. As usual, he didn't listen to me."

"Mrs. Jennings, does your husband talk very much about his work?"

"No, not really. Why?"

"Has he made frequent trips overseas in recent years?"

"Of course. He was defense secretary."

"I mean before that."

"Well, I don't know what you mean by frequent, but yes, he did go to places like Afghanistan, Israel, Haiti ... let's see, China, Russia ..."

Regan felt her pulse quicken. "Did he tell you what those trips were for? Were they related to Imhoff-Greyson?"

"He has managers that take care of things overseas, but maybe he went to check up on them occasionally, make sure everything was functioning properly. I suppose it seems funny that I never asked, but I just regarded Winston's work as his business, not mine."

Regan noticed Betty picking at some dog hairs on her pant leg, her gaze carefully averted.

What does she know that she's not telling?

"I understand, but Jon Haines has been charged with bribery stemming from his time at Imhoff. We--"

"You think Winston was involved?" It sounded more like a statement than a question; she didn't seem terribly surprised.

Then again, she'd been married to the man for more than forty years. There was probably little that shocked her anymore.

"I'm not saying your husband knew about it. We're just taking a closer look at things."

"I see. Are you hungry, Agent Manning? I'd be glad to fix you something to eat. Would you like a sandwich?"

She pitied Betty Jennings. The women wanted so much to pretend she didn't know anything and go back to baking brownies.

"I'm fine, thanks." Regan decided to shift gears. "Has Mr. Jennings said much to you about Jon and Julia's relationship?"

Regan could tell from her pained expression that it had been a sore subject between them. "Winston refuses to believe Jon meant to take Julia hostage. He insists they just had an argument, and that the FBI—your agency—blew it all out of proportion."

"So again he felt the need to protect Jon."

She nodded. "It was absurd. He went on CNN and made a fool of himself. Why he'd put his own reputation on the line like that, I can't imagine."

They heard a car pull up out front and doors slam.

Betty leaped up and glanced out the window. "Oh, here's my daughter, Kate." She looked relieved it wasn't Winston.

Kate came in the front door, trailed by two young kids. Betty introduced the two women, and Kate ordered her kids to go play in the family room.

"So, what brings you to Kansas, Agent Manning?" She sat down on the couch.

"I wanted to visit with your mother about Jon Haines. I know he came out for a visit last week; I'm interested in the family's impression of him."

"He seems nice enough," said Kate. "But obviously he's pretty screwed up. And for some reason, my dad seems to see himself as Jon's protector."

Winston Jennings' daughter was refreshingly candid.

"That's what your mother and I were just discussing, Kate. What I'm trying to determine is what's behind that."

"Who knows? I mean, Jon grew up fatherless, but I wouldn't exactly consider my dad to be touchy-feely, so it probably has more to do with their work relationship. As Dad's chief aide, Jon has always had his back—so maybe this is Dad's way of returning the favor."

Interesting take, thought Regan. She saw Kate and her mother exchange a look.

"Something else?" said Regan.

Kate leaned forward, arms on her knees. "I think we need to tell her, Mom. It's the right thing to do."

Betty looked at her hands but said nothing.

"Tell me what?" said Regan.

Betty began to weep. Kate got up and went over to her, kneeling down beside her. "Mom, you have to."

Regan waited while Betty gathered herself. She looked up at Regan and said, "I found something."

"What was it?"

"After Winston went back to Washington with Jon, I was trying to understand why. So I went into his office—where I'm not allowed except to dust and vacuum—and I started looking around."

"Tell her what you found, Mom."

Betty sighed. "I figured out his password, and I looked on his computer." Her face colored with shame. "I found …" She paused.

Get to it, Betty, I'm about to jump out of my skin here.

"I found some bank statements. From foreign accounts."

"Uh huh," Regan prompted.

"They were in Winston's name. And they contained close to one hundred and sixty-three million dollars."

Regan wanted to jump up and turn a cartwheel. "Where are the banks located? Could you tell?"

Betty nodded. "One in Austria, one in Switzerland, and one in Dubai."

"Would you show me?"

Betty stood and turned toward the hallway. "Come with me." The three women made their way to Winston's office.

"The funny thing about it," said Kate, "is that my mother hardly ever uses a computer. And then when she does, she stumbles across something like this."

It *was* pretty funny. The king of cybersecurity had just been hacked by his technology-challenged wife.

45

THE CHARTER plane had touched down at Forbes Field an hour earlier. It took less than five minutes for Winston to jump into his pickup and head for home.

With Jon locked up again, he'd decided he needed a little normalcy—away from Washington—to figure out his next move. And he needed to smooth Betty's ruffled feathers.

Winston knew he took her for granted sometimes. Ever since they first met and began dating back in high school, Betty had taken good care of him. She let him be the boss and make the major decisions, but she completely understood her own importance in the relationship. She knew he wouldn't be who he was without her, but she had the good grace not to point it out. It was just one of the things he appreciated about his wife.

He exited off the interstate and headed south. Should he stop off somewhere and buy her some flowers?

He decided not to; no sense acting like he'd done something wrong. He'd take her into town for dinner at the café instead.

On the fifteen-minute drive from the highway to his ranch, his thoughts turned to the conversation with Howard earlier. His attorney had been stunned to hear of the payoffs to foreign business consultants—especially the fact that, all totaled, they exceeded a billion dollars. Winston had explained that it was the cost of doing business, and thanks to those arrangements, Imhoff had become one of the richest companies in the world.

Howard seemed a little hurt that he hadn't been privy to the setup early on so he could protect Winston if necessary. Winston said he hadn't wanted to involve Howard because it might compromise his integrity. Instead he relied on Jon to draft the template used for the business consultant agreements, which were also run past in-house counsel.

What he didn't share with Howard was that in-house counsel hadn't been privy to the setup, either. The language was drafted in a way that appeared perfectly legal. It was the execution that wasn't.

How much did the FBI know?

Whatever it was, they weren't going to find anything pointing directly to Winston; he'd made sure of it. The only way he could be implicated was if Jon revealed his involvement, and he would never do that.

Would he?

Winston sighed and ran a hand across his head, which throbbed with tension. He needed to relax, let everything go for a day or two, then come up with a solid game plan.

Right now, just being home with Betty and Gert would do a lot to soothe his troubled soul.

⌒

REGAN COULDN'T believe her eyes. Betty had uncovered a goldmine.

"What do you think it means?" said Betty. "Where do you think this money came from?"

Skimming, Regan wanted to say. "I'm not sure, but if I had to guess I'd say it's your husband's compensation for some overseas deals that were made."

"Do you think he got it illegally?"

Yes, ma'am, I sure do. "I don't know, Mrs. Jennings."

"It has to be," said Kate. "Otherwise he'd have told you about it, Mom."

Betty put her hands to her face. "It makes me sick to think I was doing all this remodeling with money that might have been obtained illegally."

Kate put her arm around her mother's shoulders. "Dad probably cashed in some CDs to pay for that. I mean, it's not like you guys have ever been hurting for cash. But even if he *did* use some of this money, you're not to blame. You didn't know anything about it."

Betty's shoulders slumped; it looked like she was visibly shrinking. "What else hasn't he told me?"

While Kate comforted her mother, Regan pored over the bank accounts and took a quick glance at Winston's other computer files, looking for anything that appeared suspect.

"Is it okay if I print copies of these bank statements?" Regan asked.

Betty nodded. "I hope you'll be able to figure out where the money came from. If you do, will you tell me?"

"Yes, I will, Mrs. Jennings. And I'm grateful to you for sharing this with me." Just as she reached for the pages spitting out of the printer, Gertie barreled into the room, startling all three women. Regan jabbed the computer's power button to shut it down, then leaped from the desk chair. She tucked the bank statements into her waistband in back, beneath her jacket.

Seconds later, Winston appeared in the doorway.

᷿

TIME WAS running out for Dan to get his show put together. He was eager to expand the story on Jon Haines, finish what he'd started the week before.

The sooner the whole story came out, the sooner Marla would be able to begin the healing process and get on with her life. Dan hoped that life included him—at least so they could continue to explore whether a relationship between them would work. Right now she was simply too focused on her brother.

So Dan decided to focus on him, too. Jon's story, with all its drama, would have a lot of appeal to audiences. Almost like a made-for-TV movie.

A story with Pulitzer potential.

He felt a little betrayed by Nick and Regan, though; he'd been open and helpful, even coming up with names of Jennings' knee crackers, but Nick had given him little in return. They seemed to forget he had a major role to play in this case, too—that of bringing the truth to the American public. Right now, the talking heads on TV had people so confused about Jon Haines and his motives that they didn't know what to believe.

Unlike those journalists, Dan had the inside scoop. He knew what drove the man. It was a story just itching to be told.

Regan and Nick weren't the only ones investigating the facts and piecing them together. Investigation was Dan's hallmark, and as long as he didn't impede law enforcement, he was free to paint the full picture of a man who had gone from utter powerlessness to becoming a major U.S. power broker—and how that seismic shift literally blew his mind.

Dan was stoked as he went to tell his executive producer.

&

"WHAT'S GOING on in here?" Winston bellowed.

"Don't blow a gasket, Dad," Kate said smoothly. "I was showing them something on the internet. I forgot my iPad."

Regan watched Winston's face. He wasn't buying it.

"What were you showing them?" He shifted his glare from Kate to Regan. "And who the hell are you?"

"I'm Special Agent Regan Manning from the Washington Field Office."

"Why are you here?"

"Agent Manning was saying how much she loves dogs," Betty said in a trembling voice. "Kate wanted to show her a funny dog video on The Facebook."

"There's no 'the,' Mom," said Kate. "It's just called Facebook." She acted like showing an FBI agent something on her dad's computer was an everyday event. But Winston's sudden, domineering presence sucked all the air from the room, and Regan saw traces of panic behind Kate's forced breeziness.

Regan glanced at the printer and froze when she saw that one page had gotten left behind.

Winston moved over to his computer, scowling as he hit the power button to turn it on. "I asked why you're here, Agent Manning." His voice was a growl.

"I, uh, came to interview you, sir. I wasn't aware you'd gone back to Washington with Congressman Haines a few days ago, but I guess it doesn't matter because here you are."

Kate was standing closest to her dad; Regan caught her attention and shifted her gaze to the printer. Regan saw Kate's eyes widen as she spotted the paper. She darted behind Winston and grabbed it before he could turn around, stuffing the sheet in her pocket.

"What are you doing, Kate?" he said, turning. "What do you have?"

"Nothing. I thought I set my purse back here. I guess I left it in the living room."

Winston's eyes narrowed as he stared at the three of them, trying to figure out what they were really up to. "Betty, get out of my office. You, too, Kate."

Kate looked like she was going to argue and then thought better of it. She followed her mother out of the room.

"Agent Manning, I don't buy your story. Or if you did get approval to make a trip out here—at taxpayers' expense— without first checking to see if I was here, then the FBI is even more incompetent that I thought. So you have five minutes to say what you need to say before I throw you off my property and call Garrison." He and the FBI director were longtime associates, but not friends; Jennings' incessant criticism of the bureau had killed any chance of that.

Not that Tate would refuse to take his call. And Lisa Roland might be hard-pressed to explain why she approved the trip.

Regan searched her brain to come up with something that sounded plausible. "Mr. Jennings, I know I should have called first, but I was afraid you would refuse to talk to me. I thought maybe here on your own turf you might feel more comfortable visiting with me about--"

His rigid posture and piercing glare could never be construed as comfortable.

"Get to it, Miss Manning. The clock is ticking."

She took a deep breath and plowed in. "All right then, sir, I'd like to talk to you about Jon Haines. About the payments he made to so-called business consultants in other countries— payments that wound up in the hands of foreign government officials."

He moved toward her, his face reddening with fury. "You don't know what you're talking about. Now get the hell out of my house."

"Sir, we have solid evidence. I'm giving you an opportunity to--"

Winston pointed toward the door, his arm shaking. "*Out.*"

46

WINSTON'S COMPUTER warned him it hadn't been shut down properly before. Which meant it had been shut down in haste.

He found Betty and Kate in the kitchen. "What were you doing in my office? I want the truth."

"Looking at a dog video," Kate said defensively. "I don't know why you're making such a big deal out of it."

"Shut your mouth, Kate. Betty?"

"What? Kate's right; you're making a big fuss over nothing."

"You know damn good and well that machine is not for anyone's use but mine. How did you know the password?" He shifted his glare back and forth between his wife and daughter.

"C'mon, Winston, I'm not an idiot," said Betty. "Of course it's Randolph; I know how much you loved our little hometown."

He was dumbfounded; he'd assumed Betty didn't even know how to turn the computer on, much less figure out his password. She'd never shown the least bit of interest in anything involving technology. She rarely even watched TV.

"How long was that agent here?" he demanded.

"Dad, stop barking at us. You're acting--"

"I told you to be quiet, Kate. In fact, go home."

Kate's face hardened. "If Mom wants me here, I'm staying until she says otherwise."

He could barely contain his temper. "Kathryn, I'm getting fed up with--"

"It's okay, honey," Betty said to her daughter. "Your father and I have some things we need to discuss in private."

Kate searched her mother's face. "You're sure you'll be okay?"

Why the hell wouldn't she be? What's going on?

Betty nodded. Kate moved past him, foregoing the usual peck on his cheek and departing words, *See ya, Pops.*

Winston, for all his bluster, felt fear clawing at his stomach.

❧

BY THE time Regan landed back in Washington, Winston had already called to harangue Garrison Tate.

"Needless to say, the director isn't too thrilled about your trip," said Roland.

"I'm sorry if I put you in an uncomfortable position," said Regan. "But ma'am, it *was* a worthwhile visit. In fact, we hit the jackpot."

Regan pulled out the bank statements.

"My heavens ... he compiled quite a stash, didn't he?" said Roland. "Regan, I think Director Tate needs to hear all of this directly from you." She picked up the phone and called him; he agreed to see them immediately.

"Nice to see you again, sir," Regan said when they were escorted into his office. She hadn't been inside it since taking down the vice president and his oil magnate buddy two years earlier.

"Good to see you, too, Regan. I have to say, the vast majority of your bureau colleagues will never bring down even one high-ranking public official—and now it sounds like you're about to do it for the second time in two years." His smile revealed more apprehension than humor.

"It appears that way, Director Tate. I managed to obtain copies of bank statements showing that Winston Jennings has an awful lot of money socked away in three offshore bank accounts—funds his wife knew nothing about. Agent Jenesco and I will trace the funds to see if the timing and amounts match up to the illegal transactions."

"Have you obtained any other evidence implicating Jennings?"

"Possibly," said Regan.

"Here, come and sit down," Tate said, pointing to the seating area in his office. "Give me the whole rundown."

❧

ON THEIR way to interview Haines, Nick filled Regan in on the details of Jennings' protectors.

"According to Dan's sources, winning a spot on the security team at Imhoff is coveted by retiring Navy SEALs. Jennings takes only the best. They're well-paid, and their assignments often take them to hostile environments—which they're highly trained for."

"What do they do there?" said Regan.

"Anything that pertains to protecting Imhoff's assets, especially the security networks."

"Did you get any names?"

Nick nodded. "He was able to get me a pretty complete list, including the guy we already met—Boyd. His first name is Percy, which doesn't exactly beef up his tough-guy image. I'm sure that's why he prefers to be 'Just Boyd.' He's not only head of security at headquarters, he's also in charge of the field team here in DC."

"Probably the most hostile environment of all for those guys," Regan said with a smirk. "Has Dan run down any specifics on them?"

"No, I told him I'd take it from here," said Nick. "He didn't argue—he's pretty focused on getting his show put together right now."

They entered the jail and headed for the interview room. As usual, Regan would take the lead questioning their suspect; Nick preferred the supporting role.

Haines' attorney sat beside him, a guy with the unfortunate name of Ben Franklin. Regan wondered why his parents would set him up like that; life was hard enough without everyone asking if you'd flown any kites lately.

But since he was a partner in one of the most prestigious firms in town, with an hourly rate probably equal to her monthly rent, she decided not to feel too sorry for him.

"Let's get started," she said amiably. "Congressman Haines, I'd like to begin with your employment at Imhoff-Greyson. At what point did you start to play an oversight role in the company's pursuit of contracts with foreign governments?"

Jon cleared his throat. "Uh, well, from day one I knew Mr. Jennings expected me to bring my expertise to bear on the drafting of government contracts that would, uh, maximize Imhoff's advantage in overseas markets."

"And do you believe it is your drafting of those documents that led to a significant boost in the number of contracts awarded to Imhoff over its competitors?"

"I think that played a major part, yes."

"I bet Winston Jennings was thrilled to pieces."

Jon smiled. "Since that was the reason he brought me on board in the first place, I'm sure he was."

"Is it fair to say you became his so-called 'fair-haired boy' at Imhoff?"

"I don't know that I'd call it that, but yes, he valued my work. Mr. Jennings and I developed a strong and cordial working relationship."

"How long into your employment at Imhoff was it before Mr. Jennings asked you to start bribing foreign officials?"

Jon stiffened; he glanced at his attorney.

"It sounds like you're fishing, Agent Manning," said Franklin.

"Hardly, Mr. Franklin." She produced one of Weir's copies showing Haines' authorization on the movement of funds to a business consultant in China. She turned the sheet around so they could follow along.

"On this particular occasion—and we know this is just the teeniest, tiniest tip of the iceberg—you authorized a payment of two-point-two million dollars to Huang Lee, a business consultant with whom you established an agreement on September 21, 2003. See, there's your signature." She pointed to the signature line. "According to Mr. Lee, who by the way is cooperating with us, two million of those funds were subsequently paid to Cheng Wu, a member of the Chinese government, in exchange for an exclusive contract with Imhoff-Greyson to provide an advanced electronic system that would net your company more than fifty million dollars. I think a savvy attorney like yourself can see that that constitutes bribery. Heck, even I can see it."

Jon squirmed in his chair, his face losing a little of its color. Franklin waited; Regan knew he wanted to see the full scope of the evidence against his client before he reacted.

"So to repeat my question," said Regan, "how long before Mr. Jennings asked you to start bribing foreign officials?"

Jon found his voice. "We needed a foothold in China, so we provided an incentive to do business with us, that's all. The marketplace is highly competitive, and I can assure you that every American company doing business overseas is looking for ways to achieve a competitive advantage."

"Not all of them resort to corruption to get it," said Nick.

"Many of them do—but I'm not saying that's what occurred here," said Jon. "And it seems to me that you're just trying to make an example of Imhoff because of Winston Jennings' prominence. You're trying to use me to bring him down. My question to you is this: Why would you want to tarnish the reputation of a man who has dedicated his life to serving this country?"

"C'mon, Mr. Haines, let's not play that game," said Regan. "We both know that Jennings crossed legal boundaries to build a highly successful multinational company. He used you to establish the overseas framework that resulted in billions of dollars in exclusive contracts—and guess what? Despite your 'strong and cordial working relationship,' I'm sure he'll gladly let you take the fall for those bribes."

Regan actually wasn't sure of that at all.

"If you think he's guilty of something, why haven't you arrested him?" said Jon.

"Because, as you probably know better than anybody, Mr. Jennings is adept at covering his behind. So far, the paper trail keeps stopping at your feet. But we know that you didn't act alone. And if you work with us, it will be Jennings, not you, doing the bulk of the time on the corruption charges."

Jon crossed his arms over his chest. "You don't have a thing on Winston, and you want me to produce it for you. Is that about right?" A hint of cockiness crept into his tone.

Regan worried they were only solidifying his support for Winston; should they have waited until after Julia's attorney met with Jon? They took a chance on this route because Regan thought he might be more apt to choose Julia once he knew Winston had a giant target painted on his back.

"Well, I wouldn't say we don't have a *thing*," said Regan. "We have bank statements showing Mr. Jennings has deposited nearly one hundred and sixty-three million dollars in offshore accounts. Given the way corporations operate these days, he could've been awarded giant bonuses, especially with all that prominence of his, but the company's senior accountant, Mason Weir, told us Mr. Jennings' largest annual bonus was five million. Do the math, Jon. Where did all that extra money come from that he has stashed in offshore accounts—money that his wife, Betty, didn't know about?"

One look at Jon's face told them he didn't, either.

Regan's phone vibrated in her pocket; the caller ID showed the call was coming from Kate in Kansas.

"My client is not interested in building a case against Winston Jennings for you," Franklin said in a haughty tone befitting his lawyerly stature, if not his name. "And we're confident he won't be found culpable if the grand jury indicts Imhoff-Greyson. So I'd say, Agent Manning, come back when you've got something a little more concrete to talk about."

She felt like telling him to go fly a kite.

47

KATE HAD left a message to call her back. Regan returned the call right away.

"We can't let you do it," Kate blurted.

"Do what?" said Regan.

"Use the information we gave you to expose my dad. My mom and I changed our minds."

"Why, Kate? Your dad may have been involved in more than a billion dollars in illegal payments to foreign officials."

"Then you'll have to find other evidence. Ever since you left yesterday, Agent Manning, we've been trying to deal with the guilt over betraying him." Regan could hear her sniffling. "We just can't. My mother is really upset ... I never should have asked her to show you what she found. *Please* don't bring us into it."

Regan sighed. "I'm afraid it might be too late. I've already shown both Director Tate and Jon Haines the copies of bank statements."

"Did you say where you got them?"

"I told the director, but not Jon."

"Please, Agent Manning, I'm begging you. We can't let my dad know that we told you. It would devastate him. We're his family."

It wasn't surprising that Betty had had a change of heart, but Kate's about-face was surprising. She appeared to be the one person who didn't fear her powerful father—but perhaps concern for her mother's welfare trumped that.

"All right, Kate. We'll keep it under wraps for now. We won't let your father know where we got the information unless we have no other choice."

&

THANKS TO her friend in the lab at Quantico, Regan already had the results on the object she'd snatched from Jennings' front porch on the way to her rental car. DNA from the cigar butt stuck in an ashtray next to Winston's favorite outdoor chair matched the DNA the Virginia cops took from Jon when he was arrested.

It confirmed what she suspected, but the news was still a bit of a shock: Winston Jennings was Jon's biological father.

It explained a lot about Winston's behavior. No wonder he went to such lengths to protect Jon; it wasn't only about ambition, it was about fatherly devotion.

How sad, thought Regan. Jon would finally learn that his dad had been right beside him all this time, and yet they still wouldn't be able to have a true father-son relationship—unless they served time in the same prison. And they *would* do time, despite Ben Franklin's opinion to the contrary.

She shared the DNA news with Nick.

"No shit? What made you suspect that?"

"I think I began to suspect it when Jennings went on CNN and tried to defend Jon. He made himself look ridiculous—and I don't think Winston allows himself to be that vulnerable very often. He was putting way more on the line than was warranted by their business relationship. Then when Betty referred to their relationship as 'not normal,' I was pretty sure."

"You've suspected it all this time and didn't tell me?"

"If you recall, Nick, things have been a little strained between us lately. We haven't talked as much as usual."

He nodded. "Totally my fault. And I'm sorry about that, Regan."

"I'm sorry, too, Nick. We're both under a lot of pressure right now. Lots of stuff to figure out."

"That'll come later. Right now the only thing we need to figure out is how to prove our case against Jennings. So who do we tell about this discovery and in what order?"

"First we tell Lisa Roland. Then, if she approves, we confront Jennings with it."

"I hope she approves an army to back us up."

"I know; he's already pissed at me."

"What if we told Jon instead?"

Regan thought a moment. "I think it could go one of two ways: Jon wigs out completely, or he protects his daddy at all costs. Neither of those scenarios will work to our advantage."

"Yeah, but if we tell Jennings, maybe he'll feel like he has to tell Jon before we do. We might end up with the same two scenarios."

"True, but I'm thinking there's a chance we could gain some leverage with Jennings if he *doesn't* want Jon to know."

"What if we didn't say anything about it to either of them for the time being?" said Nick. "Just keep it in our back pocket until we need it?"

"Maybe you're right. Let's see what the boss thinks."

❧

DAN MANAGED to talk Stallworth into being interviewed for his show without even uttering Elizabeth Fenster's name. He figured the speaker and his reporter friend had cooled it, but the revelation of their affair was still available for leverage if he needed it.

Stallworth's only stipulation was that they not get into Winston Jennings' plans regarding cybersecurity and the potential benefits to Imhoff. In fact, he didn't want to discuss Jennings at all. He would talk only about Jon Haines.

Fair enough. Dan could save the Jennings story for another day.

He asked a few lead-in questions to loosen him up, then said, "Mr. Speaker, how did Congressman Haines manage to become a key player on your team of advisors after such a short time in Congress?"

"I've known the congressman for many years, Dan. As you know, he was a member of Secretary Jennings' leadership team at the Department of Defense, so we had occasion to interact on a fairly regular basis. I was also aware of the outstanding legal work he did pertaining to government contracts. So even though he was a freshman lawmaker, he was known and respected around Washington. I welcomed having such a bright legal mind on our team here."

"So how did you react when he took his wife hostage?"

"Just like everyone else, I was shocked. I'd been aware that there were some pressures regarding Dr. Haines' work, but I certainly didn't suspect that things were anywhere near that level of discord between them. It's a real shame. They're both gifted professionals."

"And it seems like things are going from bad to worse for Jon Haines," said Dan. "He's facing a number of charges. He's already been censured by the House of Representatives for the kidnapping incident, but if he's found guilty of other charges, won't he be ineligible to serve in Congress?"

"Only if his colleagues in the House deem him unfit to serve. The Constitution doesn't prohibit a convicted felon from keeping his elected seat."

"Boy, it seems surprising that Congress is allowed to police its own, even those convicted of felony offenses." Dan knew that was the law; he was just playing it up for effect.

"Congress and the voters, Dan. If a member of Congress is truly unfit to hold office, he or she will either be expelled or not reelected. Voters are smart; they'll take care of the problem if the legislative body doesn't."

"Sir, what do you think will be the ultimate outcome for Congressman Haines?"

Stallworth paused while he formulated his thoughts. "If he's cleared of the charges against him and could get away from certain influences ... no, strike that."

"Go ahead and start again. We'll edit that out." But Stallworth had just confirmed that he, too, believed Jon's problems stemmed from Jennings.

"I'm saddened that someone with so much leadership potential has gotten this far off track. Do I think he could overcome his current issues and eventually have another shot? It's possible, but only if he manages to avoid conviction. Things don't look good for him right now, and it's sad to see such a bright mind go to waste."

48

ON THE plane ride back to Washington, Winston replayed his conversation with Betty. She'd admitted to snooping on his computer; thankfully she hadn't found anything incriminating. At least that's what she said, and he'd never known Betty to lie to him.

Too bad he couldn't say the same about himself. His protectiveness of Jon pained her; she simply couldn't understand it. But if he told her the real reason, it would hurt her even more.

In the end, he apologized for upsetting her and assured her that his days in Washington were numbered. Soon he'd be a fulltime rancher and spend the bulk of his time at home with her and Gert, along with their kids and grandkids.

In the meantime, if she felt the urge to snoop again, there would be nothing to find. Not only had he changed his password to something she wouldn't guess in a million years, he'd saved his files to a thumb drive—safely tucked away in his pocket—and deleted anything that was sensitive.

Now he planned to spend some time at Imhoff, making sure everything there was locked down tight. With the Mason Weir issue resolved, he hoped there were no other security breaches that required similar attention.

Winston closed his eyes and breathed deeply. His blood pressure had to be off the charts; he hadn't felt fear of this magnitude since the torpedo attack in the Gulf of Tonkin when he was a young a naval officer. Just like back then, heavy artillery seemed to be coming at him from all directions.

How could he stop it before it did real damage? Before everything around him was shattered and he was left with no place to hide?

This time, unlike in Vietnam, he might not make it out.

৵

DAN FOUND six Carl Haineses. If he could locate the one who used to be married to Annabelle Haines, it could add yet another interesting element to his story—not to mention to the lives of the children he abandoned.

The first three were a bust. On the fourth one, a woman named Lena confirmed that her husband, who died more than a year ago, used to be married to a woman named Annabelle. Dan asked if she'd mind if he stopped by for a short visit.

It stretched into almost two hours, and Lena Haines couldn't have been more gracious, even fixing him lunch. He could tell she was lonely; she and Carl never had children, and she had recently retired from her job as a librarian.

"That must be why you have so many books," said Dan, gazing around. He was a fellow book hound, but his recent shift to e-books meant his condo now had décor apart from reading material.

"Yes," she said with a smile. "I guess they're kind of like my family."

It gave Dan the segue he was looking for. "Speaking of family, Mrs. Haines, did you ever meet Carl's children?"

"No," she replied. "But Carl loved his little Marla so much. He missed her."

"What about Jon?"

"Jon's not his," she replied. "Carl left Annabelle when she was pregnant with the boy, so he never met him."

"But it's my understanding your husband paid child support for both children, correct?" That was what Marla thought anyway.

Lena's face colored. "No, he didn't. He was supposed to, but Carl's work was never steady and we couldn't afford it. He lived in fear that Annabelle would tell the court and they would come after him. That's why he never tried to see Marla, even though he really wanted to."

Dan perked up. "Did Annabelle tell Carl who Jon's father was?"

She nodded. When she said, "Winston Jennings," Dan thought his head might explode.

Now he faced a dilemma: Should he share the news with Regan and Nick before his piece aired? Would withholding the information from them impede their investigation and get him into trouble?

He couldn't see how; it was a biological fact, not a criminal one.

He would tell Marla right away, though. She could make the decision about when and how to tell Jon.

Dan could hardly contain his exhilaration. The story was shaping up better than he ever could have imagined.

49

REGAN WAS soaking in the tub, mulling over her man troubles, when she got a call from Nick. "Just talked to the medical examiner. She took another look at Weir's body and found a needle mark in his shoulder she hadn't spotted before."

Regan slid upright. "I thought there wasn't any trace of poison in his system."

"Not the most common ones," said Nick. "But she's going to run tests on a couple other possibilities."

"I *knew* it wasn't a suicide. What about Jennings' private SEAL team? Have your surveillance teams spotted any activity?"

"Yep, I was just getting ready to tell you that. One of them reported a guy named David Sloan left town the day of Weir's death."

"Where'd he go?"

"Rockville, Maryland. Apparently that's where he's from; so he decided it was a good time to pay his dear old mom a visit. I've got a road trip planned for first thing in the morning."

"Want me to tag along, or is this a boys-only party?"

"I'm thinking it should be *mano a mano*. Your turn to stay here and babysit Jennings."

Regan laughed. "Okay, partner. Let me know what you find out."

ॐ

REGAN HAD butterflies in her stomach when she went to see Adam.

"Hey," he said, his voice warm with affection. "I'm glad you're here. After you left last time, I was worried that--"

"We need to talk, Adam."

He searched her face and then nodded. "Okay."

They sat next to each other in the pair of chairs in front of his desk.

"I have to admit I feel some attraction to you," Regan began. "But I can't—and won't—act on it as long as I'm still in a relationship with Jack. It feels like I'm cheating on him. Can you understand that?"

He nodded, his expression resigned. "Yes, I can. If you and I were ever to have a relationship, I'd want you to feel that way if another guy came on to you. I guess I was just eager to let you know how I feel about you—that for me it's more than just collegial. In case you find yourself single again."

"I know, Adam. But I do love Jack, and even if he and I can't figure out a way to make it work, I'll need some time to sort things out anyway—to heal."

He nodded, looking down at his hands. "Okay, I get it. I'll back off. But if anything changes ..."

She smiled. "I'll let you know. For now, let's keep our focus on the case, okay? I want us to be able to work together without it feeling awkward."

"No problem, Regan. And that ought to give your guard-dog partner some relief, too."

"I'm sure it will. So ... anything new on your end?"

"My director talked to yours, and they're feeling extremely uneasy about Jennings. If we don't have a rock-solid case, they're going to tell us to back off and leave him alone."

"We're trying to put it together, Adam, but it isn't easy unraveling all of this."

"I know you're working as fast as you can. I got the grand jury rescheduled for Monday, and since today is Friday, that means we need to have a clear picture of where we stand by later today. Can you guys do that?"

"I think so." Regan felt the vise squeeze a little tighter. She was leaving for Juneau on Tuesday.

"Hopefully the added heat will persuade Haines and his attorney to be more cooperative."

"If not, what's their defense going to be?"

Adam stood up and started pacing. "Hard to say. Haines could claim the money was used to hire consultants to help them navigate the business systems in other countries. The copies of the agreements you obtained spelled out the payoffs to the consultants but not to particular officials, so we have to be able to show the money trail. Demonstrate that the consultants weren't hired for local marketing purposes or something like that. If we can persuade any of them to testify, that's even better."

"Huang Lee is the most forthcoming, but he refuses to come here to testify," said Regan. "He'll only verify in writing that he was paid to bribe the officials. Of course Haines doesn't know that."

"I'd keep it that way. And keep trying to persuade Lee to change his mind; you might need him, especially since we won't have Weir now."

"What about Jennings' offshore accounts? The dates of the deposits coincide with the transfer of funds to pay the consultants. Is that enough proof of his involvement?"

"It helps, but I think we need more. This is Winston Jennings we're talking about—he'll surround himself with the best legal talent money can buy."

"True," said Regan. "We're contacting our counterparts in the other countries where Imhoff bribed officials, following up on earlier conversations we had with them. We're hoping to find others to come forward besides Lee. At the very least, we can build a case that Jennings was chairman and still CEO at the time when Imhoff made all of these bribes, so he was responsible for his company's actions—even if he claims he didn't know about them. But of course we'd much rather prove he was corrupt, not just negligent." The difference between killing a dangerous animal and just wounding it.

"Turn up the heat if you can, Regan. We're almost out of time."

౸

REGAN WAS mapping their progress on the white board in the conference room when Nick got back.

"Sloan claims he was already in Rockport when Weir was killed. Mama corroborated his story, of course. I've got Cutter and Grimes looking for a way to prove he got there later than what he's saying." The two agents had been on surveillance, assisting Regan and Nick with the investigation.

"Did Sloan tell you what he does for Imhoff?"

Nick gave a derisive snort. "Security. I asked what that means exactly, and he said, 'Whatever needs to be protected.' The guy wasn't exactly cooperative, but I didn't have probable cause to arrest him."

So much for *mano a mano*. A gun to the head might have been more persuasive.

"Well, at least he knows we're watching him," she said.

"Yes, he does. How's it going here?"

"Frustratingly slow," said Regan. She recounted the gist of her conversation with Adam, minus the personal stuff. "I've been contacting our counterparts overseas, but I had to quit because it's the middle of the night over there."

"Anything useful yet?" Nick munched on potato chips from the office vending machine.

"Couple possibilities. I'll follow up in a few hours."

Nick turned on the conference room TV. *Fielding Questions* was on; Dan was talking about Haines.

He recounted how Jon went from being raised by a single mother, bullied at school, to becoming a brilliant attorney, responsible for key provisions of the Federal Acquisition Regulation, and then on to defeat a longtime veteran of Congress. He managed to obtain footage and still photos of Jon that painted a graphic picture of the man. Admittedly, it was an impressive piece of journalism.

Dan also gave background on Julia and her extraordinary accomplishments and talked about the "ruptured relationship of one of Washington's most prominent power couples." With dramatic flair, he told how Jon's sister, who lived in a trailer in Manassas and who hadn't seen him in years, arrived on the scene of the hostage standoff and tried to talk him into ending it. It looked like she'd been successful, and then the house blew up. And then he focused on Jon's insistence that it was an accident and how much the congressman still loved his wife.

"The public is going to eat this shit up," said Nick. "It might even make people feel sorry for Jon."

"I feel sorry for Julia. First she's taken hostage, then she's forced to be the leading lady in a news show that feels more like a sappy movie."

The program was almost over when the journalist dropped his biggest bombshell.

"One can only wonder what Jon Haines's life would have been like if things had been different—if he hadn't been pushed around as a kid, if his mother hadn't suffered debilitating depression, if he'd had the presence of a loving father. It turns out that, unbeknownst to him, he did."

Regan stiffened, leaning forward. "Wait—he's not going to say what I think he's going to, is he?"

Dan continued, his tone serious, his eyes bright with excitement over what he was about to divulge. "A recent investigation revealed that Jon Haines is the biological son of former Defense Secretary Winston Jennings."

50

DAN'S SHOW had the effect of a major earthquake, aftershocks reverberating in the hours that followed.

As far as Regan and Nick were concerned, the timing couldn't have been worse. They were furious over Dan's brazen attempt to garner ratings at the expense of an investigation that was in the home stretch.

Regan called Marla. "Did you know about this?" Her tone was curt.

"I did; and Dan swore he would tell you what he found before using it on the air. I can't believe he didn't do that."

"What about Jon? Did you break the news to him?"

"Yes. I called him and told him the whole story." She filled Regan in on the details that Lena Haines told Dan.

"How did Jon take it?"

"I'm not sure; he didn't say much. It's a lot for him to process."

"Oh, I'm sure it is."

"It upsets me that Dan didn't tell you like he promised he would, Regan. Were you surprised?"

"No, Marla, I wasn't. We already knew. We had decided to keep it under wraps for now."

"Oh, no. I'm sorry it came out then. What will it mean to the investigation?"

"For one thing, it means Dan Fielding is definitely *persona non grata* with the FBI." Regan could barely keep her temper in check, but Marla didn't deserve to be the target of it. She took a deep breath to calm herself. "Beyond that, we'll have to see how Winston Jennings responds to having that information blasted out over the airwaves."

"I'm going to talk to Jon again tomorrow, so maybe I'll get a better sense of where he is. I'll let you know if he says anything that might help."

"Thanks."

"And Regan, I know I should be angry with Dan for lying to me, but he found out about my father—that Carl Haines died but that he always loved me. It means a lot. And his widow, Lena, wants to meet me."

Regan's anger evaporated. Marla Dunston had suffered so much in her life that she deserved any measure of happiness that came her way.

"I'm pleased for you, Marla. I really am. Maybe Willie and Emma will have a new grandma to love them."

Regan's phone indicated another call coming in. "I'm getting another call. I'll talk to you later."

The call was from Julia. "I can't believe what Dan Fielding just reported. Winston Jennings is Jon's *father*." Her tone was riddled with disbelief. "I just can't fathom ... Annabelle was with *Winston*? That's just ..."

"Unbelievable ... I know. Winston had the affair with Jon's mother right before he married Betty. Carl Haines was an enlisted man stationed at the naval base in Norfolk, Virginia, and Winston was an officer there. The relationship with Annabelle started while Carl was deployed to Vietnam—and when he came home to a pregnant wife, of course he knew the child wasn't his. She admitted to the affair with Winston, and Carl left her—but surprisingly, he never confronted Winston or exposed him as Jon's father."

"*Why?* It would have made so much difference for Jon. I can't imagine how he's reacting to this."

"Well, I was talking to Marla when you called," said Regan. "She told him, and apparently he was too stunned to say much of anything."

"I'm not surprised. Have you guys had a chance to talk to Carl Haines?"

"No, he died over a year ago. Fielding interviewed his widow, and she told him about Jennings being Jon's father. We'd already made the same discovery through a DNA test but weren't going to reveal it until we finished building our case against Jennings."

"Oh my god," Julia murmured. "That horrible man is Jackson's grandfather."

"Only biologically," Regan said. "Not in any way that matters, Julia."

Julia was silent for a moment. "I'm going to call Jon."

Regan wasn't sure how to react. She was afraid the shocking news might reignite Julia's compassion for real. Maybe make her do something she'd later regret.

But she was still his wife. It was her choice.

"Be careful," was all she said.

❧

WINSTON HADN'T seen the show himself, but Betty had.

"Why, Winston? Why didn't you tell me?"

The news of Fielding's disclosure hit him like a blow to the head, addling his brain. "I ... I ... it was a long time ago, Betty. Before you and I were married."

"Everything makes so much sense now." He could hear the anguish in her voice, and it made him feel awful.

"I'm sorry, Betty. I know I should have told you. I'm not very good at explaining things like that."

"Like *what?*" she snapped. "That you broke up a woman's marriage and then left her stranded? You couldn't find a way to tell me that?"

He couldn't tell if she was more upset that he had the affair or that he hadn't done right by Annabelle and married her.

"I didn't leave her completely stranded. I set up an escrow account and paid support for the last forty-two years."

"*Forty-two* years? In case you forgot, Winston, that's how long we've been married. You were with that woman when we were engaged. Maybe even after we were married."

"Well, I … we …"

"Never mind. I know how hard it is for you to explain things like that." She hung up.

For a long while, he sat there, stunned. Would Betty ask for a divorce? Would she try to take the ranch from him? What about his kids … what would they think of their father? Oh god, what would *Jon* think?

He'd cared for him the best he could, did everything to make sure Jon had the best life possible without drawing too much attention to their true relationship.

But now Dan Fielding had.

Not only had he caused major embarrassment to Betty and the kids, the stunning revelation would get everyone whipped up and thus make it harder for him to get done what he needed to with Congress—critical things that would make the country safer. And Jon's missteps would likely be construed as Winston's fault—as if *he* was the one who pulled out a gun and threatened to kill his wife, not Jon.

Well, now his secret was out in the open—one of them, at least. It was off his chest, for better or worse. *Let them do what they will,* he thought. *Let them come at me with guns blazing.*

He would not go down without a fight.

5 1

O N SATURDAY morning, Regan and Nick paid another visit to Jon.

"I'll help you get Winston Jennings," he announced without preamble.

Regan couldn't hide her astonishment . "You will?"

He nodded, his jaw set in a hard line. Ben Franklin sat silently beside him, hands clasped in front of him on the table.

"What changed your mind, Jon?"

"The betrayal. His cowardice. The way he used me. I'm his son, and yet he treated me like nothing more than his little puppet. I always did what he asked, and look where it landed me."

Regan nodded, not daring to say anything in case it impeded the flow of his confession. She noticed, though, that the set of his jaw was to keep himself from breaking down.

"There was always something about our relationship that seemed, I don't know, confusing. He insisted I run for Congress and brainwashed me into thinking I was some kind of political whiz kid. But I'm not. And I have no desire to be."

He paused and opened the bottle of water in front of him, hands shaking. He took a swig before continuing.

"The worst part is that because of him, I pushed away my own wife. He made me think she was the only thing standing between me and this big, illustrious career. I stopped seeing

Julia for who she was—who she'd always been." He shook his head, tears filling his eyes. "The love of my life."

Nick spoke up. "So you're ready to tell us about Jennings' involvement in the bribery schemes? You'll complete the picture for us?"

The lawyer looked over at his client. "Are you sure you want to do this, Jon?"

"I'm positive. I should have done it a long time ago."

"Okay," said Regan, "let's start with the moment Jennings first mentioned bribes."

༭

THEY WERE on their way to bring Jennings in for questioning, still giddy over Jon's confession, when Nick got a call from one of the surveillance teams.

"Hang on—let me put you on speaker so Regan can hear, too. Okay, go."

"Jennings just contacted David Sloan," said Tom Cutter. "He told him to have a 'meet up' with Dan Fielding."

"A meet up? What did Sloan say?"

"He said, 'I'll take care of it.'"

"Hmm," said Regan. "I wonder if a 'meet up' is code for stab a needle in his shoulder and poison him to death."

"Could be. We'll stay on him, of course, but you might want to warn Fielding."

"Is Sloan still in Rockport?" asked Nick.

"No, he got back to town last night. We're sitting across the street from his apartment."

"Okay, Tom," said Nick. "Keep us posted." He looked at Regan. "I thought Boyd was the guy in charge—that he was the one who gave orders to the team, not Jennings directly."

254

"Maybe something's changed. Either way, Jennings is acting like we can't touch him."

"Let's go convince him otherwise." Nick accelerated the vehicle.

"Wait," said Regan. " I have an idea. Let's go see Dan first."

❧

DAN WAS surprised when they showed up at his condo. "I figured I'd hear from you, but I didn't expect a visit in person. Come on in, guys."

"So," said Regan, "that was quite a big splash you made last night. I bet you're pretty proud of yourself, huh?"

"C'mon, Regan, it's a story that needed to be told. The public has a right to know what's going on with Jon Haines—and by extension, Winston Jennings."

"Marla said you promised to tell us before it aired," said Nick. "What, did it slip your mind?"

"No." Dan looked at his feet.

"You knew we'd tell you to hold off," said Regan. "That we're *this* close to an arrest—" She held up her thumb and forefinger. "—and we wanted to keep things as steady as possible until that happens."

"Hey, I get that," Dan said defensively. "But you need to understand what *my* job is. I have a highly rated show on NBC, and it got that way because I do what it takes to find the story and get it out to the viewers in a timely fashion. If I'd waited until next Friday night, it would have been old news."

"In this case, that might have served you better, pal," said Nick. "We think Jennings has put out a hit on you."

"*What?* How do you know?"

"We have a surveillance team on one of those Imhoff contractors you told me about. They intercepted a phone conversation between Jennings and David Sloan. Jennings told him to have a 'meet up' with you."

"What the hell's a meet up?"

"We're guessing it means you're supposed to meet up with your maker," said Regan.

"Shit," said Dan, pacing stiffly back and forth. "Can't you arrest Sloan? And Jennings?"

"We are getting ready to pick up Jennings for questioning," said Nick. "Haines is cooperating with us. But we don't have enough evidence to pick up Sloan for Weir's murder, and he hasn't done anything to you yet."

Dan gave them a sardonic smile. "I see … so you're going to wait until he kills me and then arrest him for my murder along with Weir's."

"We won't let him kill you," Regan said. "Though I have to say it's tempting."

"Listen, guys, I wasn't trying to get in your way. I told you over and over I just wanted to help."

"Great," said Regan. "Now you can help us reel in Sloan."

Dan's eyes got big. "You're going to use me as bait?"

"Yep," said Nick.

"What if it doesn't work and I *do* get killed?"

Regan smiled. "Don't worry, Dan, we have a decent track record. I'm pretty sure we can keep you alive."

52

WINSTON WANTED to see Jon to explain, but he wasn't sure how his son would react to seeing him, now that the news was out.

He paced the living room in his apartment and tried to come up with a game plan, but he had so much pent-up anxiety he felt like he might spontaneously combust. His remedy for extreme stress had always been to go for a brisk jog, but these days his knees would scream in protest if he tried that.

Instead, Winston walked to the park across the street and sat down on a bench. He saw children giggling as they tossed chunks of bread to the ducks on the pond, the silly birds dipping and flapping as the treats were launched their way. He remembered his own kids—Rob, Kate, and Kevin—when they were that age, thrilled by even the smallest things.

Had Jon been that way, too? Had Annabelle tried to make him happy, or was she already too depressed by then?

Winston thought back to when he first saw her. She was the new secretary in his office at the base, and he became mesmerized by her delicate beauty, by the sensuality of her gaze, by her lack of guile. And even though she was a married woman with a small child, he pursued her relentlessly until she gave in.

With Annabelle, he could let down his guard, take a break from being who he was. Feel safe and loved.

He knew she wanted the same in return, but she never made demands on him. So when Winston announced his engagement to Betty, she let him go—and allowed him back into her arms whenever he desired her. She sacrificed everything, while he stood by and watched the joy seep from her soul. Finally, two years into his marriage, he told her goodbye for the last time.

Now his beautiful Annabelle sat in a nursing home, her memory destroyed, unable to recognize her own children. He couldn't help but wonder how much of it he had caused—and how much of her happiness he had stolen away from Jon and Marla.

He pushed thoughts of Annabelle from his head and focused on the joggers in the park, many of them running with dogs in tow. He pictured his Gertie, lying on the porch, waiting for him to come home.

Would it still be his home now? Would his wife and kids reject him because of the secret he'd kept from them for more than forty years?

He should have confessed the affair to Betty back then. She would have been upset, but she would have forgiven him. They'd already been a couple for a long time—ever since he was a high school senior and Betty a sophomore, and then all through college. He'd strayed a few times before, but it was only about sex, not love.

Annabelle had been different. That's why he couldn't tell her.

He decided he would go visit Jon and ask for his forgiveness. He wished he could do the same with Annabelle, to help absolve him of his guilt, but it was too late.

He gazed around. Despite the turmoil in his head, the park's peacefulness had settled him. He started to get up, and then he saw the black SUV pull up in front of his apartment building. No lights and sirens, no guns drawn, nothing showy.

He spotted the red hair and knew instantly who it was. Agent Manning and her partner were just there to ... what? Question him?

He waited until they'd gone inside the building, then he rushed over to an adjacent street with heavier traffic and hailed a taxi.

ॐ

WHEN WINSTON didn't come to the door, they found the apartment manager.

"Do you know if Mr. Jennings is currently in town?" asked Regan.

"He was an hour ago," said the manager, a wiry-looking guy with glasses that were too big for his narrow face. "I was hosing off the sidewalk and he walked by me and said hello."

"Did you see where he was going?"

"Over there to the park." The man pointed across the street.

"Thanks." They ran across the street and began searching among the park visitors.

After twenty minutes without spotting him, Regan said, "Maybe he saw us pull up and got out of here."

"Let's go see if he's at Imhoff," said Nick. "At the very least we can stir up some of those GI Joes guarding the place—give them something to do with all that testosterone."

"Good idea. By the way, have you checked back in with the medical examiner lately?"

"Nope—I'll do it right now." He made the call. When she answered, he said, "Hey, Sheila, why you working on a Saturday? They paying you overtime?"

"I wish," she replied. "No, I'm working because a pushy FBI agent said I needed to run more toxicology screens in record time." Her voice carried a hint of flirtation.

"Man, I hate pushy FBI agents. Is it anybody I know?" He winked at Regan.

"Ha ha, funny guy. It's a good thing you asked me nicely. And as a matter of fact, I was just about to call you. I was able to isolate some metabolites of a muscle paralytic called succinyl choline. I found large quantities of succinic acid metabolites in his brain tissues."

"So the killer injected the muscle paralytic in his shoulder?" said Regan.

"Looks that way," said Sheila.

"Nasty," said Nick.

"Yeah, I wouldn't want anybody giving me a shot of that while I was driving," said Sheila. "Really screws with your reflexes."

Nothing like a little toxicology humor.

"Thanks, Sheila," they said in unison.

"Well, we have the *what*," said Regan. "Now we just need the *who*."

"I'm putting my money on Sloan," said Nick. "He finds Weir, jabs him with the syringe full of poison, watches him roll into the Potomac, then goes to visit mama until the heat dies down."

"But why was Weir near the Potomac in the first place? Was it just coincidence that Sloan found him there? Seems pretty convenient, don't you think?"

"Yes, I know it does, and I don't have that part totally figured out yet. I'm working on it."

"Why don't you call Jana and see what she can dig up on Sloan?" Jana was their go-to analyst at the bureau, brilliant at finding useful tidbits that eluded others.

Nick made the call and explained what they wanted. "Our system is down," she replied.

"What do you mean, our system is down?" said Regan.

"The FBI computers got hacked. Everything's down right now."

"What about the backup system?"

"It's down, too," said Jana.

"Jesus," said Nick.

They exchanged a look, each pondering the ramifications. It was frightening to contemplate. "Let us know the minute it's up again, okay?"

"Will do, guys," said Jana, signing off.

"Well, that seems awfully coincidental, doesn't it?" said Regan.

"Sure does. Just as we're about to close in on Mr. Cybersecurity himself, the bureau's computers get hacked."

"I can't wait to see Jennings' face. If he's gloating, I think we know who's behind this."

53

WHEN HE spoke to Ethan the night before, Winston explained that this new project was much more challenging—and secretive—than the one before where he just did a little tinkering with Jeremy Traynor's financials. Could Ethan pull it off without getting caught? The kid's voice held an unmistakable hint of excitement as he said, "Oh, yeah. No problem."

He was ordered not to destroy anything or capture any data, at least for now; this was simply meant to send a message.

"Cool," said the kid. Winston was thankful he was on Imhoff's payroll and not somebody else's.

A moment ago, Ethan confirmed the job was done. The FBI was back to using the telephone and typewriters until Winston said otherwise.

His intercom buzzed; it was Boyd. "Those two FBI agents that were looking for Weir the other day are here to see you. What do you want me to do?" He knew Boyd was hoping he could rough them up or run them off the property; he was desperate to get back into Winston's good graces.

Too late, he thought. Winston was already planning to make David Sloan the field team leader. For now, Boyd would be allowed to remain as onsite security chief at Imhoff because he'd been with the company for more than two decades. He deserved at least that much of a second chance.

"I want you to send them up," he replied.

Winston leaned back in his chair and waited. If they arrested him, Howard would get him released before the day was out.

His assistant buzzed him when they stepped off the elevator. "Agents Manning and Jenesco are here to see you, Mr. Jennings."

"Excellent. Show them in." He got up from his chair. "Nice to see you again, Agent Manning. I trust you had a good trip back from Kansas?"

"We'd like you to come with us," Jenesco said brusquely.

"For what purpose?"

"To question you in regard to possible violations of the Foreign Corrupt Practices Act," said Regan. "If you cooperate, we'll do so without making a formal arrest at this point."

"I'll cooperate, but you're making a mistake," Winston said. He made sure neither his face nor his voice held any trace of fear or anger. "And just so you know, I'll be putting in a call to Garrison to explain just how big a mistake it is. After I do, you two will be lucky to get jobs as security guards at the National Zoo."

"Director Tate is fully aware we're bringing you in for questioning," said Manning. "Call him if it makes you feel better, but he's not going to help you." She showed no trace of fear or anger, either. In fact, she smiled, which rankled him.

"We'll see about that." He'd wait a little while, though; right now Garrison would be pretty busy trying to find a hacker. A nonexistent one in China.

And soon Winston would have the chance to be a hero.

ॐ

AS THEY made their way across the lobby of the main building, more security guards seemed to materialize out of thin air. They positioned themselves in a semi-circle, itchy fingers on their guns, waiting for a signal from the boss. Praying for a signal from the boss.

"Stand down, gentlemen," said Winston.

Nick got a call as they were putting him in the car. Once Winston was safely tucked inside, Regan closed the door and waited outside the vehicle so Nick could fill her in on his phone call.

"That was Cutter," he said in a low voice. "David Sloan is parked outside Dan's place."

"What's he doing?"

"Nothing yet; right now he just seems to be observing. Maybe trying to determine if Dan is there."

He was; it was Saturday and they'd instructed him to stay home until they told him otherwise. If he left the house, they couldn't guarantee his protection.

"Maybe Sloan's going to hang around until it gets dark," said Regan.

"Yeah, that's what I told Cutter. I think we better alert Dan that he's out there, though."

"I agree." She climbed into the car and waited for Nick to finish talking to Dan.

"As I said, Agent Manning, you're making a serious error in judgment," said Winston. "I don't know what you think you know, but I've done nothing wrong, and once I prove that, you're going to find yourself in an extremely uncomfortable position. You still have time to reverse course."

Despite her outward calm, Regan's nerves were lit up like a Christmas tree. She and her partner had just taken the mighty Winston Jennings into custody.

If Haines had another change of heart, they were screwed. What if Winston got to him? What if Haines suffered a complete breakdown? What if …

Don't go there.

She met Winston's gaze in the rearview mirror and smiled. "You're a dear to be so worried about my job security, Mr. Jennings, but I'm sure I'll be fine. We've got a solid case."

HOWARD PERKINS kept him from saying anything, but they'd accomplished their purpose. Jennings had been put on notice.

After the two men left, Regan stood up and shook out her arms, breathing deeply.

"You okay?" said Nick.

She nodded. "The guy makes me so tense I'm afraid I'll break if I bump into anything."

"Yeah, but we've got the son-of-a-bitch worried. Did you see his face?"

"He tried to look threatening, but I could see it in his eyes — the fear about what we might have on him."

"Too bad we don't actually have a smoking gun," said Nick.

"We'll keep digging until we have the equivalent of one. Did you see how indignant he looked when I asked him if he had any involvement in hacking our system? He's quite the actor. I'm convinced he's behind it."

"And then the bastard had the audacity to say Imhoff could get it resolved for us. The guy's unbelievable."

Or brilliant, she thought. What a perfect diversion when the FBI has you in its crosshairs.

"I think we should take him up on it," said Regan.

"What, have Imhoff fix the problem?"

"Who could do it any better and faster than the one who caused it? In fact, Nick, I think we should go see the director. Get him to play along and make Jennings think Tate's going to can us—and then ask him to help identify the hacker and get the system back up. That way, Jennings will think he's won—that he's going to get away with the hacking, the bribery, and the hits he ordered on Weir and Fielding."

"Good idea—as long as Tate *will* play along and he doesn't actually believe his pal Jennings."

"He hates Jennings," said Regan. "But he subscribes to the belief you should keep your friends close and your enemies closer."

54

REGAN ASKED Roland to meet them at Director Tate's office. While they waited in the outer office, she filled her boss in.

"I sure hope you're right," said Roland. "I'd rather Jennings hacked our system to divert attention than find out it's a bunch of shadowy hackers overseas someplace who want to do serious damage."

Tate's assistant said, "The director is ready for you."

When they entered the office, he said, "I just got off the phone with Winston Jennings. He's making all kinds of threats about what he'll do to our agency if I don't get rid of the two of you." Tate looked like *he* was the one in the crosshairs.

"Perfect," said Regan.

"Excuse me?" said Tate.

"That's exactly what we wanted to talk to you about, sir. Though I have to admit I'm a little surprised at how quickly he followed up on his threat to call you." She gave the director a full rundown on Jennings' interrogation and the plan they had in mind for duping him.

Tate listened, then spent a moment silently processing, his fingers steepled in front of his lips. Finally, he glanced around at the trio, his gaze coming to rest on Regan. "I think you're on to something, Agent Manning. Using Jennings' own expertise to hang him—in effect fighting fire with fire—might be the only way we can get this done. And nothing would make me happier than to see that man put away."

"He's certainly caused the bureau enough grief over the years," said Roland. "Especially you, Garrison."

As often as Jennings had publicly attacked Tate's leadership, it was a wonder the director still spoke to the guy at all.

Regan said, "If what Speaker Stallworth told us is true, that's probably because he thinks he's competing with you. He believes they can do what the bureau does—only better."

"Yes," said Tate. "He's long pushed for privatizing national security. Ironically, Jennings' own activities of late, especially those that are illegal, point out the very reason why national security *shouldn't* be privatized. It needs government oversight to keep from being run by someone like Winston Jennings. Someone who wildly abuses power."

 ~

DAVID SLOAN was no longer outside Dan's house.

"I bet he comes back," Dan said miserably. "And I'll be a sitting duck, hoping your people out there can move fast enough when he tries to get in."

"That's why I'm staying here with you," said Nick.

"Really?"

"Yep. We considered having you leave the premises and go with Regan while I wait here, but Sloan is no fool. He's going to need to get eyes on you before he attempts to break in."

"What if he gets eyes on you, too?"

"He won't," said Nick.

Dan looked only slightly more relieved. "I want to get this over with. I have a serious case of cabin fever."

"Don't worry, Dan," said Regan. "It shouldn't be much longer; we think he'll make his move tonight. I'm sure Jennings is leaning on him to get it done sooner rather than later."

The journalist leaned forward in his chair, forearms perched on his knees. "I shouldn't have included the paternity thing in the story. It was stupid."

"Hindsight is a wonderful thing, my friend," said Regan. "But I have to agree; your story was already excellent. You didn't need the big finish."

"Well, this may surprise you, but I did it more for your benefit than the public's. I wanted to impress you guys with what I'd uncovered so you'd let me help with the investigation. I realize now it was a dumb-shit thing to do." He shook his head.

Regan softened her tone. "What's done is done. We're not going to hold it against you, Dan."

"If I live through Jennings holding it against me, you mean," he replied.

"You'll be okay. Nick will have your back." She turned to her partner. "Keep me posted, okay? I'm going back to the office to work the phones."

She intended to harass Huang Lee until he agreed to testify.

55

WINSTON'S DAY had taken a positive spin. Tate agreed to ax the two agents, saying he'd been concerned for some time about Regan Manning showing signs of being a rogue. He sounded truly apologetic that Winston had been brought in for questioning.

Perhaps best of all, he requested the assistance of Imhoff-Greyson to identify their hacker.

Winston had had Ethan include code to make it look like the hit to the bureau's computers had come from China. When the other members of Imhoff's team made the discovery, their reporting would be genuine, without any inkling of in-house mischief.

And it didn't take them long to find it.

Winston got Tate on the phone. "We found your source. It's the Chinese."

"Can you fix it?"

"Absolutely. My team is working on it now." Winston couldn't help feeling smug.

"I can't thank you enough, Win," said Tate.

"This is what we do, Garrison. This is exactly the reason I've been pushing for a public-private partnership on cybersecurity."

"I'd like to hear more about that after we get this glitch resolved. I've been given regular updates by my people on the cybersecurity task force, of course, but I want to hear about your overall vision."

"Just tell me when."

æ

"CHINA?" said Regan.

"That's what Jennings reported to the director," said Roland.

"I'm not buying it. The timing is too coincidental."

"You're probably right, Regan. But the important thing is that Winston *is* buying Tate's whole story. He thinks you and Nick are history."

"Which will make it that much more satisfying to face him in court."

"Just be careful. Until we prove our case and lock him up, he's extremely dangerous. What about your partner—any update from Fielding's place?"

"No, they're just waiting for Sloan to show up. Nick talked to his surveillance team, and right now Sloan is at his apartment. They'll let Nick know when he's on the move."

"Okay, good. Keep me updated on developments."

As they signed off, Regan took a moment to reflect on the level of support she enjoyed from her bosses—especially Lisa Roland. It could have gone down very differently.

After Regan exposed Vice President Landry Ness's involvement in a corruption scheme with his longtime friend, oil magnate Robert Carney, she pretty much had her pick of assignments within the bureau. She chose this gig in the WFO, and Roland, the quintessential team player, had graciously welcomed her, had treated her like a valued member of the FCPA task force and not someone foisted on her from the top.

The two women had a deep mutual respect from the very beginning. Regan was confident that someday, if she chose to pursue an administrative role in the bureau, Lisa Roland would extend a helping hand.

As she considered her future, her thoughts drifted to Jack.

But that would have to wait. Right now, she needed to make a call to China.

෨

IT HAD been dark for a couple hours. Dan became increasingly twitchy.

Nick put on a bulletproof vest and had Dan put one on, too. It felt bulky and uncomfortable under his T-shirt—but if it kept him alive, he'd deal with it. He just prayed he didn't take a shot to the head.

Nick peeked out a side window that had a view of the street. His demeanor was completely calm.

"Doesn't this kind of thing scare you?" said Dan.

Nick looked over at him and shrugged. "Depends on what's happening. If people are shooting at me, then yeah, it gets a little scary. But most of the time, it's a lot of watching and waiting."

"You probably prefer the action to the boredom."

Nick smiled. "I think every cop does. As long as you end up making an arrest and don't catch a bullet."

"I couldn't do it, man. Sitting around like this, waiting for an assassin to show up ... it's about to do me in. I don't know what I'll do when he actually gets here ..."

"You just need to do what I tell you. I'll handle the assassin."

Nick's quiet confidence calmed his nerves a little. "Okay."

Maybe when it was all over, he'd do a piece on Nick Jenesco—a day in the life of an FBI agent. Most people had no idea what they put themselves through.

And he truly liked the guy. Dan hoped he'd have the chance to prove to him he wasn't a complete dick.

Nick's cell phone beeped. "Yeah, Tom ... okay, good. Tail him and let me know when he's close."

A surge of fear pierced Dan's gut. "He's coming?"

"We don't know yet if this is where he's headed. He's just leaving his—"

Dan heard a pinging sound and saw Nick go down, a splotch of red sprouting on his upper arm. He stared in horror, his own limbs frozen.

"Get upstairs!" Nick yelled.

It took a few seconds longer for Dan to get his feet to move, then he darted up the steps and into his office. He crawled into the closet and started to close the door, but then he stopped.

Nick's injured. I can't leave him there to fight alone.

Dan didn't own a gun; he'd have to find something else to use for a weapon. Baseball bat? Golf club? Both were in the garage.

He grabbed a heavy crystal object from the bookshelf. He opened the door and crept into the hallway, heart pounding. "Nick?"

There was no answer. Then he saw the open front door. Seconds later, gunfire erupted.

He barreled down the stairs and then ran back up again, wild with fear. *What should I do?*

A voice in his head said, "Call nine-one-one, idiot." His hands shook badly as he dialed. Once he was assured that backup was on the way, he inched back down the stairs and peeked outside, his makeshift weapon ready to plunk someone in the head. He couldn't see Nick or his assailant; he was about to creep out to the porch when another burst of gunfire changed his mind.

After what seemed like an eternity, the shooting stopped and he could hear sirens in the distance. He backed up and plastered himself against the wall around the corner, uncertain who was left standing—and who might come through the front door.

He heard a shuffle on the front porch and waited, tense and unbreathing, his arm raised and ready to strike with the makeshift weapon. Then he saw it was Nick.

"Oh, Jesus," he gasped. "Did you get him?"

"I got him." Nick seemed to sag, either from relief or exhaustion, or maybe both.

Dan rushed over to him and peered at his wound. "How badly are you injured?"

"I'll be okay." He spotted the crystal piece in Dan's hand and smiled. "Were you using that to back me up?"

"Yeah, it's the only thing I could find. I don't have a gun."

Nick peered at it and saw that it was an award with an inscription on it. "That'd be pretty damn ironic."

Dan looked at it and suddenly realized what he meant— using an award for excellence in journalism to stop a guy who was there to kill you for something you reported. He laughed, amazed that Nick had that much presence of mind after a shootout—and with blood running down his arm.

Nick went back out on the porch to meet the cops who had just arrived on scene. With his good arm, he held up his FBI shield.

Dan could only stare as he watched all hell break loose in front of his house. Local PD, more agents, and two ambulances showed up, and people were running everywhere.

He followed Nick to the back of one of the ambulances, where Nick told a pair of cops what happened while a paramedic inspected his gunshot wound.

A metro PD detective came over and said, "Mr. Fielding? Could you come with me?"

"Yeah, just a second." He turned to Nick. "Was it Sloan?"

Nick shook his head. "It was a guy named Boyd."

56

REGAN FOUND Nick in the ER, where an attractive young physician stitched up his wound. He looked dazed and quite happy; Regan wasn't sure if it was because of the pain meds or the pretty doc.

"You gonna live, partner?"

"I don't know. Ask her."

The doctor smiled. "He'll be sore and have limited use of this arm for awhile, but he's going to be fine. The bullet didn't do any major damage."

Regan almost wept with relief.

"Luckily it wasn't my shooting arm," said Nick.

She patted his good arm. "I'm glad you're okay, Nicky."

They made small talk until the doctor finished up and sent Nick on his way. Once they were in the car, Regan said, "So what happened?"

"I'd just gotten a call from Cutter telling me Sloan was heading our way. They were tailing him and were going to alert me when he was close." He paused. "Shit, Regan, I let down my guard."

"You had no way of knowing Boyd would be out there."

"I should have covered all the bases—kept a team on him. But I was sure Sloan was the hit man."

"Like I said before, I'm just glad you're okay, Nick. If his aim had been a little higher ..." She shuddered. "How did Dan react to the whole thing?"

Nick chuckled. "He was about to wet his pants. And you should've seen what he was using for a weapon—a big old glass award he got for outstanding journalism." He started to laugh, softly at first and then hysterically; this time Regan was sure it was the drugs.

"That's appropriate," she said, laughing mostly at him.

When the humor subsided, he said, "I need to check in with Cutter and Grimes. See what Sloan is up to." With some effort, he pulled the phone from his pocket and punched in the number, then switched it to speaker mode.

"Cutter."

"Hey, Tom. Just wondered—"

"Hey, man, are you all right?"

"Yeah, the bullet went all the way through. I won't be able to arm wrestle with my left arm for awhile, but I figure it's a small sacrifice."

He'd be sacrificing a whole lot more than that for awhile, but Regan didn't want to rain on his parade.

"Hi, Tom," she said brightly. "What's our boy Sloan been up to?"

"Hey, Regan. We tailed Sloan to Fielding's street, but when he saw the emergency vehicles, he kept going. He made a big loop back to his apartment in DuPont Circle. We're sitting across the street."

"You guys have a team coming on soon?" said Nick. It was nearly midnight.

"Yep," said Cutter. "They should be here any minute."

"Good," said Nick. "We'll head that way so we can make sure everyone's on the same page."

"Nick's on meds that have him thinking he's Superman," said Regan. "We aren't heading that way; I'm taking Nick to his apartment so he can get some sleep."

277

Nick made a sound of exasperation. "I'm not tired. We need to—"

"We've got it, Nick," said Cutter. "Go home."

Regan was exhausted, too. She couldn't wait to crawl into her own bed.

She'd fill Nick in on the other stuff in the morning.

~

WINSTON HADN'T slept a wink after getting the call. Boyd was trying to be some kind of hero and had gotten himself killed.

Sloan wasn't to blame; Winston was the one who told Boyd he'd gone directly to David to take care of the Dan Fielding problem. Boyd had been miffed but had the good sense not to argue.

Instead, he tried to cut Sloan off at the pass. And now he was dead.

It meant there'd be another round of scrutiny by the FBI—but at least he wouldn't have to deal with Agent Manning. He hoped her replacement would be more properly intimidated by him.

He still hadn't been to see Jon since Fielding's story broke. It was time; he needed to make him understand why he'd kept their true relationship a secret. Tell him what a special woman his mother was. Promise to take care of him.

And try to persuade him to keep from exposing Winston's involvement in the bribes.

Without Jon's testimony, the U.S. Attorney was going to have a hard time proving he did anything illegal. If the offshore accounts came to light, that could be problematic, but he was pretty certain he was the only one who knew about them.

Winston arrived at the prison where Jon was being held. This time, he wasn't given the star treatment but simply escorted to a room that contained numerous metal tables and benches where prisoners could meet with their visitors.

He stared at Jon's face as he was brought into the room. His expression revealed little.

Until he sat down facing Winston, that is. Then the fury was all too evident.

"I'm sorry, Jon."

"I'm sure you are. You're sorry because of the embarrassment to you and your *real* family. Not because of what it's done to me."

"That's not true, son." He'd called him that many times, but this was the first time since Jon had learned it was literal.

"Don't call me that." Winston could see tears in Jon's eyes.

"Jon, if I could go back and do things differently, I would. For starters, I would have married your mother."

Jon's face registered surprise.

"I loved Annabelle more than I've ever loved anyone." The confession humiliated Winston, made him feel extremely vulnerable, but he had to make Jon understand.

His life depended on it.

"I was weak. I had been with Betty a long time and didn't have the courage to break it off. So instead, I broke your mother's heart. I don't think she ever got over it."

"No, she didn't. And because of you, our father abandoned us. That left Marla to raise me virtually on her own. She gave up her whole fucking childhood to care for me and my mother."

"I know she did, and I deeply regret that. I tried to ease the burden financially, but—"

Jon gave him a sharp look. "Marla always thought it was our dad—*her* dad—doing that."

"I set up an escrow account so it would remain anonymous."

"So you could keep your secret and go on to live your wonderful life, unaffected by what you did in a moment of weakness."

Winston's chest ached with remorse. "Believe me, I was affected. That's why I brought you into the company and tried to watch over you—make things better for you. I know it wasn't enough, and like I said, if I could do things differently ..."

The tears spilled down Jon's cheeks. "Why couldn't you *tell* me? I would have kept your secret, but at least our relationship would have made more sense to me. I would have understood why you pushed me the way you did—not as my boss but as my father."

"I should have."

"Now, because of you, my life is in ruins."

"Jon, I'll do whatever I can to turn that around. I promise you."

"What about Julia?"

"Julia is your business—I never should have interfered. If you want to try to get your wife back, I'll do whatever I can to help."

"I think it's too late, Winston. You and I both are going to prison. I've given the FBI the details about your involvement."

"Tate got rid of those two agents. Said the woman—Manning—was beginning to go rogue." He lowered his voice. "Maybe if you said she coerced you into making those statements ..."

"Claim I made a false confession?" Jon looked skeptical.

"You can say you were hurt and angry at me after hearing I was your father."

"I was."

"I know—and I'll make it up to you. But if I'm going to do that, we need to beat these charges first. We'll claim the payments weren't bribes, they were business agreements to help us navigate the culture of those countries. As long as none of the consultants say otherwise—which they won't if we pay them a hefty sum—the federal case is flimsy at best."

"What about the other charges against me? Julia will tell them I tried to kill her, and they'll probably figure out the fire was arson."

"We'll prove that Julia was mistaken. They won't find the so-called weapon because it burned up, right? And they may not be able to tell that the gas hose was deliberately disconnected from the water heater. We'll mount such a vigorous defense that the other charges will fall apart."

Jon fixed his gaze on Winston. Winston waited; he wondered if Jon could hear his heart pounding. To him it sounded as loud as a bass drum.

Finally, Jon nodded.

Winston smiled. "Thank you, son."

This time, Jon didn't protest.

57

ICK WAS taking his first Sunday off in a long while. He woke up in pain and barely had the energy to sit upright.

"Stay in bed, partner," said Regan. "I'm just going to do some follow-up. I'll check in with you later."

Nick didn't argue. It told her how awful he really felt.

Huang Lee's flight would arrive that evening. His testimony, coupled with Jon's, should be enough to point the finger straight at Jennings.

And if she could tie Boyd's attempted hit on Dan to Jennings, it would be one more nail in the coffin.

Now that the bureau's system was back up, she was having Jana put in a little overtime running down anything she could find on David Sloan. Regan needed a reason to bust him.

She also asked Jana to see what she could dig up on Imhoff's IT specialists. The timing of the system breach, followed by Winston's offer of assistance, was nothing if not suspect.

China, my ass. Regan was willing to bet the hackers were right there at Imhoff headquarters.

Yesterday, she'd put in a call to Huang Lee, not only to persuade him to fly to Washington to testify but also because he was a key player in China's shadowy underworld. If the cyber hit had come from there, he'd likely run across someone bragging about it.

Lee was okay with looking for hackers, but he'd been resistant about making the trip and giving testimony in person. She'd turned up the heat, said it would sure be a shame if his daughter was deported in her last year at Princeton.

She had to admit it might have been pushing the boundaries a little, but they needed everything they could get if they were to make the charges against Jennings stick. He wasn't a typical defendant; he was one of the most powerful men in the world.

Regan decided to head toward Sloan's place and hang out with the surveillance team while she waited to hear back from Jana. At the very least, maybe she would have the opportunity to question him.

On the way, she stopped off to pick up an Egg McMuffin and coffee. When she tried to pay with her debit card, it was declined. She tried a couple credit cards; they, too, were declined.

That son-of-a-bitch. The bureau's computers were back up and running, and now Winston was coming after her.

Regan's trip to Alaska was in two days, and she had about a buck-fifty in her wallet. She was pissed.

And hungry.

❧

CUTTER AND Grimes were back on surveillance. They whiled away the time arguing about who would make it to the World Series.

"Not a peep out of Sloan?" said Regan.

"Nope," said Grimes. "Quiet as a church mouse. Which is appropriate for a Sunday morning." He grinned.

"See what I have to put up with?" said Cutter.

Regan laughed. "Yeah, but at least you *have* your partner. Mine's home sleeping off a nasty wound."

"Is he going to be out of commission for quite awhile?"

"Longer than he thinks," said Regan. She'd been injured on the job before and learned that the mind was willing long before the body was. "He'll be on desk duty."

"Ah, hell, if that was me, I'd rather they just shoot me," said Grimes.

Cutter looked at his partner. "I can't believe the stupid shit you say. Nick *was* shot."

Grimes shrugged. "You know what I mean. I hate desk duty."

"Well, boys, I hate to break up all this fun, but I'm going to go have a chat with David Sloan." She opened the car door.

"Need backup?" said Cutter.

"Sure. How about hanging out in the stairwell?"

"You got it." The two men got out and accompanied Regan across the street.

"Tom, I'll call your phone as soon as we're inside the building and then stay connected so you'll hear the conversation inside Sloan's apartment. If you hear me yell 'Cutter,' you guys come running, okay?"

"'Grimes' is shorter," mumbled Grimes.

Regan shook her head and smiled. "We'll use 'Grimes' next time, okay?"

They were about to enter the building when Jana called Regan back.

"Hey, Jana, what'd you find?"

"Well, that's the thing. David Sloan is kind of a ghost. It looks like he went to work for Imhoff four years ago and was assigned to security teams overseas until eight months ago. That's when he came to DC."

"We know his mother lives in Rockport, Maryland."

"She has a different last name," said Jana. "Her name is Mary Allen."

"Have you done a search on David Allen?"

"Yep, and there isn't one with ties to her. Allen is a pretty common name, so it'll take too long to go that route looking for other first names. I also haven't been able to come up with a photo to run through our facial recognition software. I'll keep trying."

"I'm about to ring his doorbell," said Regan. "If I can come up with a reason to bring him in, you'll have your photo."

"Perfect," said Jana. "In the meantime, I'll get to work on the Imhoff IT people."

They took the elevator to Sloan's floor. The two men went left while she went right. She knocked on Sloan's door and saw a shadow cross the peephole. "Yes?" he said through the door.

"Mr. Sloan, I'm Special Agent Regan Manning, FBI. I'd like to ask you a few questions."

"About what?"

"Could you please open the door?"

When it opened, she found herself face-to-face with a man who looked like he was straight out of a documentary on the Navy SEALs, the very embodiment of *Semper Paratus*. Always ready.

He wore his hair in a buzz cut, and his eyes were dark and deadly. His navy blue T-shirt revealed a well-defined chest and sinewy arms. From his expression, it appeared there was little that amused him—except maybe the thought of holding a gun to Regan's head and pulling the trigger.

He narrowed his eyes and waited for her to speak.

"Mr. Sloan, can I come in? I want to ask you a few questions about your employment with Imhoff-Greyson."

He didn't budge. "Why is the FBI asking about my employment with Imhoff-Greyson?"

"Uh, well, we're questioning Winston Jennings in connection with some of the company's activities overseas, and we thought you might be able to give us a clearer picture."

"Why would I do that?"

Regan felt frustration stirring in her gut. "Oh, I don't know … maybe because you'd like to tell us how *you* weren't involved in anything illegal?" She returned his glare with one of her own, even though they both knew he could squash her like a bug if he chose to.

He hesitated a moment longer, then stepped back, making way for her to enter.

"Thank you, Mr. Sloan. Before we talk about your work overseas, let me ask: Were you outside the home of Dan Fielding yesterday?"

"No." He didn't even blink. The guy was good.

For the moment, Regan didn't challenge the lie; she wasn't ready to reveal that they'd intercepted the call.

"You drive a black Camaro, correct?"

"That's right."

"Well, we had a surveillance team on Fielding's place, and they have video of you sitting in your car outside the house."

It was a stretch; actually they had a still photo taken from an angle that didn't reveal the identity of the driver.

"Mine isn't the only black Camaro in DC, Agent Manning."

"No, but it would be pretty coincidental if someone in another black Camaro just happened to be sitting outside the home of a journalist that your boss ordered a hit on. And where a few hours later, your fellow Imhoff employee, Percy Boyd, tried to kill Fielding and wound up dead."

"Boyd's actions have nothing to do with me."

"Really? That's your story?"

Sloan's body stiffened and his glare became a little more intense. "We're through here, Agent Manning."

"Suit yourself," she said. "We'll continue our chat downtown." She reached for her Glock; attempting to handcuff him would be an exercise in futility.

In a split second, he whipped a handgun out of his back waistband and pointed it at her face.

"Cutter!" she screamed.

It threw him off for a few seconds, just long enough for Cutter and Grimes to kick open the door. They had to have been right outside in the hallway.

"Drop it!" hollered Cutter.

With three guns aimed at that well-defined chest, Sloan knew he didn't have a chance. Slowly, he bent over and placed his gun on the floor and raised his arms above his head. He kicked the gun over to Cutter.

Grimes moved over to cuff him.

"Wait," said Sloan. "I need to show you something, okay? I'm going to reach into my pocket."

Cutter moved closer, his aim still squarely on Sloan's chest. Regan's was, too; she nodded.

He pulled out a black leather case and flipped it open. "My name's Lance Allen. I'm with the CIA."

58

I'VE BEEN undercover for four years, and because of how shrewd Jennings is, I've had a hell of a time compiling hard evidence. He has other people do his dirty work for him—that way he can keep his hands clean."

"So, Mr. Allen, clearly he doesn't suspect you of being a fed," said Regan.

"Call me Lance. And frankly, I was quite surprised when he contacted me directly; always before he's gone through Boyd. Jennings said after the Fielding situation was 'remedied,' he was going to move me up. I wasn't sure what had happened, but I figured Boyd must've done something to piss him off."

"What about Mason Weir's death? Did Boyd kill him?"

Lance nodded. "He found Weir's car parked at a motel off I-95. He waited in the back seat until Weir got in, then he pulled his gun and told him to drive. When they got to that spot near the Potomac, Boyd told him to stop. He jabbed him in the shoulder with a muscle paralytic and waited until Weir couldn't move his limbs, then he climbed out, put the car in drive, and watched him roll into the river."

"My god—poor Mason." Regan flashed on how horrifying it would be to die like that, unable to move while the car slowly filled with water. "Did Boyd actually admit the whole thing to you?"

"He did. He was proud of his handiwork; thought you guys would never be able to figure out it wasn't a suicide. If I'd known ahead of time what he planned to do, I'd have found a way to stop him."

With Lance's true identify revealed, he didn't appear nearly as threatening. His eyes weren't all that deadly; but she'd been right about the well-defined chest.

"How were you going to remedy the Fielding situation if Boyd hadn't intervened?"

"I was going to tell Jennings that Fielding heard there was a hit out on him and had gone into hiding. I was going to make sure he *did* hear that and did indeed go into hiding. Of course, I didn't know you Fibbies were aware of it, too."

"Jennings didn't bother to use a secure line when he called you," said Cutter. "We Fibbies picked up the call."

"Jesus," said Lance. "He's getting sloppy. The Winston Jennings I've observed the past four years has been meticulous— *nothing* gets by him, and he is cautious to the extreme. I've been building a case against him piece by piece, getting a little closer every day, but ever since Haines pulled that hostage stunt two weeks ago, Jennings has been off his game."

"Being exposed as Haines' daddy must have thrown him off even more," said Regan. "He's scrambling to hold things together, but every time he plugs one hole in the dike, another one starts leaking."

Lance nodded. "That's why I was excited about finally having enough evidence—and why I wasn't eager to let you in. But I think it might be time for our two agencies to meld this into one case against Jennings. I'll show you mine if you show me yours." He smiled at Regan; the supposed ruthless killer actually had *dimples*.

Not that she was physically attracted to him. She had enough problems in the man department already. She was simply making observations.

It turned into a long and enlightening conversation. And when they were done, Regan was even more confident that Jennings' days as a free man were numbered.

❧

"WELCOME TO the U.S., Mr. Lee," said Regan.

"Thank you," he replied, but he looked like he would rather be anywhere else on earth. His carry-on bag wasn't much larger than a briefcase, a sure sign he didn't plan to stick around and take in the sights.

On the way in from the airport, Regan explained how the grand jury hearing would proceed the next day. "The U.S. Attorney will present evidence, including your testimony, of Jon Haines' involvement in the bribery scheme. If the jurors decide to issue an indictment charging Jennings with the crime, you may be issued a subpoena to appear later at trial—but that'll be a ways down the road. For right now, this hearing is just to get the indictment. It's a closed hearing without a judge, and Mr. Jennings won't be there—so you don't have to worry about seeing him face-to-face."

"Why couldn't I have just provided written testimony?"

"Because if you're here in person the jurors are more likely to ask questions. The prosecutor wants to give those jurors every reason to indict Winston Jennings, which isn't easy given his notoriety."

"He's a bad man," said Lee.

"Yeah, I agree. I just hope we get the chance to prove it."

"Something else, Agent Manning."

Regan turned her head to look at his face.

"There's no way it was Chinese hackers that took down your system."

REGAN STOPPED by to check on Nick. The dark circles under his eyes, combined with the heavy stubble on his chin, seriously dimmed his natural charm.

"How's the arm feeling?"

"Sore. It's hard to sleep."

"Are the pain meds helping?"

"I'm not taking them," he said with a yawn. "Don't want to get hooked and have my life turn into a bad movie about a cop who used to be pretty good at his job and then got shot and started taking drugs and went to hell in a hand basket."

"Wow," said Regan. "I see you've given this some thought."

"Yeah, well, it happens all the time."

"To anyone we know?"

"No, not really …"

"So just to cops in movies."

"Maybe. But I'm not taking any chances."

"You might change your mind after a couple more nights with no sleep, big guy."

"We'll see. So tell me what's happening out there. What am I missing?"

Regan gave him an update. Nick perked up noticeably.

"Jesus … CIA? What all does this Lance guy have on Jennings?"

"Four years' worth of stuff, including photos of Jennings meeting with corrupt foreign leaders. With Lance's evidence and our own, we'll be able to paint a pretty complete picture of the man—not only how he operates as though he's above the law but also how motivated he is by power and the way he abuses it."

"So there should easily be enough to indict him tomorrow."

"Huang Lee's testimony will help a lot. Oh, I haven't had a chance to tell you—Lee's here."

Nick's eyes got big. "How'd you pull that off?"

Regan gave him a sly smile. "I used our trump card ... hinted that his daughter would be deported if he didn't come and help us out."

"The boss is okay with that?"

"I decided not to share that with Roland—or with Tate—at the moment. I just needed to get Lee here to give more weight to our case, and there's no point in making them squeamish about how I did it."

Nick stared at her for a long moment.

"What?" said Regan.

"Nothing ... it's just, well, we're trying to prove Winston Jennings abused his power. We don't want to do it by proving you abused yours."

"Jeez, Nick, quit busting my chops. I'm trying to get this done—we're running out of time."

"*You're* running out of time. You want Jennings locked up before you head to Alaska. All I'm saying, Regan, is be careful. Remember who we're dealing with. We can't afford to make a mistake."

59

REGAN MENTALLY groused about her partner all the way home. Lack of sleep, coupled with the pain of his injury, made him extremely cranky—but it was more than that. It felt like their relationship was changing. Like he was becoming hyper-critical of everything she did.

Maybe it wouldn't be the worst thing after all if he moved home to Maine to be with Lindsay.

By the time she pulled into the parking lot at her apartment, she realized how much she'd miss him. She suspected her grousing had more to do with the fact she was famished; she hadn't eaten all day.

And there was the problem with her bank accounts. *Damn Winston.* She'd have to sort it out right after the grand jury hearing in the morning.

As she unlocked the door, she tried to recall if there was anything edible in her refrigerator. Likely she was looking at Raisin Bran again.

Once inside, she locked the door behind her and slid the chain into place. She flipped on the light and froze.

"Hello, Agent Manning." Winston sat in the corner, butt parked in her favorite chair. For a fleeting moment, she wondered if she would ever want to sit in it again—and then realized it may be a moot point.

"Mr. Jennings." She didn't bother with indignation or ask why he was there. But she took a little comfort in the fact that he looked every bit as spent as she.

She walked into the living room, perched herself on the edge of the couch, and waited. A handgun rested in his lap, his finger loosely on the trigger.

"Set your gun on the floor and kick it over to me," he said.

She removed her Glock from the holster on her belt and did as she was told.

"The one on your ankle, too."

She unstrapped her ankle holster and took it off, then kicked the smaller weapon to him.

"I warned you to back off," he hissed. "Even Tate knows you're dangerous to the bureau. You have this notion that you're above the rules."

Tate said that? Nick's words about her abusing her power flooded her brain.

She pushed them aside. "I find that ironic coming from you, Mr. Jennings. You've been operating above the law your entire career. It's my job to stop you—and make sure you get the punishment you deserve." Her voice carried no sign of fear; she would never give him the satisfaction.

"Not anymore. From what I understand, you no longer *have* a job. The director is letting you think he's playing along with your scheme, but once the grand jury clears me, you're out."

It's part of the bluff. Don't believe it.

"If that's the case, then I'm no threat to you."

"One would think so—but there's that hero thing of yours. You think if you take me down, you'll be able to keep your FBI career."

She blinked but kept her expression neutral.

He grinned. "See how it feels to have your life's work threatened? Not so good, huh?"

Not so good at all. She would almost rather take the bullet.

"What do you want, Jennings? What did you come here for?"

His smile disappeared. In its place was a mask of pure evil. "I want you gone. Out of my hair. Off the planet."

He reached into his pocket and pulled out a pair of latex gloves. Slowly, he put them on, then reached for her Glock. "They'll rule it a suicide. You couldn't take it when you lost your beloved job, so you killed yourself."

The pit of Regan's stomach was on fire. *Is this it? Has this bastard won?*

She felt a rush of fury and leaped up. "Not when the bullet is in my back." She bolted toward the front door.

With alarming speed, he lunged out of the chair and crossed the room, grabbing her arm. She pivoted and swung her other elbow as hard as she could; she heard a crack as it connected with his nose.

"Goddamn it!" He let go to grab his nose; his hands were quickly coated with blood. Regan raced to the door, hands quaking as she tried to slide the chain free.

"Don't," he said.

She looked back at him. Winston stood there, one hand shielding his battered nose, blood stains spattered down the front of his white shirt. In the other hand, he held the gun.

His eyes, and the murderous look in them, told Regan she'd come to the end of the line.

❧

NICK FELT guilty over the way he acted. He'd treated his partner like she crossed a line that shouldn't have been crossed.

But she was right, Huang Lee was a crook. If the man didn't like being threatened with his daughter's deportation, too damn bad. His testimony would help them put away Winston Jennings, and that meant they had to get him here no matter what it took.

And as for Regan's impending trip to Alaska, he had *pushed* her to go. It was unfair to accuse her of being more focused on that than their case.

He had to admit he'd been a total jerk lately, uptight over the changes that were coming. He and Regan both faced painful decisions—but rather than show compassion over her dilemma with Jack, he acted out his own fears about losing Lindsay if he stayed in Washington.

The bullet wound in his arm only compounded the discomfort that was already there. But he had no right to lash out at Regan. There was nobody more dedicated than she was when it came to solving a case, nobody more perceptive at reading people, nobody more courageous. Nobody better for a partner.

He picked up his phone and hit "Regan" on his list of favorites. After four rings, it went to voicemail.

"Hey, it's me," he said. "Just wanted to say I'm sorry for the way I've been acting lately. I know I said that before, but I really mean it, Regan. Give me a call as soon as you get this ... I'm pretty sure I won't be asleep."

Where was she? Maybe taking a bath. Or already sleeping, as exhausted as she was.

No, she hadn't been home long enough to be asleep, and she always kept her phone on the side of the tub when she was bathing.

He waited ten minutes and tried again. Still no answer. Nick began to feel uneasy.

Where the hell is she?

60

WINSTON KNEW from the moment he found her trespassing in his study that Regan Manning was a force to be reckoned with. It was the fearless way she looked at him—like she saw right through his act. He could intimidate powerful lawmakers and heads of state all over the world, but he couldn't convince Agent Little Orphan Annie to think twice about crossing him.

After the elbow jab to the nose, he should've put a bullet through her head. But truth be told, he wasn't a killer. He had never taken the life of another human being. He'd always had others do it for him.

So he found himself in a bizarre situation. He felt a grudging respect for this woman. Hell, he'd like to *hire* her, not kill her.

And she just happened to be out of a job ...

Wait. Had the blow to his nose affected his damn brain?

He shook his head to clear it. "Sit down, Agent Manning. I'm not going to shoot you." Not that he'd ruled out having someone else do it.

She gave him a suspicious look and didn't budge. Her phone rang; she made no move to answer it.

"I'm not going to shoot you." He placed her gun next to his on the end table—out of his hand and out of her reach.

She inched her way back into the living room. "What do you want?"

"A wet washcloth, for starters," he said in a nasally tone. "I think you broke my nose."

"There's … there's one in the bathroom." He followed her, blocking her path to the front door as she pulled a clean washcloth from beneath the sink and ran it under cold water. She extended her arm fully to hand it to him, keeping her distance in case he lunged.

"Come and sit down," he said.

The energy that drove him here to confront Regan suddenly vanished; his limbs felt like they were packed with wet sand. He couldn't think straight.

He wished he hadn't come. It had been an impulsive move borne of extreme anger, and now he had boxed himself in.

He'd been making more and more bad moves lately. It wasn't like him.

Winston dropped back into the chair, and Regan returned to the couch. For a long while, he was silent.

Her phone rang again. She continued to ignore it.

Winston said, "I find myself on unfamiliar ground."

She looked perplexed, unsure where he was going with it.

"You may find this hard to believe, but I've never encountered anyone like you before. You simply do not quit."

"Like I said, it's my job."

"No, it's more than that. It's who you are."

"I believe in justice, Mr. Jennings."

"Of course you do. You're young and naïve."

"And you, on the other hand, believe in the survival of the fittest. King of the jungle and all that crap. That's *your* brand of justice."

Despite her insolence, he smiled. She couldn't be certain he wouldn't kill her, and yet there she was, speaking her mind with total conviction.

"Let me tell you something, Regan. There aren't enough leaders in this world. Most people are sheep. We need innovators who improve society and, at the same time, keep us safe. That's what my company does. Your agency, on the other hand, is not only populated by a bunch of mindless followers, it's run by one. Garrison Tate is weak and ineffective."

"Because he lets people like you push him around?"

"Precisely. But you don't."

"I'm not running the show."

"Lucky for me."

"Your luck runs out tomorrow. The grand jury is going to indict you."

There was that mouth again. "I think you're wrong. Imhoff-Greyson will continue to thrive, and I'm confident I'll be running it, albeit from Kansas, for another ten years. But right now I have a more immediate situation to address: what to do with you."

&

SHE COULD only stare in disbelief. Jennings actually thought he'd get off scot-free.

And what was this weird game he was playing? She broke his nose and he started waxing about how he admired her toughness. She began to wonder if she'd stumbled into some alternate universe.

"I hate to burst your bubble, Mr. Jennings, but we've compiled a good bit of incriminating evidence against you. I don't think you'll be able to skate this time."

"What is it you think you know?" He sounded exhausted. "As I told you when you and your partner hauled me in for questioning, I did not make illegal payments to anyone."

Speaking of her partner, she was guessing it was Nick who called. Since she let it go to voicemail twice, he was probably starting to wonder what was up.

"Perhaps you didn't make the payments directly, but your people did. And we'll prove you had full knowledge of that."

He shook his head and said nothing.

Regan desperately wished he'd just leave so she could eat something and go to bed. But again, she wasn't running the show.

"Let's talk about cyber attacks," she ventured.

He met her gaze. "What about them?"

"Why did you order the FBI computer system to be hacked?"

"Don't be ridiculous."

"What would be the motivation for someone else to do it? So far, it appears nothing sensitive was breached."

"It was probably done to prove a point."

"What point is that?"

"The potential for devastating consequences without proper cybersecurity."

"And who besides Imhoff-Greyson would want to demonstrate that? It's kind of a strange marketing plan, don't you think?"

Winston shrugged. "Think what you like."

"What I like to think is that, at the very least, you and others in your company can be accused of criminal mischief. Speaking of which, I want my bank accounts restored immediately."

"No comment."

"I don't need a comment. I just need it done."

Winston sighed. He closed his eyes.

He looked almost ill, like he'd gotten himself into a situation he didn't know how to get out of. If she made another attempt to escape, would he try to stop her?

Maybe not run after her, but he didn't need to. All he had to do was pick up his gun and fire.

Regan pondered what to do. Then it hit her: she was not only a hostage, she was also a trained hostage negotiator.

"Mr. Jennings, we seem to have arrived at an impasse. What will it take to resolve this?"

He opened his eyes, observing her without speaking.

"Maybe we can wind it back," she said. "You and I are both worn out; let's just pretend this never happened."

"Why do I think that would never happen?"

"I promise it will. I'll chalk it up to an error in judgment."

Winston gave it some thought, then said, "Tell me about yourself. Where did you grow up?"

The shift threw her. She hadn't anticipated a getting-to-know-you chat.

"I grew up in Juneau, Alaska."

"What does your dad do?"

"He used to be the harbormaster. Now he's the mayor."

"Ah … a leader in the community. You two pretty close?"

"Closer than we used to be."

"I'm guessing you locked horns with him when you were growing up."

She didn't reply.

"That's probably why you're the way you are. You've challenged authority from the time you were a kid. Let me guess—your mother was subservient to your father, correct? You thought it was your job to protect her?"

It unnerved her how closely he pegged it. Well, two could play this game.

"Let's talk about why you're the way *you* are, Mr. Jennings."

"I already told you; there aren't enough leaders in the world. I vowed to be one of them."

"Tell me about Jon's mother."

Now it was his turn to look surprised. "Not much to tell. I had an affair with her; Jon is the result." He shifted in the chair.

"Were you in love with her?"

"It was lust, not love. I made a mistake."

"So you tried to atone for that mistake by protecting Jon. You hired him to come to work for you, and then you tried to make up for abandoning him."

"In a manner of speaking, I guess."

Regan could tell his feelings on the subject went far deeper than he was letting on. If she could get him to open up ...

"Where did you meet Betty?"

His face softened. "We grew up together in Randolph, a little Kansas town that's no longer there. Her brother and I were buddies; Betty was a couple years behind us in school. I started dating her when I was a senior."

"She's a lovely woman. So's your daughter, Kate."

His eyes filled with tears; she could see his lower lip start to tremble.

I'm almost there ... c'mon, Winston, spill your guts.

"I know they're anxious for you to come home."

He broke down. "I'm not too sure about that. Betty is furious with me."

"She didn't know about Jon being your son until Dan broke the news?"

He shook his head and used the washcloth to wipe away tears. Between his red-rimmed eyes and busted nose, he looked more like a washed-up prize fighter than a Washington power broker.

"So she didn't take it too well," said Regan.

"No, she didn't. And it sounded like she was equally upset that I had abandoned Jon's mother."

"Why *did* you abandon Annabelle?"

"Like I said, it was just ... " He sighed. "No, that's not true. It wasn't just lust. I loved her."

"But you didn't want to break Betty's heart."

He looked at her. "I was a coward. Marrying Betty was the easiest thing for me personally and for my career. I expected my feelings for Annabelle to go away. But after I married Betty, I realized that I would never get over Annabelle completely. She was the love of my life. I know that sounds corny ..."

"It doesn't matter if it's corny if it's the truth. And maybe if you'd been able to explain the truth years ago, to both Betty and Jon, things might have played out differently."

"I'm sure that's true. But it's too late—there's no going back."

"You're right, Mr. Jennings, there's no going back. But going forward, you can tell the truth and make things less painful for yourself and those you care about."

"I agree I made some personal mistakes, that I hurt people, but the truth is this: I have too much love for my country to sit by and do nothing when I have solutions that will make us safer. As soon as I'm able to get a new cybersecurity structure in place, one that is virtually impenetrable, then I will go back to Kansas and live out the rest of my life there. I will no longer be of interest to you or your pals at the bureau."

As far as Regan was concerned, Winston had completely lost his grip on reality. He wouldn't be going back to Kansas to live out his golden years, even if Betty *did* forgive him.

There was a sharp knock on the door.

Regan and Winston exchanged a startled glance. She moved over to the door but didn't open it. "Yes?"

"Regan, it's Tom Cutter. Grimes and I just wanted to make sure you're okay."

This was it; she could have Winston taken into custody for breaking and entering. But there was no need to complicate things; he'd be arrested tomorrow anyway.

She opened the door. "Hey, guys."

"We got a call from Nick. He's been calling you, and when you didn't answer he thought you might be in some kind of trouble. We were pretty close to your place, so he asked us to swing by and check on you."

"I'm fine. Winston Jennings stopped by for a chat—but he was just leaving."

61

AS SOON as Winston was gone, Regan called Nick and told him about the bizarre encounter.

"You should've seen Cutter and Grimes when Jennings came to the door to leave. Their eyes almost bugged out." She laughed.

"Only you, partner, would have the nerve to punch Winston Jennings in the nose."

"That's not exactly the way it went down, but it makes a better story. By the way, thanks for asking those guys to stop by to check on me. If Winston hadn't settled down, I'd have been in a bad way."

"Maybe you shouldn't have given up being a negotiator. You've got skills, baby."

"Maybe, but I never thought I'd have to use them for my own release. And besides, I like being an investigator. Right now, though, I don't want to investigate anything but my pillow and sheets."

"Well, I'm glad you're okay, partner. And the reason I called in the first place was to apologize for acting like such an asshole when you were here. Actually for the last couple weeks."

"It's okay, Nick. I know you have my back, and I'll always have yours."

"I know, I just feel bad that---"

"It's forgotten. Really."

"There's a chance you might be too forgiving, Regan. I mean, Winston breaks into your apartment and threatens to shoot you and you let him walk out the door."

"Not exactly," she replied. "I busted his nose, remember? And tomorrow we're gonna bust his ass."

෴

HUANG LEE couldn't have been more nervous if his pants were on fire.

Just answer the questions honestly, she'd told him. He was immune from prosecution.

But it wasn't prosecution he was worried about. It was Winston.

The closed hearing didn't permit anyone in the room besides Brad Culpepper, who was prosecuting the case, the jurors, and the witnesses. So they sat in the hallway and waited for word on the indictment.

Adam, who sat on the other side of Nick instead of beside her, whispered, "What do you want to bet Lee's heading straight to the airport when this wraps up?"

"That's okay, we'll have another shot at him at trial," Nick whispered back.

The door opened and Brad came out. "We got it," he said with a wide grin.

"Excellent. Did you encounter much resistance?" said Adam.

The proceedings were confidential, so Brad couldn't say too much. He said in a low voice, "A hell of a lot more than I expected. Jennings is, after all, a prominent American statesman, and his company is well-known and highly respected."

"How did you persuade twelve of them to vote for the indictment?" said Regan.

"Showed them the bank statements. It didn't persuade only twelve; it convinced all twenty."

Regan smiled to herself. At the end of the day, it was the little woman back home in Kansas who brought the big man down.

She turned to Nick and gave him a hug. "We did it partner," she murmured in his ear. "We got him."

62

O N THE long flight home, Regan tried to distract herself
by thinking about the case.

She had spoken with Julia after the hearing thè day
before, who told her that she had gone to see Jon. She told him
she would file the divorce petition in due time, but first she
wanted to help him reconcile what he'd learned about his father.
Her compassion, she said, had been freely given, without
manipulation by Jon. And she would help him get well if he told
the truth about Winston's illegal activities.

It hadn't been without great pain, but in the end he agreed;
Adam and Brad were working on his plea deal. And Jon
planned to resign from Congress immediately, a move that took
very little coaxing from Julia.

"You're an amazing woman," Regan had told her. Julia
hadn't had to lie to gain Jon's cooperation, after all—it was her
genuine love for him that did it. She wouldn't be going back to
him, but she'd be there to help him heal and find himself while
he served his sentences.

As soon as Julia was well enough to travel, she and Jackson
were going to fly out to Palo Alto for a long overdue visit with
her mother. Peter was going, too.

Regan's thoughts turned to Nick. He'd insisted on driving
her to the airport, despite limited use of his left arm. On the way,
he told her that Lindsay had decided to leave the bureau and
practice law with her mother. Once she had a chance to get

settled and see if the arrangement was going to work, he planned to put in for a transfer to the bureau's resident agency in Portland.

"But that's down the road a ways," he said. "You're still going to have to put up with me for awhile."

"Perfect outcome, partner," she told him.

Just like their case. Jennings was in custody and facing trial. Now that news of his alleged corruption had broken, she expected his detractors to come out of the woodwork. No more tight lips—which would make Dan happier than a midget at a mini-skirt convention.

Regan felt a deep sense of satisfaction. But by the time her plane touched down on the runway in Juneau, she was so crippled with anxiety she could barely stand.

She spotted Jack in the waiting area, his eyes scanning the crowd of arriving passengers. When he saw her, his face lit up.

"Hey," he said when she emerged. He pulled her into his arms and hugged her.

"Hi, Jack," she replied, voice trembling.

If he thought she sounded conflicted about seeing him, he didn't comment on it. "Good flight?"

She nodded and they moved with the crowd down the stairs to the lower level. It gave her a moment to gather herself and stop shaking.

"So how's the party prep coming? Is my mother driving you crazy?"

He smiled. "Nah, she's good. Can't wait to see you, of course."

"I'm excited to see her, too. To see everybody."

After they grabbed her suitcase, they climbed into the Range Rover, where Susie waited to greet her with wet kisses. The Golden Retriever thought the sun rose and set in Jack—

unless Regan was in town. Then her master became almost invisible.

"Hi, sweet baby," Regan said as the dog nuzzled her face, tail wagging furiously. The dog kept her head draped over the front seat, next to Regan's ear, while they drove the nine miles into town. Regan made a pretense of talking to the dog so she could steal glances at Jack.

His wavy brown locks had gold highlights from all the time he spent in the sun; his eyes were almost a perfect match to his hair. His smile, as always, was warm and inviting.

My beautiful man. How could she forget the way she felt whenever she was in his orbit? It was like he gave off some sort of mystical energy. Whatever it was, it had captivated her the first time she saw him—and it still did.

She smiled at the memory of Jack giving a talk about the Tongass National Forest to all those dignitaries during the Alaska Energy Summit. He was a natural speaker, fully at ease and able to make his listeners feel that way, too, which was a good thing since they were up on Perseverance Trail. Bear country.

"So, babe, tell me about taking down Jennings," he said excitedly. Jack could always read her like a book; he had to know her silence meant there would be some difficult conversation in the days ahead. But not right now.

Regan told him the story, hitting just the high points since it wasn't that long of a drive to her parents' house on Douglas Highway.

"Unbelievable," Jack said when she was finished. "I'm glad you're okay." He reached over and touched her leg; a lightning bolt shot through her, one with a thousand times more voltage than when Adam's leg brushed hers.

Her life in Washington seemed a million miles away. In this moment, there was just her and the man she loved. Whose heart she would break, along with her own.

Both would mend in time. They had their work.

Jack pulled into her parents' driveway. "Get ready for the onslaught."

They went inside, and Regan was enfolded in a frenzy of hugs. Her parents' Chihuahua trotted around the group, barking like a maniac at all the commotion.

"Yes, Paco, I see you," said Regan. She scooped him up and kissed his nose while Susie leaned against her legs.

"Are you hungry?" asked her mom. "Dinner was three hours ago, so I'm sure everyone is ready to eat again."

"Just some sandwiches, Carol," said her dad. "Don't put out a big spread."

"Shush, Devlin," she said. "Our daughter's home. That calls for more than sandwiches." She looked at Regan and said in a sassy voice, "Forty years of marriage and he still tries to tell me what to do."

Regan laughed as she watched her mom pull all sorts of delicious goodies from the refrigerator. She spotted her favorite seven-layer Mexican dip and realized how starved she was. She'd been too keyed up to eat before.

Colin came up and put his arm around her shoulders. "How ya doin', sis?" He kissed her cheek.

"Perfect," she replied, wrapping an arm around his waist. "I'm so glad I'm here."

"Aunt Regan, can I show you the friendship bracelet I'm making?" asked her niece, Sidney.

"Sure, Sid." She joined the six-year-old on the living room floor, along with her other niece, four-year-old Jordan. And the two dogs, of course.

Her mother brought her a plate of food and a glass of lemonade. "Here, sweetheart."

"Thanks, Mom."

"I thought we'd go shopping tomorrow, Regan, just the two of us. Pick up some last-minute stuff for the party."

"I'd love to."

As her mother scooted herself back to the kitchen to fuss over the food, Regan glanced around at her family and felt a tidal wave of gratitude. She still couldn't believe that just two days ago she'd come home to find Winston Jennings in her apartment and wondered if his was the last face she'd ever see. It brought tears to her eyes.

She glanced over at Jack, who was sitting in a chair by the picture window, watching her. He smiled.

Damn you, Jack Landis.

&

TWO DAYS later, following a spin on Jack's boat, they sat in his living room. Regan was slumped against the arm of the leather couch with Susie cuddled beside her, while Jack sat in a nearby chair. She couldn't recall a time when they'd sat together in his living room without touching. The awkward silence between them was new, too.

It was time.

"So here we are," he said at the same moment she said, "Jack, I—" They both laughed.

"We need to talk about our relationship," Regan said softly, the ache in her chest in full bloom.

"Wait," he said. "Let me just say something first. I asked you on the phone the other night if you still loved me. You said yes."

She nodded.

"So I took you at your word. And I accepted a new job."

Regan nearly fainted. "Oh no, Jack, I can't ask you to do that ..."

"It's just for a year."

She sat upright, her heart beating wildly. "What? Where?"

"I accepted an appointment with National Geographic, creating a youth education program."

"Where will you be?" She held her breath.

"At their headquarters—in Washington, D.C."

Regan burst into tears.

He got up and knelt in front of the couch, wrapping his arms around her. "I hope those are tears of joy."

She nodded against his shoulder. After a moment, she stopped crying. "Are you happy with the assignment, Jack? Is it something you really want to do?"

"I couldn't be more excited," he replied. She could tell from his eyes that he meant it. "Teaching kids about forests and how to preserve them ... man, it doesn't get any better. And being there with you ..."

"Oh, honey, it's *so* perfect! I can't believe it. I can't believe you and Susie are going to be in Washington with me. I'm just so ..." She stopped and shook her head, at a loss for words.

Her phone buzzed. It was a text from Lisa Roland. *Call me as soon as you have a minute.*

Regan was puzzled. Her boss knew she was on vacation for a week, had even told her to put work completely out of her mind while she was in Alaska and get a good rest. She'd earned it.

She leaned over and gave Jack a long, lingering kiss. "I love you," she said. "And just as soon as I get through talking to my boss, I'll show you how much."

Regan got up and went out on the deck, still tingling from the excitement of Jack's news. She watched the gulls in the cove swoop and dive as she waited for Roland to pick up.

"Boy, that was fast," said Roland.

"Yeah, well, I thought it was best to go ahead and see what you needed before I get more swept up in all the family stuff and forget."

"It's nothing urgent; I just needed to give you a heads up. With Jennings' indictment, we've got a lot of things popping overseas. You and Nick are going to be spending a lot of time traveling in the next few months, preparing the case for trial. You'll be leaving a couple days after you get back next week."

Regan felt like she'd been walloped. She and Jack *finally* had a solution, at least for a year while he was in Washington. And she was going to miss the first few months of it.

Was it some kind of weird sign from the universe?

She glanced through the window at Jack. The look on his face was one of pure, unadulterated joy.

That was her sign.

"Ma'am, can Tom Cutter go in my place? If he and Nick can conduct the in-person interviews over there, I'll coordinate everything from Washington."

"But you're more familiar with the case, Regan. You've already met a lot of the players in the other countries."

"Nick will get Cutter up to speed. Tom's a quick study. Please, ma'am, I need to stay in Washington. My boyfriend has taken a year-long appointment with National Geographic, and if you knew how hard it's been for us to get this figured out ..."

"Ah, I see."

Regan waited, silently praying it wouldn't compromise her position on the FCPA team. If it did, she had a choice to make— *again*.

"I can appreciate how difficult it is to juggle your career with your private life," said Roland. "Just ask my husband and kids. But it's my belief, Regan, that an agent who is able to have a reasonable balance between the two is the kind of individual who will be with the bureau for the long haul—who won't burn out."

"Really, Director Roland? You're okay with it?"

"I'm okay with it, Regan. Let's just say I have plans for you down the road. And I can't wait to meet that guy of yours."